LOWENKOPF AT SEA . . .

"Freddie?"

The frogman was beckoning Shelly to step from the doorway, inviting him into the narrow crawl space of the boat. Shelly hesitated and felt a warm hand close on his wrist as the frogman reached forward and tugged.

Shelly clung to his post in the doorway. "What do you think you're doing?"

The frogman yanked at him, harder.

Shelly smacked the man's hand. "Let go of me!"

The frogman let go, dropping Shelly's arm. Then, the most peculiar thing: He curled himself into a ball, drawing up his legs, and covering his face and his head with his black rubber arms.

"What the hell are you doing—" Shelly began, but never got a chance to finish.

Because at that moment he sensed rather than saw a flash of bright yellow over his shoulder and felt a searing burst of heat in the muscles of his back. Then there was a pause and a *boom* so loud it rolled over him, rattling his bones . . .

Books by Richard Fliegel

The Art of Death
The Next to Die
The Organ-Grinder's Monkey
A Semiprivate Doom
Time to Kill

Published by POCKET BOOKS

A SEMIPRIVATE
DOOM

RICHARD FLIEGEL

POCKET BOOKS

New York   London   Toronto   Sydney   Tokyo   Singapore

An *Original* Publication of POCKET BOOKS

POCKET BOOKS, a division of Simon & Schuster
1230 Avenue of the Americas, New York, NY 10020

ISBN: 0-671-68851-0

First Pocket Books printing May 1991

10 9 8 7 6 5 4 3 2 1

POCKET and colophon are registered trademarks of Simon & Schuster.

Printed in the U.S.A.

For my mother

I am grateful for the assistance and information provided to me by Robert Diamond, Mika Manty, Moira Sandrock, Eric Cohen, M.D., and especially for the generous insight and advice of Eric Rypens, M.D., to whom I owe whatever is medically accurate in this book. The lapses are of course my own.

A SEMIPRIVATE DOOM

The soft *put-put* of an outboard motor would not have been so obtrusive after all, thought Detective Sergeant Shelly Lowenkopf as the hiss and splash of their sailboat broke the lumpy purple water. A scowl like the grin of a scarecrow shimmered back at him from the muck beneath the prow—not the *prow,* he remembered, but the side, the starboard side of the boat. Or was it the port side? That word he had tried to memorize by associating the after-dinner vintage it sounded like with an imaginary glass in his corresponding hand—but which one was it? He studied both of his hands, which were large and creased with thousands of tiny lines, crissing and crossing with increasing complexity for each one of his forty-two years. The left, he felt sure, raising that hand in an invisible toast. The port was the side on the left. But facing the prow or the stern?

He couldn't recall, listening to the sibilant whisper and the thump as the fiberglass hull of the sailboat slapped the leaden water. It was a Monday night late in September, when even the most reluctant summer visitors had drawn up stakes and the weekend crowds were also in their weekday

1

homes and apartments. Only the resident boats were out, the sailboats moored to their piers and a lone trawler visible now and then among the promontories ahead. Only the flap of their sails and the smack of their hull broke the offshore stillness.

So how much more noise would an outboard really have made? The water and the wind in the tall shore grass would have covered any noise from their engine. Shelly glanced back at Homer, standing at the tiller under the moon. His glinting green eyes watched the beach alongside them—not a beach exactly, but a shore, dotted with reeds that grew down to the waterline and even hung over the rippled surface. The edge of the land snaked in and out as each bristling fist of brush opened on a hidden bay and a pier, which soon disappeared into the next nettled fingers. Somewhere, in one of these lazy inlets, Freddie "the Saw" Santino was reported to be a prisoner, held against his will on a motor launch by one or more of his own blood relatives. That, at least, was what their twenty dollar source had claimed, folding the bill into a tiny green square and squeezing it into his hip pocket. His store of information had run out after that single tantalizing tidbit, leaving the captain hungry for more.

Captain Madagascar knew as well as anyone how unreliable purchased information could be, especially information that was hard to disprove. You bought it—the snitch had to make a living, too—but you had to take it with a grain of salt and then try to confirm what you heard. The captain knew that, but couldn't pass it up. The thought of nailing Freddie Santino just hung there delectably until he decided, What the hell, let's give it a try. So there had been no choice but to scrutinize the shoreline, looking for the reported motorboat. They might have questioned the motives of their source instead, but Shelly was hardly in a position to suggest it, since it had been he and Homer who had lost Freddie S. in the first place. Well, he, really—Homer had won a flip of a coin and gone for coffee in the luncheonette when the lights in Freddie's third-floor apartment on Pelham Parkway had blinked on and then off—and the scion of New York's third largest crime family had appeared for a shadowy second and then disappeared for good.

Freddie Santino was called "the Saw" as a kindness, despite the fact that no one had ever known him to take part in the family business. It was not merely that Freddie had refused to make his bones and sign on with his older brother in the prostitution and protection rackets, preparing for the day when the old man would at last leave the reins to them. Freddie wouldn't have *anything* to do with it, not even on the legitimate side, importing nuts and olives from the Mediterranean for upscale East Side eateries. Freddie made his own way in the world, with his own hands. He had early hit upon carpentry, and it was as a builder of cabinets, mostly for stereos and television sets, that Freddie Santino earned his daily bread. He and his wife lived without children in a place on the parkway around the corner from his shop on Boston Post Road in the Bronx. Every morning Freddie would eat a breakfast of fish and eggs prepared by his wife; every noon he would lunch on sausage and onions at the pizzeria down the block from his shop; every night he would shuffle home, his cuffs spilling sawdust, to a dinner of veal and peppers or calamari or saltimbocca. Until one day, under the influence of an inexplicably romantic impulse, Freddie went home in the middle of the afternoon for a surprise lunch with his wife.

He must have entered the small apartment quietly, planning to surprise her. There were some flowers—dandelions—scattered around the floor in the entrance hallway. The bedroom door may have been open; it made no difference anyway, since the thinness of the walls would have allowed any grunts and groans inside to be heard, either way. Lowenkopf could picture it: there was Freddie, listening to his wife moaning the name of another man. What did he do? He went into the narrow drawer of the telephone table, took out a .38 caliber revolver, and emptied all six chambers into the supine form of the beefy, red-faced Neapolitan who ruled the delicatessen counter at D'Alessio's.

The screams of Freddie's wife brought the patrol officer, who found the empty revolver, which was matched, of course, by ballistics to the six bullets retrieved from the corpse. Of Freddie himself no sign was found, though his wife insisted he had marched down the stairs quite deliberately a minute before the beat cop had made his way up. The all-points bulletin turned up nothing—unsurprisingly, really, since all they had to go on was an old photograph, taken at the wedding of Freddie's niece Robin Santino to the Abolafia kid, which showed at a table of guests in the background a blurred face with a pencil-thin mustache. That was all they had to spot Freddie, when you came right down to it: five-seven or -eight, a hundred fifty pounds or so, and a thirty-year-old style of mustache. So it was with real enthusiasm that the question had been received in the D.A.'s office when Freddie's lawyer, a slimeball named Zbigniew Jones, called wondering just what sort of information they would have to hear about the Santino operation to interest them in a deal.

No one knew from whom the question had come—whether Freddie had asked in an offhand way, or whether Jones had come up with the idea himself. But it didn't take long before ears were up in pool halls all over town. Was Freddie the Saw about to make a deal? And what could he spill, if he was so inclined? Enough, it seemed, to cause earnest concern in some parts of the family—though not from the old man himself, if their sources could be believed. Freddie made no further sign of interest in a deal, and no further calls came in from Jones, who, when located, said that the only one who might know where his client was would be Freddie's elder brother, Francis Santino.

Francis was the heir apparent to the family business. No one expected his help. He had done serious time at twelve, after an Irish kid in the playground called him Frankie. He warned the kid that he didn't like that name. The kid replied, "Frankie and Johnny were lovers, weren't they?" and Francis beat his head with a Coke bottle until only the neck of broken glass was left in his hand. But he came down to the precinct house with an attorney one day, demanding to know whether the cops were holding his brother in a safe house somewhere. Shelly only wished they had one. Nobody gave Francis the time of day, of course, but the word on the street suggested he might have actually wanted to know. Freddie's father put out a generous reward for information leading to his recovery, and from the way informants were clamming up, no one had managed to claim it. Shelly knew that in a case like this, if the missing person wasn't found within twenty-four hours, odds were he wouldn't be found later. Freddie had walked away from the cop on the beat and fallen through a crack in the known world. His wife had left the apartment that night, moving in with her sister in Brooklyn. But hope died hard in a district attorney's heart, and the captain was asked to keep an eye on the place. The lights had gone on once upstairs, and had been off ever since—the only sign of Freddie Santino anyone had seen. And the two cops out front, passing the hours in a cramped Reliant, had been none other than Lowenkopf and Greeley.

So it fell to them to track him down, Shelly knew, in the beautiful logic of police tradition. And that was why he was sitting here now, straining his eyes into the graying murk where the shoreline blurred with the sea. Until the wind startled him, gusting into the sail behind him with a sudden flap of the canvas that echoed over the water like a cannon blast. So how much noise had they actually saved by going with the sails instead of an outboard, which both of them could have handled? He glanced back toward the stern where his partner crouched, fiddling with the tiller. Homer had carried the day, of course, convincing the captain that a sailboat could approach a bay without drawing the sort of attention a motor was likely to stir. But to Shelly, perched on the edge of a craft he couldn't sail, the difference in volume seemed negligible. Just making the damn vessel go straight into the wind required so much activity—swinging the sails back and forth, trying to catch the wind—that the noise of their voices alone must have drowned out any outboard's purr. Homer stood, and the brilliant white of his trunks and blue broad-striped shirt disturbed the darkness as he reached to loosen a soggy rope—a *line,* remembered Shelly, you called them *lines.* Homer frowned and motioned Shelly toward the port, or the starboard—toward the other side of the boat.

Shelly bent his head and crawled under the boom, a word he remembered as the sound it would make inside your skull if the horizontal beam caught you unaware. Now, what exactly did Homer want him to do here? Pull on a rope? Tug on a sail? Balance their weight in the boat?

"Come about!" called Homer from the aft.

Come about? Shelly looked around for something that might have supplied a clue. There was a coil of rope in the center of the boat, which he picked up casually.

Homer was pointing at him—no, past him toward the front of the boat. "Go to the jib, Shell. In the bow."

So the front was called the *bow*—but hadn't Homer called it the *prow* when he first stepped uneasily aboard? Shelly didn't stop to ask but did as he was told, taking up position beside the small sail in the nose of the boat. Then he turned for his next instruction.

Homer pushed the rudder, hanging on to the sail, and the boat started to wander. As it did, the mainsail suddenly swung from right to left, where Homer held it in place at about seven o'clock, so that the wind could rush against and past it. He waited, watching it flap, and then, as the boat lurched forward, shouted urgently to Shelly, "Sheet in the jib! Quickly!"

Shelly looked at the lax sail beside him, connected not to the central mast but to a pole that angled up from the tip of the bow to a point three-quarters up the mast. Two ropes ran from the bottom of the sail, through rings on either side of the bow. One of those ropes was close at hand. What on earth was he supposed to do with it? Tie it into a knot?

"The line, Shell!" called Homer, waving his arm. "The rope! Pull it in!"

Shelly picked up the rope tied to the sail and tugged it in toward his chest. The small front sail grew taut on his side, catching the wind and speeding their lurch to the left. Behind him, the mainsail flapped like a sheet on a wind-whipped clothesline. Homer scanned the sea, exulting in their accomplishment.

"Great!" he hollered, nodding vigorously. "We did it. You see? I told you you could sail."

Shelly looked away, not to sea, where unimaginable monsters waited for them, but toward the shore, where he longed to stand. So near yet so far, the dark mass of land slipped by in a tangle of bush and fallen trees. They passed a cove, where a rowboat dried on a cresent of mud and a sailboat rocked against the dock. And still their sailboat glided, crossing the eye of the wind. The momentum of their tack carried them past a buoy, past another tangle of growth stretching from the shore, into another little bay, where their forward motion dwindled.

"What now?" said Shelly.

Homer grinned with pleasure, "We tack . . . we do it again."

"Do what again?"

"Come about."

Sailing was a sport, Shelly knew—his partner's favorite one. But there, as in so many things, their personal preferences parted. Coming about in the salty spray would not have been Shelly's idea of a good time on a bright, sunny day in the middle of July. It was certainly not his idea of the best way to travel along the south shore of Long Island in late September, as the night coiled with a penetrating chill and the ocean at their backs turned to ink.

"Isn't there some other way to boost this thing?"

Homer shook his head. "We could turn on the engines, of course," he said, settling against the stern, "but that would defeat the whole purpose of our opting for a sailboat in the first place."

Shelly was perfectly willing to accept that defeat, but Homer tightened his grip on the tiller. Shelly looked out into the darkness before them as another clump of shore rolled past. There was an *engine* aboard? All along, while they had struggled to maneuver the sails to carry them into the wind. Not that its presence meant a lot to Homer, who would never have agreed to the sanest course and cranked the blessed thing up. There would be no talking him into it, and still Shelly would have tried, had it not been for the noise that reached his ears across the water. A groan from the wooden planks of the pier nearby, where a small motor launch lay at anchor.

"What's that?" he whispered.

But Homer had already heard it and was peering through binoculars toward the sailboat in its mooring. And then Shelly saw for himself in a shaft of moonlight what had caused the noise on the pier. Two men were dragging a third, propped between them, over the planks to the boat.

"Is that Freddie?"

"I can't tell for certain," said Homer grimly, eye sockets glued to the binoculars.

Shelly reached over and pried them away from his partner. Homer's eyes were better, but he tended to note details rather than impressions, so Shelly made the quicker identifications. Training his lenses on the men on the dock, Shelly saw a red flannel shirt, a blue flannel, a black sweater . . . Was that a sweater? It seemed to shine, like rubber. Tilting up, he saw two grizzled faces he didn't recognize, and something that mystified him: a great circle of dazzling light obscuring the third. A miner's cap? No, he made out the edge—a scuba diver's mask. Beneath it, Shelly thought he saw a pencil-thin mustache.

It could have been a shadow, he realized, as the two men

in flannel hauled their captive aboard. If only he had another second to check, but the slam of the cabin door clanged forty yards across the water.

"What do you think?" asked Homer.

Shelly grunted. "Could be. We'd better get on the radio, don't you think?"

Homer stared grimly at the power boat near the pier. He raised his ankle deliberately, pulling off one Top-Sider by the heel. "No time for that." He kicked off the other. The black water leaped and crashed between the two craft.

"You're not thinking . . . of swimming over there?"

Homer crossed his arms and lifted his sweatshirt over his head. "Don't see what else we can do, Shell. If that's Freddie in the wet suit, we'd better not lose him again, wouldn't you say? If it isn't him, somebody else needs our help. You saw them drag him aboard?"

"I saw it," Shelly admitted, "but what exactly did we see? The kidnapping of a potential informant? Or a couple of pals helping their buddy onto his boat after he's had a few too many boilermakers in the clubhouse?"

"They didn't look too buddy-buddy to me," said Homer, trying to find a place to tuck his Beretta into the waistband of his bathing suit.

"How are you planning to keep your powder dry?" demanded Shelly.

Homer weighed the gun in his hand, studied the water, and stuffed the heavy weapon into his shoe on the deck. "I'll just have to go without it."

"Homer," said Shelly, "you're planning to swim across the bay to a boat on which two kidnappers, probably armed, are planning to kill a man—without your weapon? What are you going to do when you get there? Scare them into surrendering? You can't even take your goddamn badge with you! You're not thinking professionally, here."

Homer balanced his foot on the edge of the sailboat, drawing his arms overhead for the dive. "I'll think of something on the other side."

9

"Just a second," said Shelly. "What am I supposed to do on this miserable crate without you?"

"Nothing," said Homer, checking the deck for loose lines and sails. "Toss the anchor over the side."

"And if the waves start up?"

"Ride them out," said Homer with a shrug. "Worst comes to worst, you'll capsize—that's all. Just right the craft and climb in again."

"Capsize?" Shelly stared seaward, where big black waves licked the side of the craft.

"Nothing to it," said Homer, limbering his trunk, leaning forward, springing on his toes.

"Oh, no, you don't," Shelly insisted, grabbing his partner by the shoulder and pulling him back onto the deck, where he landed hard on his seat. Shelly immediately began pulling off his own shoes and socks.

Homer rubbed his tailbone. "Now, listen . . ."

"You listen," said Shelly, fighting to keep a note of reason in his irritated voice, "somebody's got to keep this thing from floating out to sea. Or capsizing! If one of us has to swim over there, it's plainly got to be me."

It was hard for Homer to argue with that. "All right—if you feel you have to. Give me your weapon."

Shelly slapped his own Beretta into Homer's waiting hand. "It's the only way it makes any sense," he muttered, turning to the side, where the inky foam burst against the hull. Shelly unbuttoned the cuffs of his button-down shirt and tugged off his tie. He reached into his back trouser pocket and was reassured to feel a postcard still folded around his comb. He undid the clasp of his belt. Beneath his woolen pants he wore black Lycra bikini briefs, brought back by his sister Isabelle from Puerto Rico. They were nothing but the skimpiest strip of black fabric stretched between his belly and thighs—far too immodest to be worn on the beach, but comfortable beneath his pants, where he had planned to keep them. Now he stepped out of his trousers and shrugged off his shirt, leaving himself utterly exposed. A gull cawed overhead—a sound like laughter, at the sight of him, announcing him to the night.

Homer nodded—approving what, Shelly wasn't sure. He took off his glasses, folded the wire-rim frames, and settled them into the pocket of his shirt on the deck. The world around him was transformed, its rough edges blurred, the waves and sky now two hues of gray and black merging at the horizon. At the dock, the faint white mass of the fiberglass hull rocked in the distance. Shelly spread his shoulders, cracking five or six vertebrae, and then rocked forward, crouching into the dive.

"Wait!" whispered Homer as his hand caught Shelly by the crook of the elbow.

"What now?" asked Shelly. It was hard to suppress the edge of impatience in his voice while a tiny voice inside him was praying that Homer had thought of a reason for him to stay.

Homer nodded across the bay, to the boat against the dock. For an instant, Shelly didn't understand. Then he heard it: the cabin door opened with a squeak and two men tramped up from below deck, stamping their feet on the fiberglass steps. The third man was no longer between them. Shelly peered at the two blurs of flannel as they thumped onto the wooden pier and a deep-bellied laugh passed between them.

Shelly and Homer saw the two men step from the dock, landing with a crunch on the sand beyond. They saw them cross to their jeep in the parking lot, slam the doors, and rev the engine twice in the salt air. They could not see into the car, where the passenger, a grizzled man grayer and shorter than his partner at the wheel, lifted the receiver of the car phone between them and glared at the squarish silver buttons on its control panel.

"How do you work this goddamn thing?"

The driver reached over smoothly, punching in the necessary sequence. "Easy, Tuck. You don't wanna blow any circuits here."

Tuck held the receiver away from his grizzled cheek as the numbers beeped tunelessly. When the ringing ended abruptly, he settled the insubstantial plastic against his ear, waited, and muttered, "Gimme Chester."

From the sailboat about forty yards away, quiet seemed to settle over the beach. "I'll keep her steady," Homer promised, releasing Shelly's elbow.

"Thanks."

"It's the least I can do."

Shelly couldn't help but agree. He stood for a moment on the edge of the sailboat, flexing his knees to steady himself, feeling the spray and the wind. The bay water slapped at the hull below, reaching toward his ankles. The boat seemed to rock more wildly now; the gulls called for his dive. He took a deep breath and stepped back involuntarily to avoid going by accident where he intended to go on purpose—head-first into the tide. He rubbed the backs of his knees with his fist, flexed his ankle and shin. Then he crouched, close to the water again. He let it splash in his face, flecking his cheeks and nose and eyes, and shivered at the chill. The current rushed by at incredible speed and seemed to beckon him, in a dare. He recovered his balance, straightening, steady. He drew a breath as a gust passed through him and the cold air settled into his bones. There was a bitter taste in his throat, as if his Adam's apple had soured. Then slowly, as in a dream, he stretched his arms, swallowed his bile, and slipped into the waves.

2

The tide picked him up at once, carrying him past the stern of the sailboat, away from the launch at the pier. He caught a glimpse of Homer looking worried on the deck, but lost his partner from the periphery of his vision when he turned his attention to the jostling waves that seemed to flow deliberately in his way. Overhead, the stars looked like pie plates, great blurs of light splotching the sky like saucers arriving from a distant planet. Ah, the visions he saw without his glasses!

A rise of cold water caught him unaware, slapping him under the ear, drawing his notice to the wider sea around him. How on earth had he allowed himself to be talked into this—dogging his way through the night sea while a host of creatures fathoms below waited for him to fail? A swell carried him by his armpits and dropped him like a shell into the dell behind a wave crest. He chopped through with his arms, raising his elbows over the chattering foam, dropping them heavily into the ink in the wake of the swell. He made a splash but not much headway until he kicked back deliberately against the undulating surface. That helped—he seemed to move ahead. The rhythm of his arms rising above his head, slapping through the surface into the calmer water below, was somehow reassuring, as was the rocking of his two-strokes-forward, one-stroke-back progress. The cold, too, was lulling in a way, anesthetizing his muscles. The trick was not to think about it, to allow his body to do its work without the added burden of his conscious attention. To escape the unpleasant sensations splashing against his body, Shelly allowed his mind to drift—which was just what his heart had been waiting for.

He first became aware of a shadow of guilt that had been lurking at the edge of his consciousness. He had not been particularly patient with Homer, on the boat. He was well aware of that. Homer's interest in the sailboat had not been sparked by any desire for recreation, Shelly felt sure, but by an earnest belief in the advantage of sails in inconspicuousness. Policemen didn't often travel under sail when they took to the water: that was certainly true. But Homer was merely trying to capitalize on his own nautical know-how, not to show up Shelly's lack of any. He could hardly be blamed if the choice left Shelly on a craft he couldn't manage. Homer would have had to take a moment to think about other people, which was as natural for Homer as taking the time to calculate the influence of their astrological charts—and Homer was no astrologer. Blaming him for insensitivity was like blaming the north wind for its chill: considering where it was blowing from, what else could it do? You either positioned yourself to coast along in its draft or ducked out of its way. To allow himself to complain because Homer had concentrated on the details of their investigation rather than the feelings of the people involved would be to deny everything Shelly had learned about his partner in their seven years as a homicide team.

Shelly knew perfectly well, of course, the real reason for his dark mood. It sprang from the card in his pocket, folded around his comb, which should have been a cause for celebration but was just a hair less full of joy. Shelly had recognized it at once in some deep inner recess of his consciousness as a harbinger of doom, disguised as a picture postcard. It was from Mordred, ten words and an initial: "Coming home. Bad news—we need to talk. Take care, M." The promise of bad news was always disturbing, of course, but the words "we need to talk" sent a positive chill up his spine. And the final "Take care" seemed to spell out the doom of their relationship. Eight letters in two words, when "love" would have been only half the number of each. He had read the message three times and flipped the card over. The picture on the front showed a mosque embellished with mozaic tiles. Postmarked Doha. Where was that, now? Kuwait? Oman? Someplace like that. The last real letter he had had from her had come from a navy base, a fact that had troubled him originally but now seemed far more desirable a site of origin than this unknown city or state. How had she found her way to Doha? She must've met someone from the place. It didn't take him long, picturing in his mind the seam in her stockings running up into her miniskirt, to guess just the sort of person she might have attracted over there.

He noticed he was starting to drift backwards again, so he kicked the water behind with added force, propelling himself toward the pier. They had been over this ground before she left, of course, agreeing not to wait for each other, whatever that meant. It left him somewhere in the vague emotional territory between crossing off days on his calendar and forgetting about her completely. He understood that her overseas posting might be extended from six weeks indefinitely if her photos of the Persian Gulf appealed to her editor. Which, Shelly knew from her first front-page appearance, was a foregone conclusion; a shot that had to be taken from a rowboat nosed under the prow of an American battleship—a little more exciting, he had to admit, than photos of homeless squatters in old buildings, or of those buildings themselves, torched. And the exotic locale—the Casbah was over there somewhere, wasn't it? How could he keep her down in the Bronx after she'd heard Farsi?

She was coming in five days now. What was she planning to say? "We need to talk"—he didn't like the sound of that at all. But how could he prepare an answer if he didn't know her angle of attack? There was nothing he could do but wait for her to land. And then . . . well, he'd have to get there first. By the headway he was making toward the motor launch at the dock, it wasn't at all clear he would make it. The thought lent new urgency to his arms as he propelled himself through the water. With each stroke, he kicked back harder, forcing his body through the freezing water, measuring small gains by the shoreline and then slipping back again. Hypothermia could be an issue, he realized, gazing at the sailboat, strikingly small behind him, and at the pier ahead, still some distance away.

Shelly was not a strong swimmer. Yet again and again he found himself at sea. Superficially, he knew, it had something to do with the contrast between himself and his partner, whose relentless heroism was usually a pain in the ass. On a deeper level, however, it made an apt representation of his personality and situation, bobbing along in the swell of events, swimming against the tide. He crashed his arms into the waves, but the white water splashed back—he was apparently making no progress again. The muscles in his chest were stiffening, and aching, despite the numbing cold. He felt fatigue gathering in his calves and forearms, his hamstrings tightening and failing to unbunch, readying themselves to spasm. He raised his head and looked forward, then behind. Where had all this water come from? It had seemed far closer from the sailboat to the motor launch than it now seemed to either one. All he had to do was stop flailing his arms and he would sink down through the darkness to a warm tomb in the sea. He lowered his head and swam with all his might, splashing loud in his ears.

When he looked up again, a great expanse of white fiberglass loomed overhead—the hull of the launch. He treaded water a minute, one hand pressed to the smooth white plastic, shuddering from the cold. He had made the swim from Homer's sailboat; now what was he supposed to do? The hull overhead looked frustratingly high, and his arms felt heavy and waterlogged. It took him four tries before he managed to raise his hands high enough to grab hold of the edge overhead. When his fingers closed on the slippery curve, he allowed himself to hang for a moment in the icy flood, warmer than the night air through which he would have to pull himself before he could reach the deck. Then, with a desperate lunge, he threw himself on board, hanging over the side of the boat, gasping and shivering, but grateful to be feeling the pain. The air that stabbed his prickly lungs and the efforts of his heart to escape through his ribs proved he was still alive.

Scrambling over the side of the launch, he struggled for control of his autonomic nervous system, oblivious to any danger from the dock on the far side or the deck immediately below him. He concentrated on his jaw, which was trembling to its own rhythm, failing to make his teeth chatter only because he kept them wide apart. He hunched his shoulders, allowing the shaking to surge through his neck and his stomach and his knees and ankles, where it splintered into warm, tingling needles in his toes that announced the return of blood to his extremities. It was a pleasantly awful sensation, until with a start he realized that the irregular *thump-thump* in his ears was not cardiovascular, but coming from somewhere outside him.

Shelly listened, casting a policeman's eye about him at last. He looked past the long wooden dock to the shore, where a hardtop jeep sat in a parking lot, with lights on and engine running. Two shadows filled the front seat, waiting for something—for what? Their beams were pointed toward the black paved road leading away from the beach, where four green posts rusted in the salty air. There was a chain hanging from one of the posts, which had been unfastened from another, so that its links lay on the edge of the pavement near a row of white-painted rocks. But no other headlight swept down to meet it, and the engine of the jeep revved a little louder, headlights brightening for an instant as it rolled forward, climbing the hill.

They were alone—Shelly on the deck of the power boat, and the man they had left somewhere below. Unless, of course, there had been someone else waiting on the boat all along. Shelly squinted back for a sign of support, over the waves behind him. Across the water, he thought he saw the slim, pale figure of Homer Greeley perched like a figurehead on the prow of their sailboat, gazing across the bay. He would have liked to see Homer wave or indicate with some broad gesture the connection between them. But the blond detective betrayed no token of their interdependence, or in fact any interest in the motor launch bobbing alongside the pier.

Thump! That sound again. Shelly got a good fix on its direction now. It was definitely not coming from the sailboat, as a signal of solidarity from Homer. Nor was it coming from the beach, where the jeep had now climbed to a road overhead, out of sight and earshot. The beach was deserted again: the tide thundered in and then sizzled against the sand, resting momentarily and then dragging back scud lines of sand to use in its next barrage. Plenty of noise—but nothing like the thump unmistakably rising between Shelly's feet, through the fiberglass deck.

He moved to the cabin and pressed his ear to the crack of the door, listening as best he could while the night sea grappled with the sand. No good—he couldn't hear a damned thing inside. He closed his fingers on the knob, rattling the door against the frame until he stopped his elbow from trembling. Anyone inside would have heard that. He might as well take a look. He turned the knob, and the door gave way on an unlit cabin. That made no sense at all. The two men in flannel had brought a third here. What had they done with their prisoner? Or their drunken friend, if that was who he turned out to be.

Shelly climbed down the three short steps into the empty cabin, stepping on rubber mats. It was a small living space,

designed to accommodate no more than four or five, illumi-
nated only by smudges of moonlight glowing in the portholes. There was a built-in refrigerator and a table, a slab of
wood on plastic legs. Underneath the table, a jumble of
cables and tubes lay coiled and abandoned, wrapped in a
ragged old blanket. At the far end of the cabin, below the
front window, was a panel with twin engine controls and a
steering wheel of gleaming chrome edged in white by the
moon. Under the controls was a narrow hatchway door. It
was from the far side of this door that the sound came again.
Thump! Louder now. *Thump! Thump!*

He squatted in front of the hatchway. What was this—a
dog? From inside came a muffled noise . . . a voice. "Mmnf.
Hngh!"

At last Shelly understood: the captive was trapped in the
sleeping quarters, in the nose of the boat. Kneeling beneath
the control panel, Shelly tugged at the door, twisting a knob
over the handle and lifting while he pulled, until it gave—
opening onto a dark crawlspace with a gleaming protuberant
eye in its center.

The eye turned, shucking the light, blinking into darkness.
A round disk of plastic—the scuba mask. It took Shelly a
moment to make out a figure behind it, dressed in a black
rubbery skin that covered body and head so that only the
circle of glare showed in the dim light when the faceplate
turned toward the moonlight. In front of the mouth was a
plastic breathing apparatus connected to air hoses, so that
the only part of the actual face Shelly could identify was a
pencil-thin mustache between mask and mouthpiece. Shelly
stood in the open door, blocking most of the light, confronting the gaze of the plastic mask, its blankness matching his
own. Behind the plate he thought he saw a flutter, as of eyes.

"Freddie?"

The frogman shrank against the interior hull, hugging the
curve of the bow and disappearing into a black gulf of
shadow. Then, unexpectedly, a pale hand flashed—a wave?
No, the man was beckoning Shelly to step from the doorway,

inviting him into the narrow crawl space. Shelly hesitated, unwilling to cede control of the accessway, unsure what danger lay in the darkness ahead of him. But he felt a warm hand close on his wrist as the frogman reached forward and tugged.

Shelly clung to his post in the doorway. "What do you think you're doing?"

The frogman yanked at him, harder.

Shelly smacked the man's hand, bracing his own feet against the frame. "Let go of me!"

The frogman let go, dropping Shelly's arm with a shrug and moving back into the shadows. And then, the most peculiar thing: he curled himself into a ball, drawing up his legs, and covering his face and his head with his black rubber arms.

"What the hell are you doing—" Shelly began, but never got a chance to finish.

Because at that moment he sensed rather than saw a flash of bright yellow over his shoulder and felt a searing burst of heat in the muscles of his back. Then there was a pause and, as if from a distance, a *boom* so loud and insistent it rolled over him like a cloud, rattling his bones and organs, until the tiny cilia lining his lungs vibrated in rhythmic sympathy. The portholes suddenly shattered, and cold bay water poured into the cabin, filling the narrow space between the door and the place where the table had been standing. Only now its legs were gone. The brown-painted plastic supports had turned to columns of red liquid, wavering an instant before buckling under the mass of laminated wood.

The tabletop came sliding directly at him, as if in slow motion. He wondered vaguely if he had time to duck, in an instant of heightened awareness that allowed him to perceive what was actually occurring in microseconds of physical law.

In the micros before he was hit.

The tabletop crashed into him like a missile, with the force of its mass multiplied by the acceleration of the explosion beneath it. It caught him full across the chest, midway, where he heard a crunch before the weight bore down on him. As if the flash of a bulb had frozen in time, yellow turning incrementally to white, the cabin filled with brightness. And then there were no boundaries, the outside rushing in with a roar as he stumbled and then fell to his left, ear and cheek and mouth and nose—disappearing into the ink.

3

As soon as Homer Greeley saw his partner's pale body drift backwards past the stern of their boat, when it should have been striking forward past the bow toward the motor launch at the pier, he knew it had been a mistake to allow Shelly to make the trip. He was himself a far stronger swimmer, as he was a better sailor, runner, and all-around athlete—better, in fact, at most things that called for a sound body and mind. Not that there was really anything wrong with Shelly's mind—it was just quirky and rather cluttered, straying too often from the task at hand, misled by some incidental of the human condition. The clear, straight line from the fact to its corollary pleased Homer immeasurably. His partner's erratic style of thinking, which paused to take in the complexity of what passed for personal interest, made a clean, simple case horribly ambiguous. Take this one.

Shelly was supposed to swim directly to the launch—so what was he doing back behind the rudder, kicking up so much foam? Why not follow the straightest line from their sailboat to the pier? And why would he go over and under each crest instead of swimming clear through the lower part of the waves? Now was not the time to be showing off, if that was his intention. And where did he get that bathing suit? Which did nothing at all for him, of course, black against his milky skin, almost blue now in the moonlight. Still, Homer supposed it did make a fashion statement, by Shelly's standard, at least. Better than polka dots, he supposed, though a far cry from Homer's idea of a well-dressed detective at the beach.

He flipped on the ship-to-shore and put in a radio call to the coast guard station at Long Beach. They should be listening on his frequency; that was their arrangement with the captain. He picked up the microphone, depressed the button along the side with his thumb, and enunciated in a crisp, clear voice, "This is Handsome Harry, on the rigger *Houndstooth*, calling for Uncle Mac. Come in, Mac."

A woman's voice replied from the station. "Your uncle's in the can, *Houndstooth*. What's the word?"

"Looks like we might've found Little Bo-peep, in a motor launch about twenty miles east of you." He read their position off the compass, repeating it into the radio.

"Copy, Handsome Harry. Will relay, soon as the conference is over. Need any help on the dockside?"

"Couldn't hurt. And there's no way to know the shape he's in. Better send a medical unit."

"One Master Dragon and a few foot soldiers. Roger, wilco, Harry. Just tell me something." She paused, her voice softening in the static. A transition of emotional terrain—but from what to what positions? There were signs everywhere, Homer realized. He was just no good at reading them.

"What's that?"

"Are you really that handsome, Harry? That's what the girls on the first shift say. They saw you boys come in."

Now, how was he supposed to answer that? "You should know better than to believe whatever you hear, Aunt Sheila. Over and out."

He hung up the microphone, flicking off the radio with a rush of relief. He had escaped—but from what peril,

23

exactly, he wasn't sure. To avoid thinking about it further, he strolled to the place on the deck where Shelly had gone over. There was a pile of clothing at the edge, where Shelly had shucked what he was wearing like the wrinkled skin of a snake. The whole story of their partnership was there for the discerning eye, thought Homer, frowning as he squatted alongside the sloppy pile to fold each article of clothing. On top was the shirt, a cheap broadcloth with dark stains under the arms and around the neck. Shelly's tie was still looped through the button-down collar, a square-bottom knit in a loose brown weave that had dropped from the tie scene years before. The glasses were round wire-rims of unadorned aluminum; the trousers, in a nondescript beige wool, creased everywhere except down the front. Shelly wore these with a corduroy jacket whose brown wale had been flattened and faded so long it had picked up a tannish sheen. Last but not least, those brown leather shoes—the least appropriate for a day on board, with heels that scuffed the fiberglass, and soles that squeaked in the spray.

Homer wondered again how he managed with a partner like Shelly beside him when they stepped into a room. What did it do to his own look, he wondered, to be paired with such a companion? When they entered a bar, for example, did the bad guys take in his sharp threads and then lean over and nudge one another at the clashing combination at his side? Not that Shelly didn't have his good points as a cop, or in an interview, say. He was pretty quick with questions, Homer had to admit, that somehow elicited screwy answers —which opened up new avenues of inquiry for a more systematic mind, like his own. Shelly was strong on motives, too, which were not exactly Homer's own forte. But now, with nothing of Shelly on hand but his clothes, it was harder for Homer to judge for sure which way the balance swung. He looked over the bay toward the power boat and the pier, trying to make out his partner.

The binoculars were in the stern of the boat, where Homer had perched at the tiller. He settled again into his seat, fitting the binoculars to his eyes. The boat looked about thirty-two feet, twin engines, dual controls. The name in cursive script on the stern: the *Little Louisa*. A pleasure craft, as the ads called them—or a hobby boat, as Homer usually did. Probably went a mile on a gallon of gas.

Then he saw it—a white back heaving over a rise of black, surging toward the dock. It was hard to tell whether Shelly was riding the wave or the wave was riding him. Homer decided to bring the sailboat in for a closer look. Gripping the tiller, he sat forward, leaning his weight against it. Through the dark night, despite an unpredictable wind, he managed to move toward the boat, nosing in toward the docked boat with a casual, seamanlike turn. Skill—that was the important thing, whether in handling a boat on a choppy night or closing a police file. Anyone could get lucky, stumbling on a personal motive or an unearned confession. What Homer admired was method, the well-reasoned procedure that would narrow the scope of any inquiry, regardless of luck or happenstance. Like sailing a boat in the direction of choice, instead of simply riding before the wind. That was what Shelly was too willing to do—drift along with the current. As if in confirmation, his partner's pale figure was lifted up by a swell of the sea and carried away from the dock.

Homer watched Shelly struggle until he threw himself over the edge of the motor craft, climbing painfully up, where he flopped like a tuna onto the deck. Just what did he have in mind now—to wait for someone to find him? Why didn't he scramble on all fours, hustle over to the cabin door and burst in on whoever was inside? If he moved quickly and took them by surprise, he could probably handle two before the others were able to react. The others—could Shelly deal with the others, too, even if he kept his wits about him and his rhythm clean?

Homer would have had no trouble himself, given the edge of surprise. He would have slipped aboard in the cry of a gull, moving toward the cabin door silently, inexorably.

Whoever was trapped below would have been his, alone. Homer imagined his own penetration of the craft and turned up his nose at the image of Shelly's fishy arrival.

And yet Shelly managed, as he always did. He lay for two or three minutes, recovering on deck, then made his slow way to the cabin door, which opened without a struggle. Homer leaned over the gunwale of his sailboat, angling for a look, but couldn't see into the frame of the cabin doorway. So who was inside there, anyway? They couldn't have left Freddie alone, bound and gagged in the cabin. But then why wouldn't Shelly have come out again, signaling across the water for him to draw near? Homer waited, watching the closing cabin door for signs of a struggle or discovery. He edged his own boat closer, fighting the wind, which blew now increasingly cold. It took attention and skill to hold it in place. And still no hint from the cabin across the bay, of any action or reaction. Shelly had disappeared for nearly three full minutes by then. What were they doing in there—singing sea chanteys?

And then, as if in answer, a sudden eruption rocked the quiet bay, overloading Homer's senses. A blinding flash—pure yellow, it seemed, or white hot, blinding his eyes for a full two minutes before they readjusted to the moonlight. And the noise: louder than a cannon, a rocket blasting off, echoing across the bay, first from the houses on the shore, and then again from the promontory at the land's end, where a lighthouse blinked over the sea. Homer smelled powder, a stink of sulfur in the yellow smoke that billowed from the cabin of the launch. When he could see again, the inlet was afloat with half the insides of the boat at the pier, chunks of beams and wooden utensils and empty beer cans. And the power launch at the pier showed a gaping hole in its side through which it was taking on water and pouring half its innards into the bay. Homer screwed his eyes to the binoculars, scouring the wreckage, until he thought he saw amid the flotsam and jetsam a flash of milky white in a patch of black seawater, which could have been the arm of a form, supine, mouth open, rolling under the waves.

Shelly.

In a single move, Homer grabbed a preserver from the center of the sailboat and leaped over the side. As his powerful strokes carried him through the floating kitchen utensils, he collided once with an overturned pot and again with a splinter of fiberglass. A laminated tabletop passed like a shark, three-quarters under the surface, and behind it Homer saw the body. From a distance, it had been hard to make out, but when he drew near, Homer could distinguish the pale back and black trunks rolling in the waves. The sight had an unexpected effect on him: Homer found himself shouting out "Oho!" though no one could have heard him. It was a break in his usually cool reserve that scared him as much as the body did. He dived, forcing the life preserver under his partner's limp arm, rising again to the surface, where he turned the head to one side so the mouth cleared the surface, resting on one floppy arm.

Shelly was unconscious—at least. But there was nothing Homer could do to revive him then. As he slapped the lifeless cheeks without result, odd expressions began to flit through his mind. Dead as a doornail. Out like a light. Cold as a sea cucumber. There was a certain grim humor in all of them, he saw, that had never before struck him funny. Their only real hope—Shelly's only hope—was if Homer could bring him quickly enough to a warm, dry place and squeeze a little life back into him.

So where exactly were they in the drink? Too far away from the sailboat and too far below the pier. Homer's patience, which was legendary on a stakeout, couldn't tolerate the feeling of helplessness: it made him angry—at Shelly, at the launch, at Freddie Santino, and the blinding flash that had blown up in their faces. He treaded water, fighting off a rising tide of panic in his throat. If he tried for either one and failed to reach it, he would have to choose between abandoning his partner to the mercy of the waves or going down himself. The idea of his own death occurred to Homer for the first time, and it was not a thought he enjoyed entertaining. But which way to try for a rescue? The dock, so near, but so far above? Or the sailboat, floating out beyond the waves? Homer spit seawater in disgust. He had never liked ambivalence much, either.

Then the whine of a siren on the shore and a flashing red light summoned new hope in him. His radioed call to the coast guard, relayed to the captain on shore, had brought help, near at hand, on the beach. He had only to tow Shelly as far as the shore, though it seemed to recede even as he turned his head to face it. An ambulance bumped down the road. There it was: the end of his uncertainty—someone else to make the decisions.

He swam behind the life preserver and pushed against the waves which were now perversely pulling them out to sea in an unwelcome turning of the tide. There was nothing, of course, to prop his legs against; he could only kick back for leverage. But this was the kind of struggle Homer understood: you tried until you succeeded. By the time he had hauled the life preserver in to a depth at which he could stand, he heard tires crunch the sand close to the waterline and saw flashlight beams cross the waves.

"Over here!" gasped Homer, waving one hand, gripping his partner's hair with the other. They heard him; the beams converged. Shouts, and the splashing of a wader. Homer felt his own legs wobble beneath him. His right knee buckled as two men in windbreakers elbowed past him, lifting Shelly away. Homer marched behind them, plowing through the surf with the front of his thighs as his calves tingled with cold. His muscles were painfully tight, sore and chafed and raw. The headlights had multiplied, and men swarmed over the beach. Seaweed and water seemed to reach for his knees, grappling for his ankles as he climbed up onto the sand.

"Are you all right?" someone asked, throwing a blanket over his shoulders. Old and scratchy, it smelled of dog—a warm, sweet odor. He hugged it around him like a cashmere robe. People moved about in the darkness, wraiths, from the cars on his left, where a radio crackled, to the bright black bay behind him. He did not turn to face the water again. A station wagon was parked nearby—no, better still, an ambulance. Two men were crouched on the ground in front of it, kneeling in the sand. Below them was a third: Shelly, of course, who heaved and vomited water. Eyes closed. They pressed down on his ribs again, forcing out the sea, until something interrupted them, and they lifted him onto a gurney and rolled him into their vehicle.

"Come on," said a man in a blue woolen coat who took Homer by the shoulders. "Can you make it into the seat?" Homer began to resist until he understood he was to ride with them in the front cab of the ambulance.

"Of course I can make it," he planned to say, but his tongue couldn't form the words. It felt swollen with sea salt, and seemed to fill most of his mouth. He nodded, trying to show his well-being, while the man in blue wool shoved him by the elbow through the passenger door and climbed into the seat after him. In the back, the rear door slammed— they had loaded Shelly's stretcher inside. The siren started to scream, and Homer stared back blankly out the window, where silhouettes of men against the moon-white bay went wading among bits of boat.

Homer did not want to look there. He turned away with a shiver, unwilling to meet the eye of the moon, as if the long hand of the sea might reach out and haul him back. The sailboat still rocked on the black water, there, with their clothes and both of their weapons. But even those were not his concern now; other men would think about them. Homer sank back against the vinyl seat cushion as if it were feathery silk. He closed his eyes for a moment, remembered the limpness of Shelly underwater, and opened them again with horror. It surprised him to discover the strength of his feelings for Shelly, and provided a strange comfort. Maybe there was more to their partnership than he had given credit. He would have to check it out when they worked together as a team again. Which they were sure to do soon . . . if Shelly survived the ride to the hospital.

The thought made Homer remember that he had called for the ambulance for somebody else. What had become of Freddie Santino, or the man who had been loaded onto the launch? He sat forward and managed to croak, "Freddie—"

The man in the blue coat eased him back into the seat cushion. "Sit back, Sergeant. There's nothing we can do for him now."

The man glanced back into the rear of the ambulance, and Homer wondered whether he thought they had been talking about Shelly. He sat up again with a rising sense of panic. He had to explain—they needed to warn the other men still at the waterline to keep an eye peeled for Freddie. But the words were stuck in his throat. He pushed off the hands of the man beside him, struggling to communicate the urgency. But there wasn't time to shout or even to gesture before Homer felt a sharp stab in his right arm and saw a hypodermic needle pierce his flesh.

The liquid in the syringe was cool, and he was eased back into the seat cushion. He blinked as the avenues of Long Island rushed past the window in front of him, a speeding parade of homes protected by walls and stately hedges, with closed circuit television cameras mounted behind them. He leaned over a lap toward the window on the passenger side, which was halfway open. An affluent breeze crossed immaculate lawns. Privacy and comfort. In the driveways, he saw long blue cars with tinted windows. Overhead, the red glow of a stoplight was painful in his eye. He turned his head and saw a blur of mercury vapor, pink at the side of the road. Streetlights. Linked together with strands of cotton candy.

The man in blue reached forward, lifting his heavy eyelids. Homer met his professional scrutiny. He saw the man murmur to the driver, who nodded and accelerated. The hem of his coat gleamed with water.

And then he saw nothing more.

4

Shelly opened his eyes in a field of cool whiteness, taut against his left cheek and softer on his right. In his left ear he heard his breathing, an incredible sound. If he was still doing that, he was still alive. To what he owed that miracle, he hadn't the slightest idea. His last memory was the sound of rushing water as the blackness engulfed him. The aches in every sinew and synapse of his body provided all the proof he needed: it hadn't been a dream; he had come that close to death. There it was, the Big D, its wings beating close enough for him to grab a pinion. Couldn't have missed him at that range. So what happened? Its claws must have dropped him somehow, since the pressure of the sheet on his grizzled cheek told him he was evidently back among the living.

He felt a momentary sense of perverse disappointment when he realized he had seen none of the sights usually reported by watchers of that particular bird: his life hadn't flashed before his eyes and he'd seen no great blue light overhead. Maybe you had to get even closer, he thought, and experienced a warm flush of relief that he hadn't.

A shudder ran through his back, where the muscles ached

from spasms. Keep at it, boys, he thought. Keep those lungs pumping. The effort to regain control took most of his attention for the next couple of minutes. Then he blinked, trying to focus his eyes, and became aware of a powerful beast crouching on his chest. He breathed a few times, hoping to disturb it, but it just rode out the breaths. He ought to see what it was, he thought, which meant sitting up. Or at least moving his arms. They were still there, at least, connected to his shoulders—he could feel them ache to his wrists. All he had to do was stir, say, his elbows, and that would move the rest. He concentrated on his unseen elbows, trying to inch them up—and discovered something attached.

"Sergeant Lowenkopf?"

The voice came from beyond the soft white on his right, which was lifted—a pillow. From behind it, a woman in a white lab coat looked down at him. She was in her fifties, about five feet tall, with a stern, capable face. Beyond her, three others crowded around, all of them about twenty years younger than she, though equally serious, with a broad range of sympathy in their expressions. On the left was a square-shouldered woman with cropped brown hair and no makeup, who held herself aloof by tilting back her head five or ten degrees from the perpendicular. Next to her was a kid of about twenty-four with thin black hair and a delicate mouth, whose grin suggested he might just have whispered a sly remark to the redhead on his left. She didn't seem to appreciate it—her soft green eyes swept tenderly over Shelly, their sight lines crossing and somehow missing the point at which he would have come into focus. He felt a sudden need for his own glasses—*one* of them should've been able to make out the other. He didn't have them, of course, having stowed them safely in his shirt pocket, on the sailboat. He stirred and felt the powerful confinement of the sheet across his waist.

His movement was an event: the woman in front smiled slightly, lifting her brows in a show of professional kindness, and parallel curves creased the foreheads of her junior colleagues.

"Are you awake?"

She spoke with accustomed authority—firm tones, hinting at a dry humor and a quiet, self-possessed reserve. Lowenkopf raised his arm to gesture, but it was attached to a tube by an intravenous needle in the crook of his elbow.

"Uhhhnnmmm." He had meant to say, *I think so, thanks,* but it whispered out as a groan.

"Good." The woman in command nodded to her companions. There was an incredibly loud beeping in his ears, regular as an electronic faucet left dripping somewhere: *doop DOOP doop DOOP doop DOOP doop DOOP . . .*

"How's your chest?"

"Hhnngmm?"

The woman pressed lightly on his solar plexus. Her fingers were dry and warm. "Here. How does it feel?"

He paused, collecting his breath, before trying again to explain, "Unghgh ligh ungelighann—"

"Under like an elephant. I know," she said. "You have a fractured sternum—the little bone in the center of your chest, right in front of your heart. There is some indication of a myocardial contusion—that's a bruise on the heart. It can give you an irregular rhythm, like a heart attack."

DOOP doop DOOP doop . . .

Lowenkopf wasn't sure what was expected from him at that point—approval of the diagnosis or silent acceptance. He opted for the latter, since it required so much less movement.

"My name is Dr. Freylung—Margaret Freylung," the senior woman said. "I admitted you to the ICU last night."

"Dnnnghsss . . ."

"You're welcome. Dr. Goodman, Dr. Haight, and Dr. Ashbury will be looking in on you for me from time to time."

Moving his eyes from one to the other was painful for Shelly, but he did it as a politeness, in acknowledgment.

"Are you comfortable?"

He turned his head incrementally toward the gizmo at the foot of his bed, which seemed to be making the *doop*s. The woman followed his eyes.

"Like us to turn off that racket, I'll bet. Can't do it, Sergeant Lowenkopf. That's your heart."

That sound was his heartbeat? So then the silences between the sounds were what you really had to watch out for, the times it wasn't beating. He listened to a couple of *doop*s, anxiously awaiting the next.

"Do you need anything?"

"Ngmmgn glngssns," he said.

"Your glasses. Of course. We have them—recovered with your clothing, safe and unbroken. But I don't think you'll be needing them just yet."

Dr. Freylung gave him a smile of resolute courage, concluding the interview. She turned her back, and two of the others followed her to the door, but the redhead hesitated, looking back instinctively at Shelly just as he pursed his lips to say something more. She moved toward him, taking up the place Dr. Freylung had occupied, and whispered anxiously, "Was there something else?"

He hadn't realized he had moved his lips, but the evident compassion in her expectation deserved to be rewarded. There was a pleasant lilt to her voice, too—a trace of Texas. The drawl had been educated out of her, but an unexpected rhythm in her intonation made him think of horse auctions and yellow roses. He forced his head to nod a fraction, and when she bent closer, said, "Ungh pssskgrd."

A bell-shaped crevice separated her brows as she thought about what she had heard. "A passkey? You won't be needing anything like that—at least until you move out of Intensive Care. Dr. Freylung has arranged a room for you in the step-down ward on the third floor. That's just across the bridge from where our labs are, in the research annex. But you won't need any personal keys upstairs, either."

Shelly shook his head. This was going to be harder than he thought. "Ngmah pppngs pkkkah. Bahm khghm."

Dr. Ashbury glanced back toward the door, but Freylung and the others had already passed into the hall. She moved closer, one hand reaching for her mouth, and he thought he saw a tear form in the corner of her eye. He gave her his most encouraging grimace and she drew a deep sigh. "Bomb come? I don't know who has come to see you yet, though I don't think anybody's brought an explosive. But that's not really what you were trying to say, is it?"

He shook his head and a wooziness spread over him, as if he had stirred the painkiller in his veins. "Bahm khghmmm."

"Bomb *come*," she repeated, emphasizing the second syllable. "That's what you meant. Let's see, then—who has come? Your sister has been here, from the beginning. Your son, too. And a woman who calls herself his mother . . . ?"

Shelly nodded painfully. Ruth was always careful with distinctions. He could imagine the chill in the waiting room, with her on one side and Isabelle on the other.

Dr. Ashbury, encouraged by his gesture, went on, "There have been lots of people stopping by, from the police department and so on. But I'm not sure it would be such a good idea for you to speak to any of them right now."

Shelly shook his head again, and the effort hurt his chest. "Ngmah pkkkah . . . psskgrd."

"Yes, I know—*psskgrd*," she said miserably. Then, with a sudden lightening of her tone, she jotted a note on her clipboard and clutched it to the front of her coat. "It should come to me, sooner or later. We'll just have to keep an eye out until then, won't we?"

He did his best to smile as she covered him with a sheet of clear plastic attached to the top of his bed. An oxygen tent? He took a few sample breaths, felt the sharp, cold gas in his nostrils, and allowed his eyes to close.

In minutes he was dreaming about a desert sheikh, thrusting his curved scimitar through Shelly's heart.

When Captain Madagascar walked in on Homer Greeley, the blond detective was sitting up in the hospital bed, reading a report of the evidence collected two nights before in their assault on the *Little Louisa*. It was all there, just as he remembered it: the bits of fiberglass, wooden kitchen utensils, the cabin tabletop. . . . And that was what he found so curious.

The captain's expression mixed exasperation and pride as he reached forward and removed the report from Greeley's hands—just the sort of problem he'd expect from a cop like Homer. "Doctor says you're not supposed to be doing that kind of thing for a few days."

"What kind of thing?"

"Police work."

Greeley grunted. If he wasn't supposed to do police work, what the hell was he supposed to be doing the next few days? He had taken a shock to his system—all right, the system needed some time to recuperate. Which it was more likely to do with a little light detective work than scrunched up in an armchair watching old reruns of "Perry Mason."

The captain should have understood, given the single-mindedness of his own preoccupation. It was something the two men had in common: lives that centered around their jobs. It wasn't just that there wasn't much else to them—there wasn't much else to Shelly's life either, but that never seemed to lead him to the conclusion that police work *belonged* at the center of it.

There were always other concerns, other business, intruding between Shelly and a clear, untroubled focus on the case at hand. It usually had something to do with family, or with girlfriends—with *love* in one of its many guises. Homer's patience, which was bottomless on a stakeout, ran out quickly when it came to the heart. It wasn't that he didn't have emotions of his own, Homer reassured himself regularly; it was just that he couldn't stand to make a federal case of each one. Shelly seemed to live and breathe by his feelings and gut impulses. If he *felt* that a suspect was innocent or guilty, he'd ignore a mountain of real data to the contrary. That was why Homer found it so distressing when Shelly was right—not always, but too damned often.

The captain was his kind of cop, in the end: a professional, full-time clue-chewer. He ought to have understood, then, what "off duty" meant to a man like Homer, who punched his ticket but never clocked out his mind when they were assigned to a case. Madagascar stood at the foot of the bed, chewing the edge of his mustache. He must have understood . . . but he cleared his throat, pulled his shorts from the crack of his ass, and wagged his square head. "My instructions from the medicos are to keep you off active duty for a couple of days. So that's what we're gonna do. You can man a desk in the office, if you want."

Greeley knew better than to drive the captain more firmly into a position by trying to change his mind. Without a word, he reached over and recovered the report, Madagascar releasing it rather than engaging in a tug-of-war with a bedridden policeman. Greeley propped it on his lap, but before opening it, said, "It's all right if I think about the case, isn't it? That shouldn't strain me too much."

The captain shrugged. "Haven't you got anything better to think about? Or anything else to do?"

"Like what?"

"I don't know—go fishing. Take a vacation. Visit an aunt somewhere."

What the two men knew between them about taking a vacation could have been written on the front of an Easter seal, and there would still have been room for the hallelujah. But the idea of a visit made Homer think of Shelly, whom he knew he should look in on sooner or later. Which meant, at the moment, later. "How's Shel?"

"Lowenkopf? All right—they still want to watch his heart. They're moving him out of Intensive Care today. I'm putting you in for medals, you know. Both of you—him for getting wounded in the line of duty, and you for saving his life."

The phrase struck Homer's ear like a poisoned dart, and he felt a warm sensation sink through him. He hadn't really thought of himself as having saved Shelly's life, with all the responsibility that entailed. If Homer hadn't found his partner's pale body in the wreckage of the power boat, Shelly's life would have ended there: so in everything he did from that point forward, Homer had a share of the credit or the blame. The realization made him woozy—he tilted forward, catching himself just before he needed to be caught.

The captain cocked an eyebrow, fidgeted, and scrutinized Homer carefully when he sat upright. "Are you sure you're ready to leave this place?"

"Absolutely!" insisted Greeley, casting about him for the call button to ring for the nurse. "If it weren't a hospital rule, I'd skip the wheelchair ride out of here and beat a hasty retreat under my own steam."

Hardly had he pressed the button than the biggest orderly Madagascar had ever seen entered the room, pushing an empty wheelchair. His hair was cut in a military crew, and his lab coat was bursting across his chest, where spaces between his buttons showed the red and black stripes of his T-shirt.

"As you can see," said Greeley as the orderly picked him up and dropped him into the wheelchair, "they're not taking any chances with me, anyway."

Homer could see that Madagascar was trying in his awkward way to find something of solace to say. He rubbed his shoe on a leg of the bed, gripped and then released the side restraint bar when it wobbled in his hands. "Well," he grumbled finally, "at least you're still around to complain about it. Freddie Santino wasn't so lucky."

Homer was lying in wait for that. "I'm not sure, Captain,"

he said quietly, rustling the report under his elbow. He would have preferred to put off this talk until they were alone, in the captain's glass-paneled office at the Allerton Avenue precinct house. But if Madagascar was serious about taking him off active duty, he wasn't likely to get that chance—or any chance, after this one.

The captain's brow wrinkled. But he could hardly resist a teaser like that. He knew that the blond detective didn't speak through his hat; if Greeley thought he'd found something, it was bound to be worth hearing. And yet he hesitated, evidently in an effort of conscience on behalf of the invalid. Yet Homer saw his comment eat at the man's resolve. Madagascar said nothing while they made their way down the hall. At the elevators, however, while the three men stood waiting beneath the glowing red call light, the captain set down Greeley's mildewed bundle of clothes and squatted beside his wheelchair. "Why aren't you sure?"

Homer responded as quickly as if the conversation had been continuous, from the first sly comment to the question it evoked. "Because there were no bits of rubber floating in the wreckage. Shelly and I saw two men drag a third, disguised in a wet suit, onto that boat. He never climbed back on the pier. So where are the scraps of black rubber? And the plate of his face mask? Not to mention the parts of his corpse."

"Couldn't it all have been blown to bits by the explosion?" wondered the captain. "There was one hell of a cloud of smoke going up, and the ambulance driver heard the blast more than half a mile away."

"It was noisy," agreed Greeley, "and I would've thought the same thing myself—nobody should've survived that blast. Except for one thing: Shelly was aboard that boat, remember? And we know what happened to him."

Madagascar nodded. Without losing a beat of its rhythm, he asked, "What happened to him?"

"Well, he's banged up, of course. But he's still in one

piece, isn't he? Instead of all over the bay? That was the surprising thing to me, after all the noise, Captain—that Shelly came out of there with all his parts intact."

"So the diver—"

"Couldn't have been blown to bits, could he? Not if he was in that cabin with Shelly."

Either way, but not both: if the blast was powerful enough to scatter all traces of the diver, Lowenkopf should never have survived. But if it was not quite as destructive as it sounded, where on earth was the diver? Madagascar chewed it over until the bell announcing the elevator rang. As the door opened, the captain said, "So, if he wasn't blown to bits, where do you think he went?"

"The frogman?" asked Greeley offhandedly as the orderly swung him around and backed his wheelchair through the open door, and the passengers cleared a space in the center. A resident in the back row refused to be dislodged until the orderly shoved him unceremoniously aside.

"Who else?"

"To see the fishes."

The captain mused a moment too long and nearly missed stepping onto the elevator after them. He bent over the chair, his mouth forming a question. But the car was too full of passengers, who watched the three new riders with ill-concealed interest. Homer looked up and read the lines of consternation as a series of new questions crossed his boss's face.

He crossed his hands in his lap, over the report. And felt confident that his sick leave was over.

5

Chester Gafarian received two calls on Wednesday morning. The first had been routine for a man in his line of work: a corpse to dispose of, unexpectedly acquired—something he could handle by himself. But the second call was bad news, serious business, and he sank back into his chair, deciding how to manage it.

Chester Gafarian was a good middle manager. He had been a hardworking assistant to the plant manager of a mattress factory the day twenty-year-old Francis Santino stopped by to discuss an additional fire insurance policy. Chester had been nineteen, a dark young man in a soiled white shirt with bowed shoulders and a sunken chest, who had instantly respected the quiet composure of Francis's features, his steady eyes and straight nose and square, settled shoulders. Chester knew enough about clothing to admire the cut of Francis's sharkskin suit, and enough about extortion to recognize the deliberate politeness with which the offer was presented. Chester kept the factory books; by his figuring, the money Francis asked for would have been well spent, if it bought genuine safety for their persons and premises. And his personal impression of Francis Santino was that the man could deliver on his word.

The manager of the plant, however, a heavyset man named Bobby Engels, had failed to appreciate how sorely they needed the extra protection. Instead of sizing up the actual costs and risks involved, Engels made another assessment, sizing up Santino as an individual opponent in hand-to-hand combat. That, as it turned out, was the wrong assessment to make: the opportunity for personal conflict never arose. When the three men met to discuss Francis's offer, Chester didn't disagree with Engels. But the wrinkles of his brow must have revealed enough about his individual judgment to elicit from Santino an offer of alternative employment two weeks later, when the mattress factory burned to the ground.

Chester accepted it; all the diligence he had once lavished on mattresses he now invested in his new employer's enterprises. He spent the first six months learning the extortion business, and another six months figuring out how to improve it. Each of his minor adjustments in their bookkeeping system was warmly and financially appreciated. When he screwed up his courage to step forward with an idea to add personal injury insurance to the list of coverages offered by the company, he found a sympathetic listener in Francis. After all, he had said, not everybody had a place that could be burned down. When the idea paid off big among stockbroker types, Francis made him a friend.

That was how Chester thought about his relationship to Francis—a friendship, earned with trust. He was pleased with the way his own career reflected Francis's progress in the family business. He would not have called himself a lieutenant of the Santinos, since he had served in the United States infantry. He preferred the term "point man" when he led an operation such as this one: pointing out the weak spots, pointing out the strengths, pointing out the directions for the operatives. He was good at tactics, at personnel management, at coordinating efforts and expenses. Policy and strategy he left to Francis and the other silent men who gathered in his house.

Chester did not frequent the house as a matter of daily employment. His station was on Hempstead Turnpike, in the back room of a storefront florist between a bowling alley and a dry cleaner. The florist belonged to a delivery network; his phone calls came and went to every part of the city. There was a delivery van with a bright arrangement of roses painted on the side. The windows on the back doors were mirrored, it was true, but everyone knew how the sun wilted their merchandise. They double-parked anywhere for short periods of time. It was good to have a refrigerator for keeping things cold on occasions when they needed things on ice. And ready access to a wreath whenever they needed one—that was convenient, too.

Chester stroked his long face, the soft fuzz under his chin and the silky sideburns by his ears. Across the desk in front of him were spread the stock market pages of three local newspapers, with an intricate code of crosses and checks scribbled beside certain listings, charting Chester's observations of the performance of half a dozen tips. The stock market, he had realized three years before, was nothing but a wealthy man's racetrack. Instead of nags and jockeys, you had companies and CEOs, but the essential draw of both was the same. Only you didn't have to track down a bookie to collect on a winner, and stocks went up and down all day long. He was giving more and more of his time to it lately; as he sat there, he felt his eyes drawn to the change column, and pushed the paper away.

He allowed his heavy lids to close, considering his choices. How to deliver the bad news? There was always the possibility that the messenger would be confused by his message—it wasn't he, after all, who had fucked up the job on the boat. Anyone could tell that, plain enough, if they thought about it awhile. Prudence, it was true, suggested that he pass off the news to a runner. But prudence had not earned Chester the confidence of his friend, and he tapped his thin lips, considering his options. A delicate delivery might dispel some of the disappointment of the message itself—that would be better than redirecting it. He had to go see Francis himself.

When the second call came in, Chester's initial impulse had been to drive out to the house and deliver the news in person. But he wasn't looking forward to it. He hadn't looked forward to visiting the Santinos since the marriage —even earlier, actually, since the attempt on the old man's life. It had come in a local elevator: Salvatore had taken his wife Louisa for an X ray after she broke her hip, and they had walked into a wired elevator car on their way down. The bomb must have been in the control panel; Louisa must have pushed the Lobby button herself. The old man's luck had held, personally, though he sustained multiple injuries. His wife had not proved so invulnerable to violence. The blast had blown away half her face and neck.

It had taken old Sal more than two weeks to recover in the hospital—the longest time ever, which was a mystery, since he had in the past sustained far worse damage and recovered far more quickly. The mystery was solved on his recovery, when he returned to the Santino compound on the south shore of the Island with a blonde more than thirteen years his junior. Daphne Hardwick had been his nurse on the hospital ward, had seen him through the physical and emotional stress following the death of his wife, and had come home with him as his next spouse when he was well enough to return.

Chester didn't consider it surprising, in the end. The old man was still a charmer, in his way, a man who carried himself with evident power and authority. He was also a man who liked to be married, obviously, since he wasted no time in filling that position once it became available. Chester could understand that, too, imagining how he would live his daily life without Angelica in his kitchen and his bed. Who would prepare his dolmas, with lamb and beef wrapped in delicate grape leaves? Who would bathe him with a cloth before lovemaking? Who would dance with him at family weddings? No, Chester could understand why the old man wanted to be a husband again, and as quickly as possible. It was just Salvatore's choice of replacement that he questioned, as many people did—among themselves, of course.

Daphne Hardwick was a divorcée, for one thing, mother of two grown children. Her daughter Beth, studying pharmacology in Boston, refused to visit her mother's new home, choosing to believe some stories she had heard about her new relatives. Daphne's son, Eliot, two years older than Beth and slower to make moral judgments, seemed to believe his mother's remarriage opened up doors of opportunity for him; the way he treated his new stepfather suggested that he thought he'd hit upon the gravy train to the moon.

But the general uneasiness about Daphne went deeper than concerns about her children. The kitchen was her first target. Sally had to watch his heart, she announced, and banned sausage from the larder. The diet she preferred was intended for goats—bits of nuts and sticky grains and all kinds of grass. And she kept involving him in *things* all the time, activities he would never have considered. Walking, for example. Where was she going all the time, twisting her hips back and forth as she strolled around inside the compound? And then tennis: she paved the arbor at the top of the hill and installed a full-size court. Old Sally went along with her—you saw him now every morning all in white, thwacking those furry green balls around with Daphne, and sometimes with Eliot, too. It made a bad impression, Chester felt. For himself, he didn't care. But how did it look to other bosses, who drove onto the grounds and heard Sally squeaking around in shining white tennis shoes like a wrinkled Pancho Gonzales?

He wasn't going to see Salvatore, of course, but his own boss, Francis Santino. Francis took after his mother's family, the DeSotos, in tastes and temperament. In another family, he might have become a priest and joined a cloister; as a Santino, he lived in a house on the grounds, inside the same protective walls as his father. Francis once had spent almost all his time with his father. But the old man was leaving more and more responsibility to his son, as his attention fixed on his new wife. Francis still sought him out when decisions had to be made, but old Sal was showing less and less inclination to make them. So it was possible that Chester wouldn't be seeing Sally and Daph at all this trip—possible but unlikely, knowing Francis as well as he did. It was hard for some boys to say good-bye to their papas. Perhaps there was some alternative to stopping by himself into the continuing family drama? Gafarian heaved a sigh but saw no other way. This news had to be delivered in person. He jangled the keys in his pocket and headed out toward the back alley.

Near the parking lot door, Chester passed his wife's second cousin's son, Schnork, bundling bunches of new cut flowers into five dollar bouquets. He had a real flair for blending reds and yellows with white baby's breath, backing it all with delicate green leaves. It was good that someone could make a living that way, thinking about flowers. Not that the boy appreciated his position, of course—all he wanted was to get into the business. Chester had promised Schnork his shot, sooner or later. But the time had not yet come. He stuck a red carnation into his lapel and grunted at the boy, who was busy trying to slick down his hair but tipped his comb to Gafarian in a sign of respect.

Outside, in the parking lot, Chester found his one true love—or one of two, if the whole truth was known. In the garage at his home, under a custom-made tarp, was a '58 Thunderbird, a powder blue two-seater, which he drove only on sunny weekends. But parked in the shade of one wall of the lot, under a sign that read Reserved for C. Gafarian, was a 1963 forest green Delta 88, with power steering and brakes and windows—the most beautiful driving car in the world. A line from the front of the fender ran straight back to the rear, clear as a bullet line. He opened the lock on the driver's side with a thrill of expectation and settled into the vinyl seat, eyes closed. This moment—all his struggles and labor earned him this joy, and he accepted what he had won for himself. He turned the key and the engine purred. Ahhh . . . he allowed the soothing vibration to run up his spine from the floorboard and down his arm to the steering column. Then he clunked the transmission into gear and rolled out.

Gafarian enjoyed driving almost as much as dancing. Both required grace in coordination. After twenty minutes of gliding along broad avenues past neatly manicured, crisp green lawns, the Oldsmobile turned into an unmarked driveway, bumping down a stretch of asphalt until it came to a black iron gate. From here, fifty yards in from the street, one could see a wall of rough-hewn gray stone surrounding the property, twelve feet high and topped with the upraised tips of black iron spears. To penetrate the wall, a car had to pass the guard who stood inside the gate, examining by video camera all vehicles seeking entrance. Chester signaled to the guard, a man named Nick, who parted the sliding gate with a low electrical hum. Before the tail fins of the Delta 88 had cleared the gate, it began closing behind him.

There were three sizable houses on the grounds. The first, an unadorned gray two-story structure near the entrance road, housed a dozen single men who protected the larger house behind it from surprise frontal assault. In the larger house, made of moss-covered stone, the family of Salvatore dwelt in relative safety and comfort, enjoying from their hilltop a view that crept down to the sea. If, however, instead of passing the lower house, a car turned sharply right, following the road along the nearer edge of the wall, the driver would see another two-story dwelling, decades newer, built of long planks painted dull white. This was Francis's house, reflecting in its bleached aesthetic his Spartan view of beauty in simplicity. He allowed no trim at the windows, no flowers in their beds, not even a trellis on the porch supports in front, where a lone man sat in a plain wood chair. The man stood, reaching into his gray sport jacket, as Chester parked in the gravel alongside the house, cut his engine, and climbed out.

He dawdled next to his car door, to give the man a chance to see who he was. When the guard's hand reappeared from his gray sport jacket, Chester called out, "Where is he?"

The man hesitated before speaking. "Who?"

"Who? Saint Francis, that's who. Up in the big house? Or inside here?"

The man blanched at the nickname. They all called him that, Chester knew, though out of earshot, of course. Using the name himself showed he knew what they were thinking; and the fact that he never repeated it to Francis showed them that Chester could be trusted. When the man on the porch worked it out, he shook his head, stuck his thumb toward the crest of the hill, and said, "Up by the tennis court."

Chester scowled—no escaping Daphne this time around. He took a handkerchief from his back pocket, wiped his neck in anticipation, and trudged up the hill.

When he reached the top, he heard the soft thwacks and the mumble of those who were watching the game. They were all there: old Sal and Daphne, tramping over the court, Francis watching from the bench alongside while Eliot sat next to him, calling out pointers to his mother and her husband.

"No! I told you—you've got to get the racket back earlier, Sal. Show him, Mom."

Whoosh! Daphne's racket swooped at the ball, sending it spinning over the net, bouncing onto the forecourt on Salvatore's side. He lunged forward, scooping it up before a second bounce, only to float it back to her forehand. She cracked it back at him, a clean, powerful shot, low over the net.

"Good! What do you think of that, Frankie?"

Francis grumbled vaguely in reply.

His stepbrother's discomfort went unnoticed by Eliot, who leaned forward on the bony knees sticking out of his shorts and directed, "Now, Mom, move to the net! You've got to remember to press your advantage."

Salvatore glanced at him, and Eliot clammed up as the fuzzy green ball sped between them, landing just inside the line and then leaping aside, squeezing into the links of the surrounding fence. Chester Gafarian was standing on the other side, waiting to be invited into the court.

"Come in, Chester," Francis said.

Daphne, bouncing the ball before her next serve, looked over and frowned. "Hello, Mr. Gafarian. Do you play?"

"Not tennis," replied Chester, taking a fat cigar from his jacket pocket and screwing it into his mouth as he crossed to Francis at the bench. He didn't light it—he knew Daphne wouldn't stand for that—but the presence of the unlit cigar was enough to deepen her frown, cheering up Francis perceptibly. Gafarian had a condescending sneer ready for Eliot, too, which he felt entitled to by the trouble Eliot had caused him, but the young tennis adviser never glanced over to receive it. Following Daphne's lead, he concentrated on Sally, who remained oblivious to the new arrival, rebalancing the racket in his hand. He drew back his arm, stiffening the elbow, stretched it forward and back again. Daphne served, Sally returned it, and Eliot clapped.

"That's showing him, Mom."

Chester leaned toward Francis. "Could I have a word with you in private?"

Eliot looked over, interested. But Francis gave him a look that said, Stick to your tennis, and Eliot's head snapped back to the game. The old man did not like to see them "bicker," as he called it, and had even had Francis find a job for Eliot as front man for one of the family's legitimate enterprises, but the effort at peacemaking had failed, as did all efforts when the gesture of conciliation was imposed from above. As Daphne's son, Eliot had the inside track at the moment; but Francis held real power in the family business, and Eliot feared him for it. He turned for comfort to his mother, who made every effort, after hours, to discredit Francis with Salvatore. Now Francis stood with a slight nod to his father and followed the squat figure of Gafarian off the court. Daphne watched their departure with ill concealed satisfaction.

"Ready?" she said.

Sally's racket flashed nylon and chrome.

Outside the fence of the tennis court, Francis led Chester around the crest of the hill to an overgrown garden on the slope. The leaves of tall tomato plants stood listing here, yellowing in the sun. Francis seemed comforted by the shadows of the plants, seating himself in the center of a low bench, so that Chester was left standing in front of him.

"You've heard something about Freddie?"

Chester nodded. He had planned to exercise delicacy, tact, whatever. But there was nothing to do but blurt it out. "The cops . . . think he survived the blast. They think he might've swum away from the boat."

Francis cursed under his breath, an indecipherable snort of Italian syllables more like a bellow than a sentence. "What makes them think so?"

"There was a cop on the boat when it blew."

Francis looked up sharply, his eyes narrowing. Chester had his sources—that was enough, if he put his own word on the line. Protecting his own ignorance was one of the things Francis paid Chester for. Francis allowed a few seconds to pass in unallayed silence. Then he nodded, examining the ground beneath his bench. A year ago his father had worked this patch. Now the plants were dying, while the air resounded with thwacks and then silence as someone on the court missed a return.

Chester waited, listening to sighs of the plants. The two of them were alone now. There was no reason for Chester to deny himself. He took a gold Zippo from his trouser pocket, flicked the wheel, and puffed on his cigar. The smoke filled his mouth and he forced it out through a tiny space at the side of his lips. That felt cool, and the click of the Zippo in the still afternoon was a rich, comforting sound. He opened and closed the cap a few times, just to hear the noise.

Francis reached down, pinching a bit of soil between his thumb and forefinger, letting it fall back in grains to the earth. He seemed to be turning over the new information in his mind, looking for a way around it. But there was none. "Freddie, Freddie," he sighed at last. "We'll have to do something about him, then."

Chester nodded, puffing.

Francis looked up, fixing on the glint of sun on Chester's golden Zippo. His brows narrowed in concentration as if running through all the options available to them. He seemed to arrive at a decision, but when he turned to Gafarian, the middle manager saw that Francis was no closer to a plan of his own than he ever managed to be.

"Any ideas?"

Chester was waiting for the opening. "I thought we might solve one problem with another. Do you know where they took that cop on Monday night?"

"To Jude South—eight miles down the road here."

"I got another of my ideas. But it might upset things a little in the neighborhood."

"You mean—"

Chester tilted his head toward the tennis court. "A bit of trouble on the home front."

Francis squinted, watching the golden rays. They heard the thwacks again, as another volley started on the court.

Perfect timing, thought Chester. Perfect.

Francis allowed the volley to end with a distant curse from Sally before giving the green light. "You know how I like to hear *ideas,* Chester, especially from you. What do you have in mind?"

Gafarian cranked the wheel, and a blue flame danced on his lighter. "What would you say to a painful recovery?"

6

Shelly Lowenkopf did not regain consciousness while he was lifted from his bed in the intensive care unit, transferred to a gurney, and wheeled to a bed on a ward upstairs between cardiac care and the research laboratories. This was the intermediate care unit, where tricky cases no longer requiring intensive care were watched, less continuously than in the ICU but by nurses whose experience with heart patients compensated for the decreased level of vigil. Shelly did not wake up as he was moved from the gurney to a bed in the semiprivate room. But he must have been aware of the change on some level of drugged consciousness, because a strange vision entered his head with the clarity of lived experience, the sharpness of its sensory detail piercing the gauze of his dreams.

It began as a floating sensation, as if his limbs had suddenly lost the mass of their drenching in the bay. He seemed to rise from the bed, ascending effortlessly to a position just below the suspended ceiling. Beneath him, in the darkened room, his own body lay tied to the bed by a white sheet covered with a mustard-yellow blanket. In the shadows across the room, another lump lay asleep, almost imperceptible in the dimness. At the windows, the curtains were drawn, admitting no light but the soft glow of buttons above his bed, where valves for oxygen and other gases stood ready for emergencies. There was absolutely no sense of emergency now, just a calm awareness of the fragility of life and the proximity of death.

He gazed around the room from that vantage point, and felt rather than saw two other specters floating beside him. They weren't visible, exactly, but appeared as darker smudges against the darkness of the room. Into his head an idea passed, with that tingling you feel in recognizing something you should have known all along.

You fellas . . . dead? He thought, rather than asked, the question, but the two others seemed to have no difficulty picking up the message.

Uhnnn-huhnnn, the nearer smudge moaned.

Then shouldn't you be, ah, moving along to someplace else? Shelly asked, making an effort to phrase the thought in his mind as politely as he could.

We'll wait a bit, said the other one, fading in and out of the corner behind him.

For what, exactly? Shelly wondered, control of his thoughts proving harder than he expected.

The nearer presence turned toward him, but no thoughts were forthcoming. And then a gray fuzz ball of dread filled his mind and he sat bolt upright in his bed.

Me?

Shelly felt the fuzz disperse, replaced by a dull throb collecting in his head. He was no longer asleep. The room was perfectly dark—darker by far than it had seemed in his dream. So it had been a dream, after all. He sat up against the headboard, waiting for his eyes to become accustomed to the dim light of the emergency buttons. It must have been the painkillers, he decided, that accounted for the sharp hallucination. And yet it had felt so *real*. A chill ran down his spine and he tried to force his eyelids to stay apart. But even his fear could not overcome the combined influence of stress and medication. Shelly slumped again into his pillows, struggling to remain aware while the soft black darkness overwhelmed him.

When Shelly opened his eyes again, the room was far less dark than it had been before. It was positively yellow, with honey-colored blankets and a lemon-colored ceiling and glints of brilliant sunshine beating at the windows. He had to blink twice to adjust his pupils, as a flood of other colors came rushing in behind: red flowers on green stalks in pots covered with glinting silver aluminum foil. From a curved metal track on the ceiling that ran three-quarters of the way around his bed, a curtain patterned with faded blossoms swung in the draft from the window. Each pale petal struck his eye with piercing clarity, as details of stamen and pistil, root and stem, etched themselves on his retina and the frail consciousness behind it.

He sat up, squeaking the springs of the bed, rocking in their gentle undulations while the veins in his temples banged like air-filled plumbing. To steady himself, he grabbed the curved aluminum rail at the side of his bed and concentrated on the oversize red petals of a cyclamen just about to wilt. Suddenly, with a violent metal screech, the curtain whipped back on its hooks and a strangely familiar, sympathetic voice cried out triumphantly.

"Postcard!"

A woman in a lab coat was standing in front of him, not a nurse—he knew that when he saw the stethoscope looped around her neck and into her breast pocket—but a doctor, probably a resident, he thought, judging by the chart she waved on a clipboard and by the late-thirties lines in her face. Soft red curls, authenticated by the matching shade of red in her arching eyebrows, self-bitten lips curving into a gentle smile—each feature echoed in Shelly's memory, though he could hardly have named or placed her. In one of his dreams, he seemed to recall a mistress witch attended by three faithful familiars, one of whom was named . . .

"Elaine Ashbury," said the woman in the lab coat,

sticking out her hand in an egalitarian offer to shake his. "I'm not sure if you remember me—I was one of the doctors who examined you in ICU on Tuesday . . . two days ago. Along with Margaret Freylung. You talked to me."

Shelly scrutinized her sea green eyes, looking for a sign he could recognize. She looked down, embarrassed, with a sly smile, and held up a card.

"I found this postcard folded around the comb in your pants pocket. Where you told me it would be. Remember?"

He swung his gaze over to the picture postcard in her hand, which showed a mosque embellished with mozaics. Mordred's cryptic warning note. A host of worries rushed back to him.

"She must be very important to you," Dr. Ashbury mused. As his eyes moved back to her face, she added quickly, "Not that I meant to pry, of course. But . . . it was so romantic. Fighting for your life in Intensive Care, with a fractured sternum and a bruised heart behind it. Well, I hope someday that some man asks for my letter then."

Lowenkopf had no recollection whatsoever of asking for Mordred's postcard. It seemed to him most unfortunate that the depressing thing had not found its way to the bottom of the bay. But here it was in front of him, miraculously unharmed, while his body had taken a beating from the relentless waves. He tried to toss it away, but the strongest gesture his hand would make was so slight that the postcard fell to the floor by the side of his bed, face down.

Dr. Ashbury picked it up, brushed it off, and replaced it in his hands.

"There! That should keep her in your thoughts! You know, I envy her, this Mordred. But in a way, I'm grateful to her, too. When a man feels as you do about a particular woman, the hearts of women everywhere tingle in sympathy."

Shelly managed a feeble smile, acknowledging her sympathy. What he really needed was a urinal, but an expanse of cold linoleum stretched impassably from his bed to the bathroom on the far side of the room. Dr. Ashbury noticed his gaze, evaluated his medical condition, and reached for a metal container with a long neck, hanging on the bed rail.

Shelly looked at the thing as if he had never seen one before, unable to meet her eye.

"It's a urinal," explained Ashbury cheerfully. "You use it instead of trooping all the way over to the—"

"I know," mumbled Shelly, seeing no alternative but to reach out to accept the proffered device. At least she wasn't waving it at him anymore. He set it down in his lap, tapping his thumb against the edge, waiting for her to leave.

"Don't you know how to use it? The long skinny part here goes—"

"I know," Shelly said again. It was difficult enough to hold on to his self-respect while a gown flapped open at his ass; to urinate under the young woman's watchful attention was more than could be expected.

"If you use it now, I can empty it," Ashbury coaxed. And then, responding to his hangdog look, she finally offered, "I can turn my back, if you prefer."

Her tone suggested it was in reality a perfectly ridiculous suggestion, but when he shrugged and said, "Maybe," she turned her back, crossing her arms and waiting, a yard from the foot of his hospital bed.

Shelly slipped the urinal under the blanket and did his best to squash every rumble and splash of liquid against aluminum. When he had finished, he offered the brimming vessel to Ashbury, who seemed to sense it behind her and turned to accept it.

"Now, isn't that better?"

Holding the container in her right hand, she reached over his bed with the left to recover the postcard, which had fallen into one of the folds of his blanket. For a moment Shelly thought she might spill its contents on his blanket. But she handled it skillfully, despite her concentration on the postcard. With an admiring glance for the mosque on the front, she set it upright on his night table by leaning it against his water pitcher.

He gave her a forced half smile in response, an expected demonstration of gratitude for her help with his personal habits. It wasn't much of a smile, really, but it lifted her spirits immediately.

"There we are! You see what a little picture postcard can do! The healing power of a loving heart! You're on the road to recovery, Sergeant. I can feel it."

Dr. Ashbury, evidently having satisfied herself with her contribution to his health, skipped out, urinal in one hand, clipboard in the other. Shelly turned his attention to the card on the night table, blowing at it repeatedly. It took all of the breath that was in him, but when the laminated cardboard finally fell forward onto its picture, he sat back against his pillow with a sense of real accomplishment.

There was a cough behind him, and a clearing throat.

"So the affair wasn't exactly everything the lady believes," a voice from across the room insinuated. "A tad less romantic, maybe. She dumped you, eh?"

Shelly looked over at the other bed and saw an elderly gentleman in striped pajamas propped on his pillows, regarding him through one screwed-up eye. The other lid was closed, as if in sleep, with no effort of the cheek required to keep it shut. A moment before, there had appeared to be nothing but a scrambled pile of blankets on the bed. Now the one good eye fixed him with a piercing glare from beneath a shabby thatch of white hair.

"I wouldn't say she dumped me, exactly," Shelly began, in a ridiculous defense of Mordred.

"No? Then what would you say happened? That she wandered off at the oasis for a camel hair coat?"

"I don't know what actually happened. But I'm guessing some sheikh noticed her, and—"

"Oho!" The geezer laughed noiselessly after his snort. "A sheikh led her astray. Let me tell you a story about a man with a horse. You got a minute for a story, don't you?"

It was hard for Shelly to insist he had some more pressing engagement. "Go ahead."

"I'm a taxidermist, see? At least I was before I retired. But one day I'm in my shop and this fella come dragging in. He looks like the saddest human being on the planet, by the redness of his eyes and the bags under them. I figure it's a pet job, you know? Stuffing Tabby or Fido. I was close. Only better.

"This man walks up to the counter and makes like he's gonna talk, but nothing comes out of his mouth—he's too choked up. So he lays this envelope on my counter and takes out a five-by-seven glossy of a horse, a beauty of an animal. Maybe six years old. The man gets a gander at the face and his eyes fill up with water again. He turns his head away, and when it comes back to face me he's worked up the courage to ask if I can save it.

"I could stuff it, of course, but that's not what he asked, is it? I can see that he's dying to lay his story on someone, so I give him the green light and ask why.

"So he tells me. It seems he and his wife have been having this little three-way thing with the animal in the photograph. But there was an understanding between them: neither would have sex with the horse without the other, too. One day the poor son of a bitch comes home to find his wife has broken their bargain. So what does he do? What any red-blooded male would do, given the same situation: he pulls out a gun from his dresser drawer and shoots the horse!

"Can't you just picture the scene? It's afterward—the horse and the wife are lying in bed together. Smoking. The guy comes in, sees them together, and pulls out his gun. The horse says, 'Now-w-w W-w-wilbur, it's not w-w-what you think!' The guy shuts his eyes and blows the beast away.

"Now what was the sense in that, exactly? Did he think the horse had seduced his wife? 'H-h-hey, baby, w-w-whadda w-we need your hubby for, anyw-w-way?' Of course not! Only to a guy, any guy in love, it's always the other guy's fault, not hers. His own gooey gumdrop would never do something like that, not to him! So he shoots the dumb animal."

Shelly clucked and shook his head.

"So what were you saying about that sheikh?" Before Shelly could find an answer, the old man's silent laughter racked him again. "Not so romantic as the doctor thought, now, was it, after all? Still, I suppose it was decent of you to say nothing and leave her illusions intact."

"I wasn't trying to be decent," Shelly said hoarsely, lacking the strength for a more vigorous protest.

"That's usually the time most people succeed," said One-Eye. "You take Ms. Sawbones, there—if you had thought about it, you would've realized you could've worked on her, turned her sympathy for the separated young lovers into something less distant but just as tender. And you mighta tried to do something not at all so decent."

Shelly thought about the tender look in her eye when Ashbury held up his postcard.

"You think so?"

The man laughed. "Didn't think of it, huh? Well, don't waste too much time regretting it, either. You woulda fucked it up, for sure."

Shelly leaned back into his own pillow. This was his roommate—an old man with a bitter laugh, whose plan for passing the time on his back was to torment his fellow patients? He wondered why they called them semiprivate rooms. Wasn't privacy something you either had or didn't have? If a white-haired old man listened in on every word that passed between you and your doctor, was that somehow more private than two or three other patients listening in at the same time? The hospital room itself created an intimacy between roommates Shelly wasn't sure he appreciated. How many of Screw-Eye's personal friends had ever seen his striped pajamas? Lowenkopf had never seen the old man before—he didn't even know his name. And yet they would be spending the night together, sleeping in the same room.

"What's your name?"

"Debs," the old man replied, "Marvin Debs. No relation

59

to the great Eugene—although I did hear him once deliver a speech in a union hall. What an orator! When he raised his voice, the windowpanes rattled in their frames. And when he pounded on the lectern, you felt it right through your folding chair."

Shelly was wondering how much of an orator Marvin himself would turn out to be. He had an itch for conversation, that much was clear. But did it go on all day and night? "You never know," he said, finally. "There might be some old family connection running back a few generations."

Debs shook his head. "Not even the same name, really. My papa changed it from Debrisi when we reached Ellis Island."

"Russian?"

"Georgian," Debs corrected, with a squint. "It may be the same to the Americans, and especially to the Soviets, but not to the people of the eastern Black Sea area."

"Is that where Georgia is?" Shelly asked. "I thought it was somewhere in the middle of the Soviet Union."

"Between the Black Sea and the Caspian," Debs replied, his chest visibly swelling with ethnic pride. "West of Azerbaijan, north of Armenia. You've heard of those, haven't you?"

Shelly nodded.

"Their national identities are like straw compared to the Georgian. How can I describe the country? There are mountains, but not like the ones you see here, or anyplace else, beautiful mountains that rise from Tbilisi like angels ascending to heaven. Look: in a pasture on a mountainside, a monk and a huge shepherd dog tend a flock of sheep; cedars line the slope to the village below, where the people play the balalaika and the drum. The men, as everyone knows, are the fiercest fighters in Europe, who have learned a little from the Russians, a little from the Arabs, and a lot from one another, you see. When it comes to cultural heritage and military prowess, the Georgian people are unequaled on this earth."

Shelly nodded—what else was there to say? All he had known about the Georgians before was that they ate a lot of yogurt and lived long lives.

Debs nodded back at him. "You in the army?"

Shelly shook his head. "Why?"

"The doc called you a sarge, didn't she?"

"Police. A detective sergeant—Shelly Lowenkopf. I'm a plainclothes cop."

"No kidding? Solving murders and stuff like that?"

Shelly wasn't sure he actually solved all that many, but the man had the general idea.

"Like that."

"Say," said Debs, leaning toward the foot of his bed to reduce the distance between them, "you're not on duty now, are you? Checking out the ward after the break-in this morning?"

Shelly lifted his gown to testify to the authenticity of his infirmity, when his professional antennae began to tweak. "What break-in?"

Debs sat back, figuring. "Of course you couldn't admit to it if you *were* undercover. You'd have to ask a question like that one, all innocent-like."

"No," said Lowenkopf. "I'm on the level, here. Was there a burglary on this ward?"

Debs grinned. "So you don't know nothing about that, huh? And you just kinda want to hear what I know about it?"

"As one roommate to another—"

Debs gave him an exaggerated wink. "Sure, just roomies throwing the old bull around. We talk a little about women, about names, about Georgia. Now you work the conversation around to the talk on the ward. All right," he said, lowering his voice, "you wanna hear about the robbery, I'll tell you what I know." He grinned. "Like you said. Just one roommate with time on his hands to another."

7

Shelly had expected to yawn his way through hours of boredom during his time in the hospital. A little local burglary might be just the thing to exercise his professional talents. Besides, what was the alternative? To dwell on his dream-time premonition of death? He glanced up toward the ceiling and wondered what it was that led him to call it a premonition. Rather than pursue that line of inquiry, he propped his back against the bars of the bedstead and turned his attention to Debs. He would have liked to raise the upper half of his bed, to improve his angle, but didn't want to allow any delay that might give Debs a chance to reconsider how frankly to tell his story. Shelly probably didn't have much to worry about on that score. His roommate evidently liked to talk, often and at length.

Debs crawled forward to the foot of his bed, from where he could see a bit farther down the hall outside their hospital room. The fact that Shelly could see none of it didn't deter him from stretching his arm and cupping his fingers into a visual representation of a turn. His other arm was hooked by an intravenous tube to a bottle on an aluminum stand near the head of his bed. But that didn't stop his edging forward to the full extent of the tubing.

"If you take a walk down this hallway out here," he began, "and keep going past the elevators, you'll turn a corner and come to a glass door at the end of the corridor. It's got letters etched on it, and won't open, even if you kick it. It's locked. On the other side is a bridge, like, that jumps to the next building. That's what they call the lab, the place where the docs do their experiments—for their own personal research, see?"

He seemed to expect an answer. "I can't see it from here," said Shelly, "but if you say so, I believe it's there."

"It's there," said Debs. "I saw it."

"You were there?"

"My doctor takes me down there from time to time, to have them run some tests on my chest. Not that they ever get them straight, either. They're either jabbing me in the arm, looking for a vein till the whole damn thing turns blue, or zapping me with gamma rays till my nose hairs fall out—I ain't got all that much on my head to start with! I can't understand why they pass these ham-fisted incompetents through med school in the first place."

"What's wrong with you?"

"Nothing."

"I mean," said Shelly, "what are you doing in that hospital bed?"

"Oh," said Debs with a wave of his arm signifying pay-it-no-attention, "my heart is too big."

Shelly glanced at the scowling old man, who didn't seem to be joking. The irony, it seemed, was bigger than Debs, a medical commentary on his personality that went right over his head.

"So they take me down to the lab now and then, to see if the bug juice they're dripping into my arm is making any difference." He shook the intravenous tube at his elbow and the bottle hooked to his aluminum stand rattled overhead.

"And that's where someone broke in?"

Debs smiled, feeding out his details like a fisherman angling for a bite. "Nope. But I can see how you'd think that—if you didn't know any better."

"I don't."

"Of course not. But no one broke into the lab itself. The break-in occurred at the icebox in the hall."

"The icebox?"

"Where they keep the samples."

"Of what?"

"You know."

Shelly sighed. "No, really. I don't."

"You're gonna make me say it, huh?" Debs regarded him with bitterness, shaking his head in confirmation of a private thought about cops. "All right, then—they broke in and stole some of the scum they keep in there. Is that what you wanna hear? You get your jollies doing interviews or something?"

"The scum?"

"You want me to tell you what scum is now? Forget it. You can be the most innocent fucking cop in the world, you've still got to know what scum is."

Shelly tried to piece together what he had learned. Someone hadn't broken into the laboratory but had been granted access to the corridor, only to break into a refrigerator full of frozen semen? It sounded less and less like a burglary and more and more like a prank by an overstressed intern. Shelly understood how a person might need a release after all those hours of practicing medicine, but his interest in the case nonetheless dwindled.

"Any practical jokers on the staff here?"

Debs's expression implied that he did not care for the implications of that question. He rolled over, turning his back on Lowenkopf, sulking for a while. Shelly enjoyed two or three minutes of beautiful silence before his roommate mumbled, "Practical jokers? You'll have to find out, won't you? But not from me. That's all I'm going to tell you about the robbery, Officer. If you're still interested, why don't you ask Ashbury about it?"

Shelly had begun to thank his lucky stars, when the name of the pretty resident struck his ear. "Dr. Ashbury? Elaine? Has she got something to do with this?"

Debs frowned. "Who do you think works in that lab? Just the technicians and rats? All of these residents do! But you've got no way to know that, have you?"

"No."

"I didn't think so. Then neither do I. Listen to me, like an old woman, going on and on. Gossiping about other people's business."

A fine time to think about that! After all the man had blabbed. Now that he knew Ashbury was involved, Shelly wanted to hear more about the affair—the burglary, or act of vandalism. As a matter of professional interest.

"Look," he said gently, "let's say I was here, undercover, on a case. Would that make you feel better about it?"

"I dunno."

"Let's say . . . let's just say I needed your help on this job. Would you be willing to lend a hand?"

Debs looked over his shoulder at Shelly. "Like how? What could I do?"

"You could start by telling me what you know about the break-in at the icebox."

"All right, now," said Debs, turning toward him, evidently pleased that the charade was over. "What d'you want to know?"

"Just start at the beginning," said Shelly with a sigh in his best professional intonation, "and tell me in your own words everything you saw and heard."

Debs opened his mouth to begin, but hesitated. "Don't you need a pad or something?"

"I'll remember. Talk."

Debs sat up, his spirits restored. "It was Tuesday, the morning before they brought you up here—two days ago. I was in the lab for a reading of my ticker—they do that on a table. Freylung is my doctor; she was assisted at the examining table by Bruce Haight and your little sweetheart, Ashbury."

"Ashbury is not my—" Shelly started to say, but Debs waved his objection aside.

"No more denials, please! Not while I'm testifying." Debs held up one palm to restrain further debate, but it hung in the air as if he were taking the oath.

Shelly's impulse was to explain that this hardly amounted to testimony—but he restrained himself.

"Well, then. I was lying on the table with my shirt up over my pupick, rolled between my armpits, when we hear this scream from one of the other labs. And I mean a scream— no little mouse squeal but a full-fledged holler from a full pair of lungs. We all three look toward the door and in comes Marsha Goodman, holding this test tube of milky liquid as far away from her lab coat as her shaking arm allows.

"She points at the stuff in the tube and says, 'This isn't my semen!' I was about to remind her that nobody thought it was, when Freylung steps forward, prying the tube from her clenched fingers and holding it up to the light. 'How can you tell?' she asks Goodman.

"Marsha stamps her foot. 'I ought to be able to tell my own research materials, don't you think?' she says. 'I spent four hours separating these samples last week. You should see them under the microscope now! Can you explain to me how sperm cells stripped of their chromosomes managed to grow their DNA chains back again?'

"Goodman reaches for the tube again, but Freylung holds it away, out of arm's reach. 'Could you have mixed up the samples?' she asks at last.

"Goodman gives her a look of such contempt and then points a finger at poor old Haight. 'He did it!' she says, 'and I can prove it, too. Make him provide a sample of his own and we'll match it to the stuff in this tube!'

"Brucie turns pretty pale at this suggestion, but Freylung

steps between them. 'Marsha,' she says, 'Bruce may have a warped sense of humor, but he's not the only man who had access to the freezer. There's Martin, for one.' He's the orderly who helps out around here. 'And Mr. Griegg.'"

Since the information was not immediately forthcoming from Debs, Lowenkopf asked, "Who's Griegg?"

"That's just what Goodman wanted to know," said Debs with a grin, his narrative pause having paid off handsomely. *"I* knew—he's the janitor who cleans up on this floor, after daylight hours. Goodman kept concentrating on Haight. 'Then they'll all have to provide samples,' she says."

Debs was about to go on, but bit off his next sentence when an orderly entered, a giant of a man. He seemed to realize that his entrance had interrupted their conversation, but made no excuses for his interruption. Debs said nothing but mouthed the name Martin, watching silently as the big orderly in the military crew cut emptied the trash from beside Debs's bed and crossed over to Lowenkopf's to do the same. Lowenkopf's trash can was unused, but the man removed the plastic liner anyway, crumpling it in his enormous hand and replacing it with an identical one. He met Shelly's eyes after the pointless substitution with an unwavering, heavy-lidded stare.

"Hospital policy," Martin said, as if that explained it and, glancing back at Debs, left with their garbage.

It took Debs a moment to recover from the intrusion. "You can't be too careful around here," he said, with a significant lift of his eyebrows.

Shelly nodded. "You were telling me about the burglary in the lab down the hall."

"Right," said Debs, brightening. "Where was I?"

"Marsha Goodman was demanding some of the janitor's—"

"Not just his," Debs said, opening his palms in a gesture that took in the entire room. "She wanted samples from all of the men who came within squirting distance of her test tubes. You can guess how I felt about it, sitting on the table there, just inside from the icebox. Not that my feelings would've counted for squat, of course—we're just patients here. It was Freylung whose feelings made a difference. And—bless the woman—she didn't like Goodman's idea any better than I did.

"Freylung shook her head, bunching up her lips, like, in wrinkles. It looked for a minute like she was considering it, until she said, 'We can hardly demand a sample from every man who might have come through here, Marsha. What about Mr. Debs, on the table here? Do we demand a sample from him?'

"I'll tell you, they could've demanded all they wanted, they weren't about to get one from me. Goodman stares at me, and I can tell she reads the resolution in my eye because she turns back to Freylung, steaming.

"'So that's all we're going to do—shrug our shoulders and forget about it? Is that your proposal, Dr. Freylung?'

"You can tell Freylung is not crazy about her tone of voice, but she's a cool customer. 'I don't see what else we can do about it, now, Marsha,' she says. 'I'll take it up with Bixby'—he's the hospital's chief of services—'but I don't really see what he can do about it, either. I doubt if he'll want to waste much resources on tracking down a practical joker. It's hard to see why anyone would want to risk so much'—with a hard glance at Haight—'just to infuriate somebody else. But you have no real proof that anything has actually been tampered with. Test tubes *are* mixed up, on occasion, even by you.'

"You can imagine how Marsha responded to that piece of news. But whatever you imagine, it was better. At first she bit her lip, turning all shades of purple and red. And then the dam broke—those years of med school and internship and residency, all those lonely hours in the lab came pouring out in a tide of bitterness—at Freylung. Goodman accused her of indifference, resentment, and finally the topper: envy of the brilliant prospects of her own research compared to Margaret's dry spell these last few years.

"Freylung took it like a battleship. When the storm was over, she just said quietly, 'Why don't you take the rest of the day off to consider the offense that has been committed against you and the offenses you have committed against others.'

"Goodman spun on her sensible heel and walked out of the hospital. Freylung held herself erect, keeping her eyes straight ahead. Ashbury and Haight looked awfully embarrassed, counting the tiles in the linoleum. Freylung glanced at her watch and excused herself with dignity. The other two mumbled, 'Of course, Doctor.' It was hard to tell who was more anxious for the parting. I wasn't, of course—I wanted to hear more. But as soon as Freylung was gone, Haight wheeled me out."

Debs stopped, watching Lowenkopf for a sign of confirmation. The man expected him to know most of the story, Shelly felt sure, and was waiting to see how his own account jibed with those of the other parties who would no doubt be questioned on this case. But Lowenkopf had not heard anything about the incident from any other source and could only nod his head vaguely.

"That was a very straightforward account," he said finally. He was looking for just the compliment Debs was expecting. "It'll provide a good, impartial version to keep in mind when we question the other participants."

"What others?"

"Freylung and Ashbury and so on."

Debs smiled. "You can huddle with Ashbury as much as you like, Sergeant. But you're not gonna get much from Freylung, now, are you?"

"Why not?"

The man scowled again. "I thought we were all through with that sort of fun. Everybody on the ward knows already, Sarge, there's been neither sight nor sound of Margaret Freylung these last two days. She's disappeared."

8

Homer Greeley's desk in the big, open detective room at the Allerton Avenue precinct house stood nose to nose with Shelly Lowenkopf's, so that the two policemen usually sat facing each other across a double expanse of desktop on which the battle of their personalities played itself out in paper clips and plastic trays. On any given day in their working relationship, Homer's desk was a model of organization: neatly labeled trays in translucent black plastic, stapler and pencil cup aligned with the rectangular box that used magnetic force to dole out paper clips one at a time. On Shelly's side of the dividing line, the weather was evidently different, since only a storm of terrible magnitude could have produced the disarray of sheets from various case files, dotted with dull-pointed pencils and clips untwisted from their useful shape to make a menagerie of creatures that never stood upright. The message Shelly's desk sent to suspects and complainants couldn't help but undermine the carefully laid plan of Homer's own. Stability, resolution, order—these were the things their workplace should have communicated to people passing through, the things Homer's desk was arranged to express. But what was Shelly's

desk whispering on the side? Even Shelly's typewriter—
Homer's own sleek IBM was bolted to his desk return,
where it could reliably be found when he needed it. Shelly's
manual Remington seemed to wander, beginning the morning at the very front edge of the desk, where Shelly usually
drew it, half into his lap, while he typed; but it ended the day
in one or the other back corner, its rubberless back leg
anchoring slips and scraps of paper, casting its round
shadows over the line between their domains.

The contrast was sharp enough on most days, when
Homer was deeply engaged in the logic of a case and Shelly
was worrying about his family. But Homer had been
confined to the precinct house these last two days, with
nothing much to do but answer telephone calls and rearrange the order of his desk. Each time he printed his name
on an inch of masking tape and affixed the new identifying
label to the bottom of a Scotch tape dispenser, he would
glance over at his partner's desk, where a ring of Scotch tape
lay unmounted on top of a pile of file folders, its loose end
stuck to the numbered part of the label on the topmost file.

This was going to have to stop, thought Homer, a sentiment shared by most of the people who regularly worked in
the precinct house. Each of them had at one time or another
complained to the captain about an improvement Greeley
had made to an office system for which they were responsible. Homer had, for example, arranged all of the paper in
the Xerox photocopier cabinet by size and color, with the
long legal-size sheets on the lower shelf and the letter-size
paper on the top. It was true, as he had pointed out, that this
prevented the longer sheets from hanging down over the
shorter ones. But since he had done it by fiat, explaining the
advantages of the new organizational plan by a memo in
everyone's mailbox, Dolores had wasted a run of three
hundred short sheets before noticing the improvement. She
explained her mistake to the captain, of course, who shook
his head and added her story to the ones he had heard about
Homer restacking bottles for the water cooler and reassign-

ing boxes in the mailroom. Now he watched through the panes of his glass-paneled office as Greeley, at his own desk oblivious to the gritted teeth around him, squeaked his top drawer for the twelfth time—pulling it out, adding a drop of oil to the track, pushing it in again, then repeating the process. Madagascar winced at a particularly unnerving squeak and reached for the stack of new cases collecting on his desk.

He tapped a finger on the glass panel until he caught the detective's eye. When Homer rose and headed for the office, a sigh went up from the personnel around him. Madagascar was satisfied with the early results of his decision—it was the rest he felt uneasy about. Medical orders were to keep Greeley at a desk. But to do that would be to drive the rest of them away. So he hit on a compromise: a case that demanded nothing strenuous but sent Greeley outside the precinct house, into the fresh air. He looked through the first three files quickly: a mugging, a domestic beef, a robbery. The last one looked like a candidate—someone had broken into a coin collector's shop and stolen a pair of shoes. No way Homer could overexert himself on *that*.

"Yes, Captain?" asked Greeley, standing in the doorway as if reluctant to enter.

Madagascar wondered what the hell he was so anxious to get back to—oiling the bottom drawer? But he settled on the flowered cushion on his own hard chair and motioned for Greeley to do the same with another, across the desk. There was no cushion on the other chair, of course—in little ways like that the captain underscored the hierarchy of authority in his office and his precinct.

"How are you feeling, Sergeant?"

"Pretty good, sir. I've been noticing a strain on my eyes from reading under the fluorescents out there. By my count, almost a third of the tubes are flickering. I plan to take that up with Janitorial, once I stop my desk drawers from sticking."

Madagascar was sure he knew just how Janitorial would

react to Homer's constructive criticism. "But, ah, setting aside the lights for a moment, how are you *feeling* now? After the shock in the water and so on?"

"You mean psychologically? I've been sleeping better the last two nights. But I'm still a bit reluctant to step into a bathtub."

"I mean, do you feel up to a case, or not?"

"A case?" Homer leaned back in his hardwood chair, crossing his legs. He picked a lint-ball from his trouser knee and said, "I believe I could handle one now."

Madagascar threw him the file and avoided meeting his eyes. "Take that one."

Homer opened it, removing the single-sheet report, signed by the robbed coin collector. He glanced over the first few lines, caught the general drift, and held up the page between them. "Think I can manage this alone, Captain?"

Madagascar wasn't sure if Homer was serious, but never liked to see his cops lone-wolfing a case—too easy to get caught with your pants down that way. And yet this was Greeley's chance to tackle a case without Lowenkopf; the captain could understand how he'd be looking forward to that.

"I'm sure you could manage it, Sergeant. But it's a good chance to train one of the younger men, wouldn't you agree? Talk over the lineup with Sergeant Binkler and give one of the uniforms a break."

Greeley didn't rise at once from the chair, but Madagascar could see his mind was already on his choice. There were some good potential partners among the first-year men, and here was a chance to train an officer the way Homer thought they should be trained. He said, "Any of them?"

The captain nodded. "Take your pick."

Homer arose, excusing himself, and departed. Madagascar felt a twinge of guilt for the unsuspecting officer Greeley would put through his paces. But, considering the air of relief settling over the squad room as Homer passed through the door, that lone officer would have to put up with the strain. He had no doubt that partnering with Greeley could teach him more than the next two detectives put together— Homer was that good at solving a case. It was just a matter of surviving the lessons one at a time, and staying on the force.

Homer Greeley did not really need to confer with Sergeant Binkler in selecting the first-year patrol officer he would take under his capable tutelage. He did go to see Binkler, who was responsible for assigning street patrols and knew the personnel as well as anyone. But Greeley didn't pay much attention to the slow drawl of the sergeant as he ran through the qualifications of his first two candidates. He didn't pay much attention until Binkler, clearing his throat, started on his third suggestion for the plainclothes assignment.

"There is one other choice you might consider," the portly sergeant observed, contemplating his clipboard. "Not exactly the easiest partner to get along with, but someone who'll never let you fall asleep on the job."

After Shelly, that was just what Homer was looking for—someone to hold the line for him, for a change. "Who'd you have in mind?"

"Morganthal."

Greeley pushed a rotary-dial telephone across the sergeant's desk. "Make the call."

Officer Jill Morganthal did not like to be interrupted in the middle of a case and would have frowned when the call came in from Binkler had her professional standards included a frown as an option she allowed herself in response to an order from a superior officer. As it happened they did not, and so, when the dispatcher relayed to her the sergeant's summons to the precinct house, she abandoned her one-woman surveillance of the corner candy store and turned her squad car homeward with a squeal that impressed the old women knitting and gossiping in front of the butcher shop next door.

Officer Morganthal did not have time for knitting and gossiping in her own life. To another officer, the neighborhood she patrolled might have seemed a sleepy backwater of the Bronx, where shopkeepers opened their shops in time for the morning rush to the subway station, where the stores were thinly patronized by housewives and elderly until three o'clock, when the schools let out and teenagers and younger adolescents began filling the pizza shops and music stores, dropping candy wrappers and plastic soda cups on the shop floors and sidewalks, until the evening trains brought their parents back to the neighborhood. But that was not how Officer Morganthal saw her beat.

Jill Morganthal had grown up in such a neighborhood, where her mother still lived in a rent-stabilized apartment over a barbershop. Jill knew those shops, both the front rooms and the back, where children on rotating stools might serve to cover a bookie joint or loan shark's operation behind a beaded curtain. The candy store she was watching was a typical example: why so many men trooping in and out? True, each of them emerged with a newspaper under his arm. But were those papers their reason for stopping— or was there a darker purpose? Officer Morganthal couldn't be sure, of course, unless she watched the place more or less continually. She couldn't request backup, of course, until she had something more to go on. But she was more than willing to get what she needed, because each hour spent in her patrol car across the street from the candy store brought her sixty minutes closer, she felt, to her immediate career ambition—an assignment with the plainclothes boys in Investigations.

Now she wondered about this Detective Sergeant Greeley, who had requested her as a temporary replacement for his regular plainclothes partner. She had heard about the explosion on the boat and the officers who survived it. Was Greeley the one blown into the bay or the partner who saved him? She hoped for the latter, of course, having identified with the rescuer rather than the rescued when she first heard the story. She had an idea who he might be: the blond detective who kept glancing over when she spent an afternoon looking through a stack of reports about arrests in and around the candy store. Hadn't he asked what she was doing and raised an appreciative eyebrow when she answered him? Even then she had recognized in his expression a potential boost for her career. Industriousness, professionalism, personal initiative—those were the qualities her inquiry implied. It was just that sort of casual impression, Morganthal believed, which could raise a cop from patrol officer to the ranks of the plainclothes in record time.

To turn the temporary assignment into a permanent one she would need a case flashy enough and thorny enough for her to show what she could do with a really intractable problem. A case that knitted their brows and kept them guessing, with tricky motives and no clues at all to follow. She could discover her own, interpret them, and track them down to the perpetrator—that was how she planned to make a name for herself. She might have felt a twinge of guilt for the other one—Lowenkopf, was it?—in whose place she planned to stake her claim. But this was her chance to be noticed, and Jill Morganthal was determined to make the best possible use of the detectives' unfortunate accident at the dockside.

It wasn't as if she wasn't qualified for the plainclothes job: top of her class at the academy with special training in forensics and firearms, and undercover experience as a decoy on a sting operation in the park. She had taken every opportunity to prepare herself for this chance, and every cell in her twenty-two-year-old brain was ready to show its stuff. What she needed was a sympathetic appraisal by a superior officer who appreciated the exercise of deductive reasoning, patience, and persistent police work. Someone like Sergeant Greeley.

Jill Morganthal had heard about Homer Greeley from the other patrol officers when she was first assigned her locker in the Allerton Avenue precinct house. His green eyes and blond hair would have made him a topic of conversation in any women's locker room, but the talk about Homer usually began with his prowess on the investigative scene. Jill thought him the most methodical, unrelenting, and penetrating investigator in the precinct house, and followed the record of his collars the way teenage boys tracked the batting statistics of baseball players. She would have been pleased to be called into plainclothes for any occasion, but the prospect that her partner might be Greeley himself positively gave her chills.

When she entered the squad room at the precinct house, she saw at once that she had been right. The blond detective leaned back in his chair, picking something from the herring-bone knee of his suit pants. In the center of his agreeably neat desk, a file folder lay open with what looked like a single sheet of paper inside. The lack of extensive documentation was her first disappointment, but Officer Morganthal was always slow to draw a conclusion. A single sheet of documentation might mean the very beginning of a case that would prove gratifyingly thick when they closed it. She had spent more than twelve hours in the street outside a candy store, on the strength of her suspicions about the place. She could certainly work up a respectable file on a case that had actually been assigned.

Greeley looked up as she approached and waved her into the chair beside his desk, where suspects sat while he typed up their vital statistics, and where complainants sat while making their complaints. Jill would have preferred to occupy the other chair, behind the desk facing Greeley's, but was willing to wait until she had demonstrated she deserved that seat. For the moment, she sat where he suggested.

"Sorry to call you in on such short notice," he said, "but Sergeant Binkler didn't think you would mind."

Binkler? Did she owe him for this, too? Of course she didn't *mind* a call into plainclothes—even Binkler would have to know that. Or was this some kind of test dreamed up by Greeley himself? She decided to nod without comment until she saw where the conversation was headed.

"You don't mind, do you?" Greeley asked.

"Not at all."

"Good. You're taciturn—I like that. My regular partner is sometimes given to . . . volubility. The peace and quiet will be a welcome change in our car."

Officer Morganthal made a mental note of that remark. She would have liked to ask about the case, but held her tongue.

Greeley gave her a moment to respond and seemed pleased when she chose to refrain. He rocked forward in his desk chair, picked up the single sheet of documentation, and handed it to her. "This is our case," he said, "a burglary. Not much to go on and not much to do. Why don't you look that over and see if any questions occur to you?"

She read it carefully, looking for a question he would judge smart. The case seemed depressingly straightforward —a stolen pair of shoes. What on earth could she possibly ask to show him her talents on this?

"The only thing I don't quite get," she said finally, "is why you called for my assistance on this. Why didn't the captain let you handle this on your own, Sergeant Greeley?"

"That," he replied, "is an excellent question—probably the only one on this case. But please, call me Homer. We probably won't be working together long enough for you to repeat the whole title."

"All right."

"And I'll call you Jill, if you don't mind. Now, is there anything else before we visit the scene of the crime? To set your mind at ease or clear your sights?"

She shook her head, keeping her lips buttoned. Her mind was more than at ease already; it was positively abuzz. And her sights were quite clear, thank you—she would be sitting behind that other desk, one way or another, before Sergeant Lowenkopf recovered enough to return from the hospital.

Visiting hours at South Shore Hospital were formally from one to three in the afternoon and informally during any other hours that a visitor could slip past the nurses at the desk by the ward elevators. For some reason, the staff felt that their honor was bound up in their duty to keep visitors off the wards at unofficial hours, and so the watch on the elevators kept a priority higher, for example, than the patient call buttons or the cardiac monitors in the hall.

Or so it seemed to Lowenkopf, who, if he lay in absolute silence on his back, could make out the noises of his own heart monitor, stationed next to his door. Debs had been rolled out around ten o'clock after being prepped for surgery, so there was no one to distract Shelly from the life-and-death monotony of the machine tracking his heart-beat. Every now and then, there would be some irregularity in its *beep-beep* rhythm—a pause or a triple *beep*—which would scare him thoroughly, disturbing the rhythm of the monitor even further. It was most disheartening to listen to the static of his own apprehension. He would wait a few minutes, holding his breath, then press the call button for the nurse, who would not arrive for another four or five minutes. For each of the first three times it was a different nurse, whose head would appear in the threshold long enough for him to explain, "The monitor skipped a beat."

The first nurse, an Austrian woman in her fifties who looked as if she could wrestle Mike Tyson to the floor, ordered him not to worry about it, which filled him with fear. The machine was ticking along again, concealing its darker purpose—no wonder she wasn't worried. In half an hour, he'd be dead and she'd tell the doctor on call there had been no warning.

He said, "You didn't hear the change?"

"There's no one to cover the desk," she replied, "and it's perfectly normal right now. Forget about it!"

A few hours later the second nurse, a young man named Miguel, wheeled the monitor into the doorway where Shelly could see it. "See those peaks?" he said, outlining the rise and fall of Shelly's heartbeat on the small screen. "They look just fine, Sergeant Lowenkopf, just fine."

Shelly swallowed hard. "Now they are. They must've been jumping all over a few minutes ago."

Miguel shrugged. "There was no one to cover the desk. That's the policy, man." He said it in apology for forces beyond his control. Shelly couldn't help wondering just what they were covering the desk *for,* other than the health of their patients.

The third nurse, on the same shift as Miguel, was a large black woman in her early forties. She entered the room, setting hands on her hips at his bedside. "What's the matter, Sergeant? Why do you keep pushing that call button? Think we've forgotten about you in here?"

"The monitor . . . it skipped two beats and then honked out three loud ones in a row."

She nodded, raising his head with one hand and fluffing his pillow with the other. "Those machines do that every so often, don't they? Scares the bejesus out of people." She picked up a newspaper from the floor and quartered the want ads, sticking a stubby pencil into his fingers. "Why don't you do the crossword and let me listen to the beeps? That's my job. If you keep on doing it, what will they need me for?"

The name on her pin was Verna Jeffries, and Shelly decided right then that she was the nurse for him. She spotted the look in his eye and shook her head. "Oh, no, don't you go asking for me, now, whenever you need something. That just increases my load on the ward, that's all—not the best way to reward somebody for taking time with you."

That made sense to Shelly and he didn't call the next three times the monitor's rhythm jumped its two-beat track. Debs was carted back into the room around midnight, utterly unconscious. He lay stiller than in sleep, his limbs flopping as the big orderly hauled him onto his bed. The grim face of the Georgian émigré seemed to suggest all the suffering of his people at the hands of the Khazars, the czar and then the Bolsheviks. And yet he clung to life, his lips blanched from surgery but still firmly pressed, lest his soul slip out through his mouth. Shelly heard his own vulnerability beeping on the monitor.

He tried to forget about it by writing a letter, but that only made him think of the postcard from Mordred. She hadn't even said exactly when she would be arriving. But what did that matter? Whichever day she landed, there was no chance he would be out of the hospital in time to meet her at the airport. It occurred to him she might read his absence as a sign that confirmed what she had been feeling overseas. He wanted to make damn sure she didn't read it that way. So he set to work on his letter, trying to put down in blue ink on yellow paper all that he felt for her.

By the time Elaine Ashbury stopped by, just before breakfast, he had written only "Mordred" at the top of the page. He had tried at first "Dear Mordred," but crossed it out at once, since it sounded under the circumstances too much like "Dear Jane," the salutation that always marked the beginning of the end. He had opted for something more romantic, next: "Mordred dear"—and again blackened it out with his pen. That sounded like a lecture from a grown-up to a daughter on how to behave and, given the twenty years or so between their ages, not the shrewdest association to invoke. He had gone back to the first form, writing "Dear" before crossing it out again when he remembered his objection to the word. A helluva tricky choice. He settled on just plain "Mordred." Now, where should he go from there? Ashbury found him staring at a perfectly clean page with one word at the top.

"What about the date?" Ashbury asked, announcing by that gentle suggestion her presence behind him.

Lowenkopf folded the page in half, effectively ruining yet another attempt. He couldn't send Mordred a creased letter. And now that he had to write it over again, "Mordred" alone sounded awfully impersonal for what he had in mind.

Dr. Ashbury said, "Verna tells me the cardiac monitor is driving you crazy. That true?"

He hesitated, reluctant to be tagged a complainer. "It does kind of remind me of my peril."

She nodded. "That happens sometimes. The last thing that heart of yours needs now is additional stress, so I'm going to have the monitor on this end disconnected. Instead, we're going to listen in by telemetry—a radio signal to the nursing station, where the monitor will be. You can stow the little sender box in your holster, if you like."

The tug of a weight under his shoulder was always comforting to Shelly. "Is it as . . . reliable?"

"Yes," said Ashbury, frowning at his new source of anxiety. "There's no reason to worry about that, now—the whole point is to try to relax! If it makes you feel any easier, I'll have somebody come in here a couple of times a day and listen to your heart through one of these."

She held up the nose of her stethoscope.

"Would that be you?"

"Unless you'd rather have somebody else. Dr. Freylung

assigned your case to me because I took such an interest in your personal belongings—looking for that postcard."

She couldn't stifle a charming smile, and Shelly remembered her kindness in recovering it. "Thanks again."

Her smile became rueful as her eyes wandered toward his lap. "I'm not so sure. Are you up to answering it already?"

He tore the creased page from his writing pad. "Apparently not." He crumpled the sheet and aimed for the trash, missing the can. Ashbury picked up the uncrumpling ball and smoothed it out against the hard pad in his lap.

"If you have something to say to her, you'd better say it," she warned him. "You can't expect the girl to read your mind—or even your heart."

"It's too late," Shelly said with a sigh. "There's nothing left to say. I'm a dead duck, waiting for the ax to fall."

"Of course there is," said Ashbury, sitting on the foot of his bed, crossing her legs. "You've got to write about your feelings. You do have feelings for her, don't you?"

"Too many."

"Describe them to me."

He took a deep breath. "What you've got to understand is, she's young. Younger than me by fifteen years—maybe more. Even younger than you."

Ashbury smiled at the compliment. "Thank you."

"That makes me feel guilty just taking up her time. I keep feeling she ought to be with someone her own age, someone who can give her what I can't."

"And what's that?"

"Youth—in return for her own. Sure, I know a few things these young kids don't, and maybe even understand her better. I'm certainly willing to put her before me more than any of those bozos. But what is all that on one end of the scale—maturity, appreciation, affection—compared to that one thing on the other end—youth? I'll tell you what I think: even when my side has real money going for it— which I don't—and wonderfully dignified looks—which, again, I don't—it doesn't make the least impression. The scale tips in favor of youth every time."

Dr. Ashbury gave him a look of such sweet understanding that it melted for a moment the icy grip of impending doom on his heart. "I'm with you on that," she said. "You're talking to someone who knows only too well what you mean! I'm thirty-eight years old, Sergeant Lowenkopf. Have you any idea what those numbers mean to a woman? Every tick of fading youth registers in my cells. Do you know what my research is all about?"

He shook his head.

"Cell regeneration. I'm trying to find a way to take a bit of genetic stuff from an old dead cell and implant it in a new young one, to read the genetic code of the old cell in building a whole new life. I'm still working with rats now, but one day soon—we'll see. You don't have to explain to me the attractions of youth! I know them well! But let me assure you: there is life yet in old war-horses like the two of us. You are a dear man, a sweet man. I'd fall in love with you myself if my work left me time to fall in love with anybody.

"Now you write your letter and see what happens."

Shelly was speechless with amazement. In the time it took him to recover, she withdrew from the room. He watched her go, each step assured, confident, and sexy, even in her shapeless lab coat. He couldn't help wondering what was beneath it. He looked back at the pad in his lap and found that writing a letter to Mordred was more difficult than before. He tossed his pen on his nightstand, where it knocked over the postcard of the mosque.

By the time lunch arrived, Verna had indeed come around to disconnect his cardiac monitor, allowing him his first untroubled breaths. "Now you eat this," she said, "and we can pull out the other thing and get those damn tubes out of your arm. How would you like that?"

He loved it, and her for arranging it, and turned to his lunch with a triple motive for eating. His worrying had worked up an appetite, which vanished completely once he removed the plastic lid from the plates. A green bowl of smashed peas, another of orange—sweet potato? carrots?—and a plastic cup of applesauce with an aluminum foil seal. Was he supposed to eat this stuff? There were two containers of liquid. He opened the juice, drained it, and turned to the milk, his thirst unquenched. The single-serving carton was warm in his hand. He could drink milk ice cold, as he preferred it, with crisp chocolate-covered doughnuts, or he could drink it heated, to help him sleep. But warm milk in the middle of the afternoon—whose idea of a lunchtime beverage was that?

He picked up the milk carton, shook it, and resettled it on the tray. He sniffed at the bowl of green, sniffed at the bowl of orange, tore a white plastic spoon from a clear plastic bag, and ate the applesauce. The taste of the sweet mush on his tongue sparked his appetite again, but he couldn't quite find what it wanted. He hesitated, spoon poised over and between the two bowls of green and orange substances. He put down the spoon, picked up the milk carton, felt its warmth again; put down the milk carton, picked up the spoon, wavering over the bowls. And that was how Isabelle found him when she burst in with a big straw totebag over her forearm and a paper shopping bag over her wrist.

"Hello, Shelly!" she called, too lightheartedly, dropping both bags on the mattress by his feet. "I stopped off at your apartment and picked up a few things you might need. And added a few of my own."

Shelly grunted his appreciation. It was nice to see his sister again, and the bags she brought were a treat, but her energy was tiring him already. And the clock had barely reached 1:15.

"Let's see what we've got here, now." She gazed into the shopping bag first, as if it held a hoard of treasure and she couldn't decide which golden cup to seize first. She pulled out his bathrobe, a red plaid flannel affair worn to the point of embarrassment. She helped him sit up and slip his arms into its torn sleeves.

"I couldn't find any pajamas in your drawers—you don't sleep in any, do you? So I stopped by Joe Tuckman's and picked up a few pairs. Can't go around in your underpants here." She glanced around the room, sizing it up for formality, noticing Debs on the other bed for the first time. The old Georgian lay inert, his mouth open. "He asleep?"

Shelly nodded.

"That's nice. All right, now, are you ready for the good stuff? There's not a lot to do in this place, so I thought you might catch up on your reading."

She reached deep into her shopping bag and produced a stack of paperbacks, which toppled over onto the blanket. She had evidently been standing in front of the M's, because the novels that came tumbling out were by Lia Matera, Sharyn McCrumb, and Dallas Murphy. She tapped the last with her index finger.

"This one's by a playwright. Did you know that? I asked a woman at that mystery bookstore by my place what she recommends, and she gave me a few suggestions. This one"—holding up Bob Campbell's *Alice in La-la Land*—"is about toughs and low-lifes, she said, just your sort of crowd. And here's a good title, don't you think?"

It was *First Kill All the Lawyers,* by Sarah Shankman, writing as Alice Storey. Shelly didn't have the heart to tell his sister how many of the books he had already read, so he nodded again, smiling weakly. "Thanks—"

"Wait!" she said, forestalling his gratitude, "there's more. Nobody can read just books." Then the magazines came, a second stack reflecting her tastes rather than his own: *The New Yorker, the Atlantic, Newsweek,* and *Vanity Fair,* with a *Playboy* thrown in as a gesture toward the differences between them. These were followed by newspapers, including, he couldn't help noticing, the one that published Mordred's photos as well as the *Times, Newsday,* and what must have been Isabelle's personally thumbed copy of the *New York Review of Books.*

Shelly dropped his hand on the pile. "Thanks, Iz—"

"I'm not finished yet," she interrupted him, reaching into the bottom of her shopping bag for a small cassette player. And there were cassettes, from his apartment: Thelonious Monk, Charlie Parker, Sidney Bechet, Bix Beiderbecke, Gene Krupa, Anita O'Day, Ella Fitzgerald, and Billie Holiday. She stacked them beside the magazines, but they too toppled, sliding down the glossy surfaces to the floor and under the bed.

Shelly leaned over the side, reaching for the cassettes and trying again, more forcefully. "You're an angel, Isabelle. You shouldn't have—"

"One more thing!" she cried, turning with alarm to her straw bag. "I almost forgot about these."

As if for the encore of her magic act, Isabelle pulled a bouquet of fresh-cut flowers from the straw. Carnations, mostly, in strange shades of blue and purple as well as red. She stood for a moment holding the stems, casting about for a vase, before reaching for the call button and buzzing for assistance.

"They don't always come right away," Shelly warned her in a plea for modest expectations.

His sister shook her head, keeping her thumb pressed on the call button. "You have to know how to ask, Shell."

A nurse appeared immediately: the Austrian woman, who marched into the room in evident indignation. But she had not counted on Isabelle, who, though slender, stood her ground as firmly as a lightning rod in a storm.

Their eyes met for a instant fiercely, but it was the nurse who broke away. To cover her retreat, she scowled a few times and demanded, "Who's been ringing that bell?" She tried with her glance to direct the question toward Shelly.

But Izzy moved to protect her brother, raising the device in her fist. "That would be me. Could you bring us a vase for these flowers, please?"

The nurse scowled, but Isabelle raised her thumb over the button and the nurse disappeared, returning a moment later with an aluminum pitcher.

"Those buttons are for the patients to use," she said sourly. "Patients only."

Isabelle replied sweetly, "Thank you."

The nurse turned to leave, but Shelly said, "Do you think you could help me with this bed? I've tried to raise the upper part, but it seems to be stuck."

The nurse was clearly tempted to walk out on them, but her professional code restrained her and she approached the head of the bed. She pressed the same button that Shelly had tried, with the same lack of result. Then she gave the bed a kick, which failed to stir the mechanism into action. "It's stuck," she said at last, abrogating with that diagnosis all personal responsibility for treatment.

"We're aware of that," said Isabelle. "Could you have it repaired?"

"I'll see what I can do," the nurse said, taking advantage of the opportunity to give them the slip. "It could take a while to get through to maintenance. They're backlogged. And there's no one to cover the desk right now."

"But you'll make the call right away?"

"I'll make the goddamn call," snapped the nurse, muttering a few syllables under her breath as she exited.

Izzy turned to Shelly, victorious. "You see? It's all in how you ask."

He nodded, but she seemed to expect more. So he gave her his halfhearted smile again, wondering just how much hostility the staff would be nursing toward him as a result of this splendid success.

10

When Homer Greeley and Jill Morganthal arrived at the tiny coin shop on Fordham Road, they were immediately impressed by the security evident from outside the store. Not only was there an accordian-style sliding gate that covered the plate-glass window with crisscrossed steel bars, but the door itself, recessed two or three yards from the street level, was made of reinforced glass and bolted to its hinges. The sign overhead was certainly discreet, a lone word, *Coins,* obscured by a thick blanket of dust that had evidently been left undisturbed so as not to call attention to the store beneath it. The proprietor, Mrs. Geffelman, clearly expected her clientele to know where to find her with very little in the way of public announcement.

And yet the thief had used no subtlety in his assault on the shop. The accordian gate had been hacked through at the center, and the door was shattered and then smashed repeatedly beside the knob until a hole had been cleared in the wire-webbed glass large enough for a hand to pass through and undo the lock from inside. Morganthal stuck her own hand through the glass, noting its size in her book—the thief's weight could probably be guessed from the maximum circumference of his palm.

Homer watched her with satisfaction as she flexed her palm, congratulating himself on his choice of replacement partner. Here was someone with real commitment to the art of police work. He was impressed that she thought to measure the size of the hole and was willing to stick her own hand among the jagged shards. He felt also a nudging little regret that he hadn't thought to do it first himself. Passing his wrist through a circle of broken glass was just the sort of measurement he usually thought to take at the scene of a crime.

But regardless of who had collected it, they had a clue as to the size of the thief, or at least the circumference of his fist. There had to be an average proportion between the size of the hand and one's height: a watchmaker should be able to give them some idea of the range. Now, what else could they glean from the exterior scene about the party who committed this crime? Every perpetrator left his signature on the scene in little signs that could be picked up like tiny hairs and examined under a microscope or deduced from the obvious personal choices. Homer usually concentrated on the former and left the latter to his partner, but felt confident he could handle Shelly's province, too, in his absence.

What would Shell have noticed about this perp? To begin as Shelly did, with the obvious, the burglar must have been very strong or very determined to have hacked his way through the steel and reinforced glass. But which? Homer imagined Shelly beside him and tried to picture the scene: the perpetrator standing on the empty sidewalk, smashing away at the gate. He must have made quite a racket on the deserted night street. There was an alarm, too, which would have been blaring, and a halogen streetlight less than ten yards from the storefront, so the thief would have been visible to any passing patrol car. So much vulnerability would have spoken to Shelly of motive—desperation.

Whatever he wanted from inside the shop, the thief must have wanted badly.

"Shall we go in?" asked Jill.

Homer opened the door, listened to the tinkle of its bell, and held it for her. Jill hesitated, shrugged what-the-hell, and entered the shop before him.

Inside, a short woman in a knitted suit hurried to meet them as they entered. "You are police?" she said, with an expression of hopeful expectancy. Her hair was cropped short, totally white, and her eyes nested with wrinkles. But her blue eyes were clear and sharp, watchful and alert.

Jill had changed from her patrol uniform into a skirt and sweater from her locker, so the old woman's guess had more to do with her wishes than with any evidence she noticed about them. Unless it was that air of moral authority, Homer thought, which sometimes gave away even the most impeccably disguised undercover officer. He carried it, he knew—she might have sensed that about him. But it was usually experience in the criminal element that taught you to pick that up, and Homer began to wonder about the woman's personal past. Something in her aspect reminded him of the theater, and he concentrated, trying to determine what is was. If she had worn a big scarf in striking colors, or if her hair were upswept or flowing down her back, he would have been satisfied. But there was nothing particularly dramatic about her plain blue suit, evidently crocheted by its wearer without niceties except for the tiny fancy stitches around the buttonholes. Until she offered her hand with a sweep of her arm and he realized the size of her gestures was the thing: she was playing for the back of the hall. Homer made another of his unconfirmable hypotheses and suspected Mr. Geffelman might have been nearsighted.

"Mrs. Geffelman?" he asked. "I'm Sergeant Greeley. This is Officer Morganthal."

Homer took a good look at Morganthal as he introduced her, wondering what sort of impression they made together. In the past he had seen her only in uniform, and most of his attention now was given to her clothing. She wore a plain woolen skirt in a light shade of gray with delicate blue stitching at the waist. She had picked up the blue in her choice of sweater, an acrylic blend that showed her torso to good advantage but ended at the throat in a cowl that made her slender neck seem much too skinny for her shoulders. There was a faint red stripe in the weave of her skirt—he looked down quickly and was relieved to discover she had not chosen to make more of the stripe by opting for red spikes. Her shoes were charcoal, a sedate low heel, over uncomplicated gray hose. Her only pieces of jewelry were silver earrings and a watch with a black leather band. The total impression was of a teacher, or perhaps an assistant principal, a fashion statement she maintained by the shoulder-length flip of her brown hair and some insecure dabs of shadow and mascara. Her hazel eyes, however, were uncommonly steady and calm—all right, he decided generously, an elementary school principal.

"Thank you for coming!" Mrs. Geffelman exclaimed, ignoring Jill but seizing Homer's elbow and leading him deeper into the store. It was a messy place, the left side of the shop dominated by a long glass display case in which were laid out coins of various sizes on a blue velvet backing. The wall behind the counter was hung with unframed posters of postage stamps—special issues from the post office and a few ancient advertisements in foreign languages. The faded colors of the posters and the dust on top of the display case made Homer wonder if coins and stamps were no longer the bread and butter of her business. Their replacement was in evidence along the right-hand wall, where giant frames on metal racks sagged under the weight of huge photos of Marilyn Monroe, James Dean, and Fred Astaire. On both sides of the poster display were rotating racks of postcards, black-and-white stills from movies, and famous publicity shots. Homer saw Betty Grable flirting over her shoulder, Rita Hayworth kneeling on a bed, and Clark Gable at a poker table grinning from ear to ear. On an old wooden desk was a display of pins and earrings, as well as ankle and wrist bracelets strung, stamped, or engraved with the images of former movie stars.

"Nice, huh?" Mrs. Geffelman said.

Homer pursed his lips.

But the real prizes were in the back of the store, locked in a display case guarded by the cash register, a venerable machine. Arranged with care and identified by stiff white cards, hand-lettered in a graceful calligraphy, were a few relics of the film trade that had somehow or other fallen into this place. On the top shelf was a woman's hat in white silk with a patterned lace veil; beside it stood a card that announced it had been worn by Norma Shearer. Sharing its shelf of honor was a worn silver dollar marked "George Raft's." The shelves below held other items, attributed to celebrities whose names Homer failed to recognize. Who were Margaret Lindsay and Donald Crisp, Betsy Blair and George Marion? Beside the counter was a rack of clothing, mostly overcoats, feather boas, and hats. Homer glanced through the double-breasted jackets with padded shoulders but saw nothing that he could wear, then squatted beside the case, eyeing George Raft's dollar.

"Is that the one he flipped—"

"In *Quick Millions*. The very same."

"How do you know?"

"I have an affidavit from an attorney who sold the estate of a gangster who bought the coin in a charity auction. Donated with a letter from Mr. Raft's widow. Would you like to see it?" Homer wasn't sure if she meant the paperwork, but she went behind the case and brought out the coin with reverence, laying it in its purple velvet box on the countertop. "It's the first piece of cinemabilia I acquired, accidentally. Boy, did it open my eyes! Just having it here brought more people into this old shop than in the last ten years of Jacob's trade."

Homer wouldn't touch the coin, but hovered over, inspecting it. "You sell a lot of this stuff?"

"The real things? Not much. But they lend appeal to the other items, the buttons and posters. Those giant posters on the rack there, that's where the money comes from. People worship them like idols. And do you know why? Because that's what they are—pictures of real-life gods."

Homer made a doubtful face, and the woman raised one gnarled and spindly finger, beckoning him to follow her to the rack of movie posters. "Look at them carefully: each one personifies a quality. This"—holding out a photo of Fred Astaire dancing with a coat rack—"isn't that the image of grace most people hold in their minds? Listen to Baryshnikov and those other ballet dancers—who do they say inspired them to put on dancing shoes? This man, that's who! You want the picture of youth? Right here!" She smacked the photo of James Dean. "And here you have female sex, in the flesh!" Her hand slid over the glossy paper, tapping at the cleavage of Marilyn Monroe, who stood slightly bent, leaning forward in the updraft.

"People used to worship the god of this and the goddess of that, paint pictures of them on cave walls, or carve their faces into totem poles. Now we call them movie stars and turn our technology on them. But we still worship them the same way—silently, in the dark, gathered together. My husband's trade was hobbies: coins and stamps. He never made a living at it, really. I trade in religion. You know what I found out? Religion is better business than hobbies."

Jill, who had been wandering around the store during this recitation, ended her tour behind the counter, near the silver dollar that made George Raft a star. She studied it carefully. "Was this coin in the display case last night?"

Mrs. Geffelman nodded. "Always."

"And it wasn't stolen?"

The woman raised and dropped her arms as if to ask *who could understand the mind of a thief.* "Almost nothing was stolen—just one pair of shoes. They were supposed to have been worn by Fred Astaire, but to tell you the truth, I have a little doubt about that pair. The woman who sold them to me showed me papers, but I don't remember seeing a pair like them in the movie."

"And that was the only theft?"

"The burglar went through the register, of course. And ransacked the papers in the back. But I don't keep cash in the store overnight. The door and gate—those are the expensive losses."

"The thief opened the register?" asked Homer, his clue radar sounding. But Jill was two steps ahead of him, already behind the machine.

"Which button?" She had a handkerchief ready and a small plastic evidence bag.

"This one," said Mrs. Geffelman, pushing it and springing the cash drawer with a crash and a bell. "But I've touched that already a dozen times this morning. I have to do business here, don't I?"

Homer and Jill exchanged frowns. They weren't going to get fingerprints from that. He peered into the back of the shop. "You said the burglar went through your papers, too. I take it you meant the affidavits?"

Mrs. Geffelman smiled bitterly and shook her head. "That would make sense already! Those are worth something, if you also have the items they identify. These were just papers—sales slips, receipts, inventory records. Nothing worth a penny to anyone but me."

"Are any of them missing?" Jill inquired. Homer noticed that his new partner was evidently right beside him on the same logical trail.

"No, just dumped all over the floor. I've been rearranging them all morning. I can't remember each and every document, of course. That's six months' worth of business transactions. But nothing's missing, as far as I can tell."

"Except," jumped in Homer while Jill was still forming her next question, "those shoes worn by Fred Astaire."

"Maybe worn by him."

"Either way, they're all we have to go on," Homer persisted. "And the thief took the affidavit? The one you had from the woman, describing the shoes?"

Mrs. Geffelman shook her head. "He did not. And without it, they're worth no more than your shoes—less, by the look of your tassels. What are those, fifty, sixty dollars?"

Homer was about to object strenuously to her undervaluation of his footwear when Jill reclaimed control of the line of questioning.

"In other words," she said, pausing to make sure that Homer was listening, "somebody sawed through a steel gate, smashed a hole in a reinforced door, stuck a hand through a jagged ring of glass to get inside here—and then ignored all these precious coins and souvenirs, walking out with a single pair of shoes . . . of doubtful origin?"

Mrs. Geffelman raised her shoulders in a stage gesture of bewilderment. "That's the way it looks, doesn't it? But it makes no sense at all. Only a collector would take so much trouble for something with so little monetary value. But anyone who collects seriously enough to care about those shoes would know enough to doubt their authenticity. Now, how do you figure that one?"

Homer knew how he usually went about it: clue by tiny clue. But Mrs. Geffelman was asking about motives again, which were usually Shelly's department. Why did people do things? He never liked to speculate. Out of habit, Homer turned for a response to his partner—and found Jill looking back at him with an equally quizzical frown.

Chester Gafarian did not like to be away from his telephone during the crucial early phases of a plan of his own, but lunch was a devotion he observed with regularity. If he didn't, there would be irregularity, he liked to say, with more than a grain of truth. Angelica worried about his health, bent over a desk all day long, and made him promise to stretch his legs at least as far as the diner. In accord with her instructions, he had a salad every afternoon, with black olives and big chunks of feta cheese to give it flavor. She allowed him an ouzo besides, but he never drank one in the middle of a job. And he had to admit, each afternoon when he returned to work, there had to be something to what she said—the change of air and exercise always made his muscles more limber and his head clearer when he rang the little bell dangling over the door on his way back into the flower shop.

Schnork was not in today—of course, Chester had given him a little errand to run. So there had been no one to answer the phone during his lunchtime absence. That was not a problem, however, since Chester had invested in an answering machine. He was dead set against mechanical toys for their own sake and refused to bring in a fax, but felt it only responsible to make use of new technology when it increased his responsiveness to his employer's needs. An answering machine certainly did that. Francis was not pleased the first time he heard the outgoing message, recorded by Schnork, which began with a song about a dandelion by the Rolling Stones and followed with a quip about "saying it with flowers." But Chester had changed the message to something more dignified, and the music to Jerry Vale, and had counseled Francis about the advantages the machine provided an operation such as their own. Francis had recognized the wisdom in Chester's words a few days later when a warning was left by Ricky Tick about a raid on their Long Beach office. Francis had insisted that all their shops put in a machine the following week. That was the way it worked between them, Chester understood: he had an idea, persuaded Francis not to interfere, and then allowed him to believe that the insight had been his own in the first place.

Now he tapped the little button on the front and listened to the stories on the tape.

There were two messages on the machine, according to the glowing red digit in the LED readout on top. The first was a hang-up, a dial tone followed by a recorded announcement from the phone company. The second he had expected —the caller had left his number, as if Chester didn't have it inscribed on his memory already, let alone in the Rolodex on his desktop. He hadn't forgotten about that little matter, but could tell by the strain in the recorded voice that it was time to make a reassuring follow-up call. His scheme was moving ahead right on schedule; no point in letting any of the elements slip out of line.

When he opened the door to his inner office, Chester's face lit up at once. There was nothing he liked better than a present, really, wrapped in beautiful paper and tied with a bow—unless it was a surprise present, which he enjoyed more. And that was just what was waiting for him in the center of his desk, in dark blue paper decorated with tiny white snowmen. He was aware that a man in his line of work needed to be careful about these things, and Chester recognized his obligation to Angelica by taking his metal detector from the closet and passing it over the package before touching the curled white ribbon. But caution was one thing and paranoia another—when the detector indicated there was no metal in it, he pulled the satiny edge and tore through the paper.

Inside was a pair of shoes, the old saddle kind, with brown flaps covering the laces and yellow leather at the heel and toe. He recognized them at once as dancing shoes, an old pair, made of butter-soft leather, polished to a glaze. Chester stuck his hands inside the shoes, and felt a stiff card in the left one, on which had been printed in graceful calligraphy, "Worn by Fred Astaire in *Swing Time*, 1936." At the bottom of the box, stuck in the folds of red tissue paper, was a smaller card of the kind enclosed by florists in gift bouquets. Along the top, a printed family of swans swam in blue water. Below, printed in a big, childish hand, were the words "Please accept these as my apology, to show you that I tried." It was unsigned, but Chester had no need of a signature—he knew the author.

He unlaced the shoes and stuck his feet inside. A little snug, maybe, but a helluva gesture—he had to hand that to the kid. Perhaps it wasn't such a bad decision, after all. Everyone was entitled to a little patience when their first efforts failed. It depended on what you did with the second. Chester realized he was going to have to think of something to say to Angelica, but if things worked out all right, something was certain to come to him when he needed it.

He dropped into his chair and dialed home. They would go dancing—he could try out the shoes. There, on the dance floor, he could whisper whatever he liked without her raising a ruckus. After all, Schnork was his cousin, too. Chester had taken him under his personal protection and promised to look out for him. And he was looking out for him, already. There was a career in this business, a good one. Wasn't that why they had come to him in the first place? When a little real money starting rolling in, her cousin would have nothing to complain about.

She picked up. "Hello? Who is it?"

Chester said, "Me."

"What is it?"

"I want to take you dancing tonight."

"Why?"

"I feel like it."

"Why?"

"Don't you want to? You like dancing."

"Sure I want to. What's not to like? But there's a reason, isn't there?"

"What makes you think so?"

"Because I know you, don't I? But if you don't want to tell me now, I can wait. You're gonna have to tell me sooner or later."

She hung up. Chester thought about his decision and decided again that it had been the right one to make. The kid kept nagging him for a chance, and this job was just his size—and not too risky, either. As to the outcome . . . well, he hadn't brought back what he was sent for, had he? But the failure of his first attempt wasn't his fault, and he was trying to set it straight this time, wasn't he?

Chester tried a fast shuffle on the linoleum floor, watching the gleam of his shoes. The gift showed some style. He hadn't expected it. Schnork showed promise—if only he would do something about his hair.

It wasn't that Schnork Szabo hadn't tried to do something about the mass of black hair that stuck straight up on the front of his head like the spines of a frightened porcupine— it simply made no difference. No matter what lotion, unction, or formula he tried, his hair recovered its upright stature sooner or later. It was just a matter of time: mousses were overcome in mere minutes, while a thick slab of petroleum jelly might take a few hours to neutralize. He had been to a succession of barbers, hairstylists, and even doctors specializing in hair problems. The haircutters all promised to fix his condition with the right style and conditioners, and usually had him looking pretty good by the time he stood up from their chairs. By the time he had made his way down the street, however, his hair would begin to reassert itself, and the rearview mirror inside his car always reflected his ultimate defeat. Doctors were hardly sympathetic; after trying to grow hair on bald heads all day, their usual advice was to enjoy what God had given him.

But it was not so easy to enjoy unruly hair—not for Schnork Szabo. It was interpreted by his family as a sign of indifferent self-discipline bordering on rebellion. His mother said it revealed his Hungarian Gypsy blood; his father pointed out patiently that there was no Gypsy in him. Either way, it was a symbol of the wildness that both agreed was in him, though Schnork was in all other respects a model of behavior. He applied himself in school and earned A's and B's on his tests, though his teachers usually knocked him down a grade on his final reports. They saw him sitting there with his wild hair waving like the crowd at a football game doing "the wave," and couldn't believe that it hadn't been he who sent spitballs at their backsides when they turned to their blackboards.

Women also suspected him. The message in the tresses that stood up from his forehead was that here was a man who would come to no good; either because of his own inability to take control of his life or because of the ill will of others who misjudged him, Schnork was not regarded as the man to entrust with their future and that of their children to come. Rivals could score easy points by making jokes at the expense of his hairdo, and Schnork soon suffered from the lack of self-confidence that a few such experiences could exacerabate. Hair aside, he was not a bad-looking kid, with black hair and olive skin and brown eyes the color of cherrywood. But none of that seemed to matter, since no one ever looked past the crown of spikes on his head.

Gabor Szabo always had sympathy for his son. But as the junior man in his Parks Department office, he could hardly find a job for him when the boy left school. It had fallen to a cousin on his mother's side of the family to give Schnork his start in the business world. Chester Gafarian was a name that Gabor Szabo heard only when his wife compared him, unfavorably, to the husbands of the other women in her clan. Schnork had also heard these unflattering comparisons, and although his sympathy went out to his father, the underlying message was all too clear: to win the heart of a woman, and to overcome the obstacle of his hair, he would need to do what Gafarian did—make a lot of money.

He had taken the job in the florist's shop because Chester had told him to take it. But he had learned without surprise and in short order that flowers were not what made Gafarian such a good provider. He almost called his father with the news when he learned about the business that had treated Uncle Chester so well. But, with a shrewd understanding of his parents, Schnork knew that his father could not keep the information to himself and that his mother, if she knew, would no longer allow him to follow Uncle Chester's example. And Schnork wanted to be like Gafarian, not merely because of the money Chester accumulated and the status it lent him in the family but also because he had achieved his success despite a cowlick that stood out from the crown of his head like a dandelion sprouting a flower. Chester provided a model that Schnork could emulate and escape the predicament of his cranium.

Schnork did whatever Chester told him to do. His confidence was in obedience: sooner or later, if he followed every command, Gafarian would feel responsible for Schnork's well-being. And when he did, he would have to arrange what Schnork desperately wanted—a chance to prove himself in the business. For the sake of that opportunity, Schnork was prepared to rearrange flowers with a concentration unmatched even by the Japanese. He was prepared to make deliveries, carry lunches, and pick up suits at the cleaners; he was prepared to press those suits himself, if necessary. It was a strategy of servility. He watched it taking its toll on Gafarian, as each humble service rendered him more and more into Schnork's debt. Until the day arrived when Chester could no longer stand to take on additional obligation and gave him his first illegal assignment.

Schnork was determined not to screw up his chance to prove himself a criminal. After eight months of earning his shot, he was not going to disappoint Chester and himself. The job was easy enough: he stood on the sidewalk in the light of a streetlamp, sawing his way through a steel gate, punching his way through a door. It seemed to Schnork that his determination protected him—no passing cars stopped to ask what the hell he was doing. Not that it would have mattered if they had. Schnork would have given them his untroubled expression, which always proved enough to send them away.

And that was why it agonized him to discover it wasn't there—the thing Chester had asked him to retrieve. Schnork was not by nature a ruffian: there was no reason to trash the place, once he had made sure the object was gone. But he had felt a need to carry something back to Chester as a token of his good faith in the endeavor. His eyes lit on the dancing shoes in the counter by the register, reminding him how much Chester liked to dance. So he took them as a consolation gift and left them on Chester's desk along with a humble note of apology. They ought to buy him a little time, at least, to prove himself. Enough to follow up his hard-earned lead.

He had cleaned out the cash register to throw the police off the scent, though it had hardly any money in it. He had just grabbed the cash then, and was now counting out the bills for the first time as he sat in his Dart. Forty dollars: twenty in singles, two fives, and a ten. Just enough for a sales clerk to make change in the morning. He folded the bills on top of seven of his own and stuffed them back in his pocket. He had to work fast, to make up for his failure. If he succeeded, there would be no shortage of money in the future.

He looked up as a window on the second floor rattled from within, shutting with a squeak. Was she cold up there or what? He waited for a second, watching the venetian blinds through the panes. Then a second window closed, at the northern corner, and Schnork smiled. She was moving toward the front of the apartment now, which probably meant she was going out. Three minutes later his suspicion was confirmed, when the woman who had taken in the paper at apartment 2C stepped from the building lobby. She was pushing a cart full of laundry, like a baby, in a basket. Mrs. Pilson—at last. Schnork glanced at his watch. He had wasted half of the morning and most of the lunch hour waiting for her. He would have to work fast. He still had to stop by the printer and make a delivery.

Mrs. Pilson lowered her laundry cart from the sidewalk to the street, crossed to the other side, and strode off at a brisk clip down the pavement. Have a good time, Schnork thought as he waved after her while she disappeared around the corner. We'll take care of the home front while you do the wash. He gave her a moment to forget her soap powder and run home for it. When she didn't reappear around the corner, he cranked up his window and reached into the backseat for a pair of garden gloves and a rolled-up towel. It was heavy and he shook it, reassuring himself by the clunk of his tools inside. He wedged it under his arm and climbed from the Dart, locking the door behind him. He fished in his pocket, found a quarter, and fed it into the meter. He turned the knob and the needle jumped—an hour. That should be more than enough.

He glanced in both directions down the block, making one last check at the corner. Then he put on the garden gloves and stepped into the street, crossing briskly toward Mrs. Pilson's vacant apartment.

12

Thom showed up at the hospital near the end of Izzy's visit, as she was rummaging for her car keys in her bag, making noises about leaving. He stood on the threshold of the room, hesitating until Isabelle walked over to escort him to the bed. "Thomas! Come here! It's so nice of you to come and visit your father. Uh, where's your mother, dear?"

She looked past him toward the hall, as if expecting to see Ruth behind the boy. From the grim resolution on Isabelle's lips Shelly could see she was preparing to resume whatever battle had waged between them while he lay unconscious in the ICU. But that didn't prove necessary.

"She'll be back to pick me up in twenty minutes," Thom said with an affected shrug of eleven-year-old indifference.

"So soon?"

"That's fine," Shelly protested, "more than enough time." A strange brew of feelings bubbled in his chest, blending shame, that his son should see him in so reduced a condition, and joy, in the boy's presence. There was a flavoring of relief, too, that Ruth had been willing to acknowledge the occasion by allowing him to visit. He watched his son approach the bed with a wary eye on the intravenous contraption. Shelly stirred his arm at the elbow, and the connecting tube wiggled.

"Pretty creepy, huh?"

Thom nodded, looked into his father's face, and then smiled, catching on that Shelly was joking. But he didn't like the looks of the contraption any better for the levity, and moved around to the other side of the bed, anyway. "How long have you gotta be hooked up like that?"

"Until I can eat. Which could be some time, judging by what I've seen of the food so far."

The boy gazed over toward Debs, who was sleeping with his mouth open like a corpse.

"Why don't we take a walk down the hall?" Shelly suggested, raising himself with an effort. "No reason for us to wake the dead, is there?"

Thom shook his head, staring at Debs.

Isabelle said, "I've got to be off. Why don't you walk me to the elevator?"

They did, and when the doors closed on her last blown kiss, Shelly suggested he and Thom continue on down the hall to the research laboratories in the annex. He thought Thom might like to see one of those, if they could get in. Thom shrugged, which Shelly interpreted as a yea vote, and the two Lowenkopfs shuffled toward the bridge between buildings, with the wheels of the intravenous stand squeaking beside them.

As they walked down the hall, it was clear to Shelly that every effort had been made to stave off the presence of death. The machines of science were the first line of defense, beeping and glimmering defiance. There was no sign of blood or bodily fluid on any of the staff, whose spotless aquamarine uniforms demonstrated their allegiance to the living. Sterilized bottles and cotton products and paper-wrapped steel instruments were stored in the closets like armaments stockpiled against a siege. And yet, what a museum of death the hospital actually was!

Every room accommodated a pair of potential specimens:

heart disease dominated, but likely victims of stroke were on hand, and several varieties of cancer. The room next to the elevator had a kidney patient on a dialysis machine, and diagonally across the hall, someone was moaning and gripping her stomach. They were prepping one old alkie for a liver shunt—an operation they thought might give him a few months longer. His coughing came from deep inside, an intermittent rattle like the hiss of a snake that had swallowed a live rabbit. The enemy had breached the walls, and no one seemed to have noticed. Shelly remembered the beeps of his own heart throbbing with more than a little trepidation.

Thom didn't seem to notice all the mortality, his attention engaged instead by a series of children's crayon drawings, framed in glass, on the wall. They came to the end of the hall where a glass door was etched with the name *LDS Research Facility* and securely locked. They hesitated at the entranceway for a moment, Thom studying a train in the last of the drawings, when Bruce Haight came rushing down the hall, the lab key tight in his hand, extended like a divining rod before him.

He fit it into the glass door and fumbled with the lock, anxious to get it open. He passed his clipboard from his right hand to his left, still couldn't manage, and offered it to Shelly beside him, muttering, "Hang on to that for a minute, will you?" Shelly was not given an opportunity to agree before the Masonite board was thrust into his hands. The lock slipped and the doctor recovered his clipboard, glancing quizzically from father to son before disappearing through the door.

Shelly didn't mind the slight; he planted his foot on the threshold and held the door for Thom. On the other side was a short hallway, very bright, lined on the left and right with windows. It was a sort of bridge between buildings, linking the patient care building with another, shorter, structure, whose top story was level with the third-floor ward. On the far side of the bridge was a glass door, unmarked and unlocked, which led to a perpendicular corridor. To the right this corridor ended at a single door, from behind which emerged shrieks and howls and the squeak of metal—all the sounds of a torture chamber. Thom pressed his nose to the window in the door with Shelly behind him, and the blur of movement inside became discernible. Directly in front of them were stacked thirty small cages of white rats and diminutive mice. To the left of those cages, a flat table with a paper cover and a glinting aluminum rail served to mark a gap in the evolutionary scale: on its far side, larger cases held shapes that looked like children in the darkness, until they leaned forward, baring their teeth and screeching, and revealed themselves as chimpanzees.

Thom looked at his father, who nodded, murmuring, "Monkeys." The boy clung to the glass, watching the restless beasts jump up and down in their cages. Shelly leaned over again and whispered, "Why don't you wait here?"

Shelly headed toward the far end of the corridor, hearing yips and woofs behind him. Dogs, he realized, probably off to the left somewhere, out of sight from the hall. At first he was concerned that their barking might alert Haight. But when the resident failed to appear in the corridor, Shelly understood that the noise was something you lived with and learned to ignore—and it provided good cover for the clinking of the pole against the intravenous bottle running into his arm.

Shelly passed the entrance hall and surveyed the other end of the corridor. There were five laboratory rooms and a big steel-and-glass refrigerator. Haight's voice was coming from an open room two doors down on the left, loud enough for Shelly to recognize only his characteristic whine, the tone of a man who considered himself perpetually mistreated. Shelly didn't quite know what he hoped to hear, but his professional instincts provoked him: a doctor had disappeared. He edged closer to the door. Beyond it, against the opposite wall, was the refrigerator, and he could see a large examining room at the end of the hall. That was probably where Ashbury and Freylung examined Debs the day Goodman found her samples tampered with. Shelly would have liked a look around in there, as he would have liked a quick search around each of the laboratories. He did not stop to think about his own status in the hospital, the lack of any formal charge or complaint, or what he would say to Haight if the resident confronted him in the laboratory hall.

The first door immediately to his left had Freylung's name stenciled on it, just below a square of double glass. That would be her lab, of course, the first and largest encountered by a visitor to the annex. If Haight's door was the second one, ajar on the left, then Goodman and Ashbury were probably installed in labs on the right. Shelly stretched his neck, trying to make out which room was Elaine's and whether she was actually inside. But he didn't get a chance to find out, because at that moment he heard an unmistakable change in the pitch and volume of Bruce Haight's telephone voice.

"Just how long do you think that'll be?" Bruce said, trying to whisper but losing control of his volume so that his thin whine became audible.

The answer to his question from the other end of the line was evidently complicated, or so Shelly assumed from the length of the silence that followed, and unsatisfactory, judging by the indignant pleading with which Bruce next responded.

"But you told me you would take care of it! You said that two days ago. Now you want me to—"

Shelly felt a touch at his elbow and turned to see Thom, who had evidently grown bored with the animals. Shelly placed a finger on his lips; the boy's answering gesture, a thumb wagging over his shoulder, was clearly intended as a suggestion that they should leave. Shelly shook his head, poking Thom's chest and pointing toward the door. Thom stepped back but held his ground: if Shelly wasn't leaving, he wasn't either. So they both heard Haight's next exasperated whimper.

"But for how long? I can't keep something like that under wraps for more than a couple of days."

Thom mouthed, What's he talking about?

Shelly shrugged, shaking his head. He glanced toward the exit again, but Thom only crossed his arms.

Bruce's nervous laugh reached them seconds later, trailing off into a halfhearted boast. "Hell, yeah, there's plenty of deadbeats around here. But they're not all the same kind. We lose one on the table every now and then, and a few even go in their beds. But, Jesus, Ches," he said, dropping his voice, "this is murder."

Shelly stepped back from the door, forgetting about the tubes in his elbow. They tugged at the bottle, which rattled against the stand, tipping it over. He caught it as the top of the metal frame crashed into the wall. A moment later, Bruce Haight's head appeared at his door.

"What are you doing out here?" he demanded.

Shelly's first instinct was to say "Police" and reach for his weapon. But his hand felt only the radio transmitter in his holster, wired to his heart. Where his departmental badge should have been was only the thin cotton of his open-back hospital gown. He had an idea how unimpressive an impression he made with his rear peeking out behind him.

"Looking for Dr. Ashbury," Shelly said.

"She's your doctor," growled Haight. "You don't go paying calls on her. You're Lowenkopf, aren't you?"

Shelly nodded. Haight glared at Thom, who stepped closer to his father. "Nice animals," the boy said.

"Keep away from them," Haight responded. "They're subjects, for research. Nothing to get sentimental about."

The boy looked at his father, who was eyeing Haight evenly. The doctor met his gaze for an instant, did not seem to enjoy it, and broke away.

"You'll have to leave," he said.

"We're off," said Shelly.

Haight turned back into his room. Shelly waited until the doctor was out of sight. Then, holding Thom's hand, he strode down the corridor, his intravenous stand tagging along like a third wheel. When they cleared the bridgeway door and found themselves once again face to face with the children's art on the ward, Shelly began to wonder just what it was they had actually overheard. Already his memory was growing ambiguous, a doubtful source of information and an even more doubtful source of evidence in court. He remembered five essential words: "Jesus, Ches, this is murder." But even his own immediate self-reflection started to poke holes in his story. Long experience enabled him to anticipate what a defense attorney, strolling back and forth with his hands behind his back, would do to his testimony on the witness stand:

"*Now, Sergeant, you reported overhearing the suspect say, 'Jesus Ches'?*"

"*Yes.*"

"*Then would you mind telling the court—who is Jesus Ches? A new divinity? Or couldn't he have said Jesus Christ?*"

"*Not the way I heard it—*"

"*You were ill, weren't you? With a tube in your arm? At less than full operating capacity?*"

"*My hearing wasn't affected by the—*"

"*You were listed on the precinct roll as medically unfit for duty. Were the precinct records fraudulent?*"

"*Of course not.*"

"*And you were on medication, weren't you? Wouldn't you assume another man in your position might be functioning at less than his best?*"

"*I suppose. But—*"

"*So you might really have overheard the defendant say, 'Jesus Christ, this is murder.' You ever hear anybody else say that, Sergeant? Ever say it yourself?*"

The prosecuting attorney would have to bring Thom in as a corroborating witness, and Shelly wasn't prepared to expose his son to that experience. What was more, he wasn't sure that anything sinister had actually happened to Dr. Freylung. People disappeared all the time, turning up two days later, suntanned and carrying conch shells under their arms. The doctor was probably on a beach somewhere, soaking up the rays, relying on her residents to cover for her. In the old days, it wasn't even considered a missing-persons case until twenty-four hours had elapsed. Now those rules didn't always apply—for a disabled person, say, or a missing child. But a competent physician was presumed to be able to take care of herself, lacking evidence to the contrary. So what was he getting so excited about? He felt the answer lurking in the back of his skull: too much interest in Ashbury—and behind that, the darker dread of what Mordred was coming to say.

"Let's go back to the room," he said, putting his arm around Thom. The boy's brow creased for a moment but he said nothing, and Shelly was glad for his confidence.

As they passed the elevators on their way back, Miguel was manning the desk. He reached under the counter when he saw them and said, "Sergeant Lowenkopf! Do me a solid, will you? Take this to your roomie?" It was a newspaper, rolled up and secured with a red rubber band. A cursory glance told Shelly that Debs would be happy to see it—he could tell from the lettering that it was apparently the *Georgia Gazette*.

"Sure."

He tucked the newspaper under his arm and turned toward his room, but Thom hung back reluctantly by the elevators.

"Gotta go now, Dad. Mom'll be waiting out front. You know how she is when she's blocking traffic."

Shelly remembered: twenty minutes. Was that why Thom had gestured to leave the lab corridor? He gave the boy a hug and a kiss on the top of his head.

"Thanks for coming."

"Sure. It was, uh . . . fun."

The elevator took him away, and Shelly wondered, *fun?* Was that what you called sneaking around a hospital?

Listening in on private phone conversations? Overhearing what could have been a confession? He shrugged. It was life with Shelly Lowenkopf, and to a eleven-year-old boy, sure, that might be fun.

When Shelly entered his room, Debs was sitting up, drinking a cup of black tea. "Georgian," he croaked, his voice still sore from the forced oxygen he'd received on the operating table. He wiggled the plastic stirrer. "Best tea in the world."

Shelly tossed him the paper. "News from home."

Debs reached for the bundle anxiously, the sudden movement causing a wince of pain, which he ignored. He unsnapped the rubber band, straightened the front page, then stared at Shelly with an expression of incomprehension that was slowly transformed into a grimace of joy.

"Good news?" Shelly asked.

Debs turned to him, speechless, with tears in his eyes. He looked back at the paper again, to make sure of what it had said, then took a deep breath, his chest swelling and swelling with each effort to express what was inside.

"Freedom!" he cried in a whisper. "Freedom!" The utterance cost him dearly and he shut his eyes, raising his face to heaven. His arms shook as he clutched the newspaper in a frenzied grip.

Shelly peered at the incomprehensible headline. "Who's free?"

But Debs couldn't answer: the emotion was too much for him. It surged through his hands, crushing the newsprint, and raced through his shoulders and his heart. His lips trembled, parting ecstatically. And then one eye suddenly opened as if he had noticed something, and the look of transport on his face turned to fear. His upper torso continued to shake, but the rhythm changed, increasing from a tremor to a lurching spasm. He tumbled forward, tearing at the robe over his chest.

Shelly didn't bother with the call button—he hollered

until Miguel appeared. The young nurse took one look at Debs and sounded the alarm, and in a matter of minutes the room was full of medical staff and machines.

Bruce Haight entered and took immediate control, issuing commands to the others. They fixed electrical nodes to Deb's chest, cleared away, and Bruce zapped him with current. Twice. Then they stuck a long needle into him.

But it made no difference: the enlarged heart had burst with a surfeit of national pride.

13

When Helen Pilson returned from the Chinese laundry, pulling her empty cart behind her, she found the door of her second-floor apartment unlocked. The Pilsons had only one lock on their door, the kind that came with the apartment and had to be locked with a key. Helen thought back, pursing her lips, and distinctly remembered setting aside her laundry cart, finding the key in her handbag, and locking the door behind her. And now the knob opened in her hand?

Helen was in her middle thirties, with brown hair that hung limp no matter how she cut it. She wore a plain print dress and a knit sweater, bunched up at the sleeves. She took pride in her good common sense, her ability to keep house, and her loyalty as a wife. She had no personal interest in collecting anything, but had thrown in her lot with her husband. If something was threatening Arthur's things, it was threatening her, too.

She stepped into the apartment fearing the worst. She had known this would happen sooner or later. Hadn't she been after Arthur to install a dead bolt, or at least an automatic lock, now that his collection was finally growing to a point where someone might actually be interested? But Arthur had shrugged and shaken his head, examining some piece of junk through a glass and filling out one of his index cards. Now someone had come into their home—she could feel it in the air. A minute later her suspicions were confirmed when she saw the cabinet doors in her kitchen hanging open, revealing her plates and drinking glasses, and the nested pots and pans beneath her sink.

She looked around for a desperate moment before realizing that nothing had really been disturbed. The plates, unbroken, were still stacked on their shelves; the cookware had been rearranged but replaced in the same general area. A most considerate intruder it must have been—neat, even. That reassured her some and gave her the confidence to venture farther into her apartment. The wreckage was worst where she expected it, in their bedroom and in Arthur's study, the little room she had hoped might be a nursery, twelve years before. The child had never come, and Arthur had filled the room with his collection—first photographs of film stars, starting with Rita Hayworth, then items that had belonged to this one or that: a glove from Susan Hayward, two cuff links with the initials of Tyrone Power, a tie said to have been worn by Leslie Howard. Three of the walls were lined with metal bookcases now, each shelf crammed with shoe boxes, carefully identified in Magic Marker. For each acquisition he filled out a crisp white card, recording a description of the item, the price he had paid for it, and the shoe box in which he had stored it. When the metal shelves of the study were filled with boxes, he had started on the shelves in their bedroom closet. The closet was a mess now, Arthur's shirts and jackets dumped unceremoniously on the bed, his shoes strewn about the floor. The burglar hadn't taken the time to straighten up after himself in here. But this was nothing compared to the chaos of the study itself.

As soon as she entered the room, Helen knew that the disorderliness would cause Arthur more grief than the loss of whatever had been stolen. Half a dozen shoe boxes had been emptied on the floor, torn, and flattened. Another dozen were still on the shelves but had evidently been searched and rearranged—large items mixed with small ones, a confusion certain to upset Arthur. All over the floor, wherever she stepped, were things you might find in the catch-all top drawer of a desk: pens and marbles, a lighter and a tie clip, elaborate hair ornaments, and a thimble. And each one, by its displacement, might have been severed from the history that gave it value. She was standing in the middle of a heap of things of great value to her husband, afraid to set down the heel of her foot lest she ruin something salvageable from the wreckage of their burglary.

There was a piece of writing paper under the toe of her shoe, embossed with the initials N.S. She picked it up, uncreased it, and tried to rub off the smudge. Arthur would know whose paper it was, without a doubt—she hoped. Poor Arthur! She stood for a moment, surveying the damage, pitying her husband in advance. The devastation would cause him anguish at first, but he would get over it, once the shock of violation wore off and he came to terms with what remained, one item at a time. The painstaking recovery would be a healing process for him. For herself—she did not want to think about what it would mean to her. She walked to the telephone and called the police.

Homer and Jill were munching a late lunch when the call from the precinct house came in. Homer had intended to make their first meal together something of an occasion and had called in a reservation to his favorite seafood place on City Island. But Jill was determined to do some real investigating before they put their feet up to talk over what they had learned, and insisted they catch a fast bite within earshot of the car radio. Her vote was for pizza. It took all Homer's persuasive power to convince her to drive down to Burke Avenue for some slices from his favorite pizzeria. He went inside while she sat in the car, waiting for him to bring a thick, square slab of Sicilian for himself and a regular pie-shaped slice for her, with two super-sweet grape drinks in cone-shaped paper cups. They had hardly begun to eat when the radio call came through, vindicating Jill in all her stubbornness, or so she obviously seemed to feel. Homer sighed, gobbled his Sicilian in half a dozen bites, and gulped down the grape drink. Jill watched him chew each cheesy bite with unspoken impatience in her eyes, until he wiped his mouth on the waxy white paper and threw the car into gear.

When they reached the Pilsons' apartment building, Helen was waiting for them in the lobby. As they pulled up at the curb, they saw her through the plate-glass window that looked out over the street. By the time they reached the outside door, she was already holding open the inner door for them. Homer glanced back at the Reliant and wondered just what it was about the car that seemed to announce their profession to even the most untrained civilian. How did she know they were police? Remembering Mrs. Geffelman, he realized it had to be their appearance rather than their car, but a glance in the glass as he passed through the door convinced him it wasn't *his* suit. He looked over at Jill Morganthal, took in her sweater and skirt and brown leather bag, and wondered again about her.

"I didn't touch anything," Helen Pilson said, spreading ten fingers apart to demonstrate her hands-off caution. "If there's anything your experts can learn from the condition of the place, it's still up there."

Homer was about to tell her he wasn't sure that any technical experts would be called to the scene, when Jill asked, "Can you tell us, ma'am, just what was stolen?"

"Well, *I* don't know, of course," Helen said. "Only Arthur could tell you that."

"Fine," said Jill, looking around the empty lobby. "Where is Arthur?"

"At work," said Helen. "I didn't want to tell him about this until there was something hopeful to say about his chances of recovering what was stolen."

"There aren't going to be any chances, ma'am, unless someone can tell us what's missing."

Helen pursed her lips, considering the alternatives, until at last she nodded. "All right, I'll call him. But don't blame me if he's a little emotional about it."

Helen called her husband from the pay phone around a corner from the elevator, returning a few minutes later to say Arthur was on his way. He worked in an eyeglass store on Gun Hill Road and would be home in less than twenty minutes. Under Helen's expectant scrutiny, Homer could not resist calling the crime scene unit for a fingerprint expert to dust the Pilsons' apartment. Arthur and the lab man arrived within minutes of each other, and the party of five went upstairs together to the second floor.

Arthur Pilson was a heavy man, dressed in a brown suit a few inches too small around his waist. He held himself together with effort, unwilling to express his grief until he understood the extent of his loss. He swallowed often as the elevator ascended, a lump in his throat rising above the knot of his tie each time he did.

The exterior apartment door showed no prints other than Helen's when dusted, though the lock did indeed show signs of having been picked. When Homer signaled to Arthur that they were ready to enter, his keys shook in his hand until his wife took them away from him. In the kitchen Helen's were again the only prints. The thief had evidently taken the trouble to wear gloves, which meant, Homer thought, that they had called down the fingerprint expert for no reason, except to prove there had been no reason to call him.

While the police went over the kitchen, Arthur glanced toward the bedrooms several times, drawn to the worst of the damage but afraid of what he might find there. Homer noticed his gaze and suggested, "Why don't you go on ahead? See if you can figure out what's been taken. Just don't touch anything in there, and we'll be right behind you."

Arthur nodded, accepting the suggestion as a command.

He swallowed again, his face growing pale as he prepared to confront his destiny. Taking his wife's hand, he headed for the bedrooms with faltering steps.

Homer started to follow them, but Jill took the fingerprint man by the arm and led him back to the front door. Opening it again, she squatted alongside, estimating the distance from her elbow to her ear and then, pointing to a space about a foot above the lock, said, "Try there."

The fingerprint man looked for confirmation to Homer, who shrugged. Jill frowned, and the cop knelt, dusting the door where she indicated. It was too high, Homer knew, for them to find fingerprints there, so he was more than a bit taken aback to discover a strange imprint on the metal under Jill's hand.

"What's that?" he asked.

The fingerprint expert shrugged, shaking his head in silent incomprehension.

"An earprint," Jill explained, with the barest trace of smugness. "I read about them in the *Police Journal*. They've had some success matching them to perps lately. Why don't you get a Polaroid of this one?"

Suddenly there came a howl of pain, and the three officers looked up, trying to place its source. Homer was the first to realize it was coming from inside the apartment. With his hand on his automatic, he ran inside, found the master bedroom empty, and entered the smaller one, where Arthur Pilson knelt in the middle of a junk-strewn floor, hands covering his face, wailing.

"My God!" cried Pilson, racked by convulsions of sobbing. "God in heaven! God! What have they done?"

Helen stood over him, patting his shoulder, repeating, "Now, Arthur. There, there. There, now."

Pilson looked up at her, his face red as a cherry, his eyes swollen, tears running down his cheeks. The horror he felt was etched in his face, from the crow's-feet at his eyes, past the corners of his mouth, to the line of his trembling jaw. Arthur had abandoned all attempts to maintain control of his emotions and was weeping uncontrollably, allowing all of the painful disappointment he had ever felt about the empty nursery to express itself now in his loss. His wife, hovering over him, was herself shedding tears of sympathy for her husband, whose cries were her cries, too, and those of their unborn child.

Homer didn't have the slightest idea what sort of gesture he could possibly make, and the unbridled howl of human suffering cut through him like a knife. This was when Shelly would have stepped in with some ridiculous question that would have drawn the attention of the sufferers away from the cause of their pain. Homer couldn't for all he was worth think of a question that would serve. He began looking around desperately for someone to fill the void, and just then Jill came into the room behind him.

"What on earth is all that racket?" she said.

Helen turned to her, and Arthur raised his pathetic face to her as well. Homer would have given his right arm for Jill to have said something comforting to them then. She looked at each face: Arthur's, Helen's, finally Homer's. She seemed to know that something was expected of her. And Homer could see in her features a reflection of his own feelings—knowing that something was expected was not the same as knowing what to say.

"Any idea what's been taken yet?"

Arthur stared at her for a full minute before responding. "My dice!" he said. "The ones used in Nathan Detroit's floating crap game in *Guys and Dolls*—gone! The sword wielded by Jose Ferrer as *Cyrano de Bergerac*—stolen! Who—who could have done this to me? He might as well have thrust that sword through my heart! My combs—all of them—taken! The comb used by Edd 'Kookie' Byrnes on 'Seventy-seven Sunset Strip.' Is there another one like it? Not to mention the b-b-back—" He couldn't go on.

"He had a whole collection of backstage combs, used to dress the hair of movie stars," Helen said sadly.

"Garbo!" exclaimed Pilson, suddenly recovering use of

his tongue. "Nobody ever saw her, but I had a decorative comb she wore on screen in *Camille*. And one from Dietrich —and Cooper—and James Dean . . ." His voice trailed off and Arthur burst into another round of sobbing.

The fingerprint expert came in with a shrug, and Helen gave them all a glare of barely concealed contempt. "I think you'd better go now," she said. Her tone suggested there was nothing else she believed they could do.

The three professionals exchanged uncomfortable glances. They *couldn't* leave then—they still had a job to do. And nothing made them want to do it more than the suggestion that there was nothing they could actually accomplish.

Arthur started to whimper, unable to maintain the intensity of his grieving. Helen held him, patting him about the shoulders and head. "There, now," she said. "There."

"I'm s-sorry," said Arthur, catching his breath.

"It's all right," Helen said. "Everything. We're going to be just fine."

Arthur nodded, gripping her hand.

They did not get an accounting from him of what he thought was stolen for another hour, at least. It took Helen the better part of a half hour to calm him down and to convince him that he could do something to help recover what had been taken from him. Homer bit his tongue to refrain from reporting how long were the odds against recovery; and he shook his head at Jill to prevent her from doing so.

The fingerprint expert dusted the room and was out of there as quickly as possible. Arthur's howl of pain had soured him, too; something about their handling of the case made him feel as if his own part was less than honorable. Perhaps it was simply because all of them knew they could hardly promise any relief to the pain Arthur evidently felt—especially, as was soon clear, without fingerprints to go on. Homer found a scuff mark in the Pilsons' bedroom closet, which under ordinary circumstances would have made him feel he had made his unique contribution. It was a heel mark near the hem of one of Helen's dresses—a neat bit of observation which, to his satisfaction, even Jill Morganthal had overlooked. But that did not seem enough this time, with the emotional end of the whole business so plainly unattended. He had never missed Shelly more than he did each time Arthur Pilson whimpered.

Afterward, when they had learned from the wretched collector all he had to offer, Homer drove Jill back to the station house and punched them both out for the night. And that was when Homer's brain really started working again —when the horror of Pilson's anguish finally subsided. In Homer's jacket pocket was his notebook with the list of items Arthur had realized were missing. But which had the thief come for? All of them? Or one of them in particular?

Remembering the scene in Mrs. Geffelman's shop, Homer inclined toward the latter. After all, the thief had left plenty of valuable merchandise. His motive couldn't be purely monetary. He had taken the shoes, but he was obviously after something else, too. It occurred to Homer that they had two inventories to compare, which just might be related. It was possible at least that the item for which the thief had come to Pilson might have been the same one he hoped to find at Mrs. Geffelman's shop on Fordham Road. Mrs. Geffelman had mentioned a file of receipts, records of her sales and purchases. What if those records listed an item stolen from Pilson?

He remembered the scattering of cards on the floor and fit his time card back into the rack. If the thief had come to Geffelman's place looking for something in particular and had failed to find it, what was he likely to do? Just what Homer himself would have done: look for a clue as to where it might have gone. For some reason the thief had thought at first that the item could be found in Mrs. Geffelman's store. Since it wasn't there, he'd figured she must have sold it and that the customer's name might be in her file of sales receipts. The thief could have taken the card, of course. But that would have called attention to it. Better would be to read the name of the purchaser, and mix the document back into the mess of cards on the floor.

Not much of a chance, really; mostly conjecture. But it was worth driving by for a fast check through Mrs. Geffelman's file. A flutter of guilt touched Homer as he climbed into the Reliant without Jill. He was just going down to the shop again; he felt no real need for backup. Jill had certainly performed well enough that day, but there was no reason to demand she work overtime on a couple of burglaries—minor ones at that, in which only small amounts of money were involved.

Homer drove to Fordham Road and was encouraged to find a light still on in Mrs. Geffelman's shop. He parked the Reliant and, when the door closed snugly behind him, felt as unencumbered and good about his work on this investigation as he had felt since accepting the assignment from Madagascar. At last he and his partner weren't tripping over each other's heels in a rush to do the same things. He walked into the store, heard the bell ring overhead—and saw Mrs. Geffelman and Jill Morganthal behind the glass counter, going through a box of sales receipts.

14

There was a certain resemblance, Shelly decided, between the flurry that followed an emergency on a hospital ward and the one that followed a death at the scene of a homicide. In both cases, a variety of experts congregated around a body, examining and poking and finally inserting something into it, while at the edge of the circle, Death watched the proceedings, looking for a recruit. From his bed across the room, Shelly had an excellent view of Haight's attempt to revive the lifeless Debs, an impressive effort, which stimulated in Lowenkopf some grudging respect for the resident, despite what he had overheard in the lab. The man was a doctor, saving lives, whatever else he was up to on the side.

When the resident gave up, and Debs lay zapped, punctured, but still dead, Haight left him to the orderlies, who loaded him onto a gurney and bore him away. That was another difference, Shelly realized, as the medical professionals cleared out, turning their backs on the corpse. His own colleagues were more comfortable with the dead, squatting alongside them to begin the painstaking collection of nail scrapings and fibers that might supply a clue to the guilty parties. There were no guilty parties here in a hospital, where people died every day, where a man who had just come out of surgery after an operation on his heart might reasonably be expected to die of complications. The autopsy by a staff pathologist in the basement would confirm that Debs's heart had given out.

Or were there? After the gurney had gone, Lowenkopf swung his legs over the side of his bed, ignored his slippers, and went to the dead man's bedside, reaching down for the crumpled newspaper that had slipped beneath the bed. He could not read the headline but decided to hold on to the paper for a while. He was sure that the doctors would get to the bottom of things, but it never hurt for someone to be a little suspicious. That's what you get, Shelly thought, when you let a cop near one of these scenes.

He tried to distract himself by reading his own newspapers, but found it difficult to concentrate. The world outside the hospital was too far away, except for the Persian Gulf, which was too close to home. An article on Moscow caught his attention. He looked up to ask Debs a question—and saw the stripped mattress, still unsheeted, with the caseless pillow and the blanket folded on top. Like the bed of an air force pilot shot down over his target. Shelly returned to his newspaper but kept glancing over, expecting to see his roommate's wrinkled face frowning on the pillow, and felt each time a little drop in his own heartbeat when he discovered Debs wasn't there. That little drop disturbed him, given his own diagnosis, and Shelly put away his newspaper, shucking a superstition that what happened to Debs might just as easily happen next to him.

He dozed for a while, awakening at dinnertime, when Martin bumped his bed with the food cart. Shelly was startled to see someone else sitting on Debs's bed, which had been remade while he slept. The sheets and pillowcase were on, while the woolen blanket had been stripped off again and dumped in a heap on the floor. It was not Debs, of course, but a kid with no appetite, who stuck his fork into one of the compartments of his tray and sniffed the orange stuff on the tines. But the tray gave Shelly hope, because in the central section was a tempting breast of skinless boiled chicken.

The meal under the plastic lid on Lowenkopf's own tray was no improvement over lunch—green mush, orange mush, and yellow applesauce, with no boiled chicken breast —but he ate it all anyway, his appetite sharpened by his determination to have the intravenous tube removed. Verna came in to collect his tray, saw the aluminum sections scooped clean, and clapped her hands at his accomplishment. She unstuck the medical tape in the crook of his elbow and pulled out the intravenous needle, then covered the wound with a cotton wad. He was free, disconnected from the wheeled stand that had followed him everywhere, carrying his clinking bottle. But even that did not succeed in lifting his spirits. He flexed his newly liberated arm, making great circles in the air beside him. Verna watched approvingly, coiling the intravenous tube around the bottle, still hooked to its stand, when her attention was drawn to the sound of another cart at the door.

It was Martin, the big orderly, pushing another patient on a gurney. He had missed the angle necessary to clear the doorway, and the cart was stuck in the hinges of the door. All Shelly could see of the patient was his head, which was wrapped around the temples, over the crown, under the chin, and across the nose with thickly padded bandages. Dark eyes looked out between them, blinking baldly— without lashes on the lids or brows above them.

Martin struggled through the doorway and braked the gurney at the foot of Debs's bed. It took him a moment to notice the blond kid watching him from beneath the sheets of the formerly empty bed and another to find the words to respond to this unexpected complication in his instructions. "What's goin' on here?" he finally said to the boy. "Who're you?"

The kid looked up from his dinner tray, revealing a face

about twenty years old, entirely speckled with freckles and framed by ragged blond hair. "I'm . . . Nieff," he said, placing both hands on the front of his nightshirt as if to make certain that he was indeed the same fellow as the last time he checked. The gesture seemed to lend him confidence. "Howard Nieff."

The orderly shook his head. "You're not supposed to be in that bed."

"I'm not?"

Martin stepped outside the room, checked the number over the doorway, and reread the instruction slip he had taken from his pocket. "According to this"—he lifted the wrist of the man on his gurney, read his plastic bracelet against the name on his slip, and turned back to confront the kid in the bed—"you're gonna have to get out of there."

"Martin!" said Verna, shaking her head. "What's the trouble now?"

The orderly clearly did not enjoy having his instructions questioned, particularly by a nurse. But he wasn't exactly sure how to proceed, either. "This bed was vacated earlier today," he explained. "I'm supposed to move Dr. Haight's patient down from the fifth floor." He thumbed toward the man on the gurney, who looked to Verna to confirm his claim.

"It seems that the bed has been reassigned already," Verna pointed out. "We can't just toss this patient into the hall, can we? Who is *your* doctor?"

The question was directed to the blond patient in the bed, who had just the presence of mind to stammer, "Marsha Goodman."

"Dr. Goodman? Well, her lab is in the annex at the end of this floor, too. So Dr. Haight will just have to walk upstairs when he needs to visit his patient. Take him back to the room he came from on the fifth floor, please."

The orderly checked his paperwork doubtfully, raising the document as if to show it to her.

Verna never gave him the chance. "Thank you, Martin,"

she said with a stiff smile, a shade more forcefully. The difference in intonation might have been missed by anyone unfamiliar with doctors and nurses. But Martin heard it clearly and, mumbling under his breath but without further discussion, wheeled the gurney with Haight's burn victim back out of the room.

"Thank you," said Nieff, clutching his sheet to make sure he could hold on to it.

"Don't be silly," said Verna. "We can hardly have patients wandering the corridors looking for a place to lie down. It's just that Dr. Haight. His lab is on this level, and he likes to gather his patients around him." For the first time she seemed to notice his lack of a blanket and the woolen heap on the floor. "What have you been doing with your bedding?"

Nieff glanced down at the blanket under his bed as if he had never seen it there before. "It's made of wool, isn't it? I don't use wool."

She picked up the blanket, folded it, and put it away in the closet. "You might've said something, Mr. Nieff. We can find you another, if you're allergic."

"Oh, I'm not allergic," he said, turning back to his plate. He didn't eat anything, just forked the boiled chicken breast a couple of times, sniffed his sweet potato again, and pushed the tray away.

Verna brought over a synthetic blanket from the closet, saw his tray, and frowned. "Is that all you're going to eat? Peas and two bites of yam?"

"I'm not very hungry," Nieff said.

"Then exercise! And eat some chicken," Verna insisted, tucking in the new blanket. "That's protein—it's the only way you'll ever get well."

"I don't eat chicken," Nieff said.

"Are you a vegetarian? Why didn't you say so? We can get you a vegetable plate instead."

"Thank you."

She carried the tray of boiled chicken out of the room.

Nieff watched her disappear through the doorway and craned his neck to follow her down the hall. Then he slid down below the smooth hem of his new blanket into a position that bore a striking resemblance to Debs.

Shelly would have liked to sleep again himself. The absence of tubing at his elbow meant he could turn and toss as much as he liked. He removed the cotton ball from his elbow, examined the spot of dried blood, and raised both arms above his head—because he could do so now, unencumbered. But the mock yawn made him no sleepier, and when he closed his eyes deliberately, they opened on their own.

He turned back to his newspaper, picking it up off the floor, but the feel of the paper in his hands reminded him of the one he had recovered from under Debs's bed. Shelly had stowed it safely under his pillow for the moment; perhaps Homer could get it translated, if he ever stopped by for a visit. It made him feel he was doing something for his departed fellow patient, his former roommate. For the first time he had a sense of what former prison cellmates might feel toward one another: an ambivalent mix of the need for privacy and a peculiar intimacy imposed by their sharing a semiprivate room.

The news of the world was fraught with peril, and worrying about international conflicts was the last thing he needed for his heart. He concentrated on the local news instead. A picture on page three caught his eye: in the Soundview section, in the southeast Bronx, some tents had been erected in an empty lot between a Housing Authority development and the Sound. The picture showed a woman on a stool beneath the flap of her tent, with a boy beside her, holding a pail. All around them, tall grasses blurred the edges of the photo, with a grasshopper in the foreground— the ghost of a grasshopper really, just an unfocused suggestion of mammoth insect life in an urban jungle of weeds, with two indigent people utterly overlooked.

At first Shelly thought he recognized the woman; he soon

knew that he didn't, but couldn't shake the feeling of something familiar about the shot. His eyes wandered along the border, and suddenly he noticed something that sent a hot current racing through his nerves.

It was a physical shock, a sensation that clenched his jaw and his stomach, filled his lungs with breath, and doubled the beat of his heart. He felt it pounding out of control and heard it against his rib cage, fueled by the adrenaline that surged through his toes and fingertips with a warm, tingling flush. He had to quiet it, to calm its beating, or he would end up like Debs. Shelly lay back against the stack of his pillows, covering his solar plexus with his hand.

He fell asleep that way. He was awakened some hours later by Elaine Ashbury, who was trying to nudge aside his hand so that she could listen to his heart with her stethoscope. When she saw his eyes open, she took his wrist, counted his pulse, and jotted a note on the chart in her clipboard.

"I understand you had some excitement in here." She was dressed in street clothes: blue blouse, denim skirt. "How are you doing?"

"You tell me."

She folded and stuffed the stethoscope back in her medical bag. "Your heart sounds fine, so far. Let's hope it stays that way. How're you feeling?"

"A bit uneasy, really," said Shelly. "Debs—the man in the other bed—went down right before my eyes. One minute he was sitting there reading, and the next . . ."

"He wasn't," she said simply. She looked down, only too familiar with the experience.

"He wasn't *anything*," Shelly replied with a shiver. "I've seen a lot of them ten minutes afterward, but I don't usually see innocent people go down for the count."

"Not a pretty sight, is it?"

"Not as pretty as some," he admitted. "Like the one I'm seeing now, for example."

She deflected the compliment by changing the subject,

kicking some of the newspapers at the side of his bed into a neater pile. "You do like your newspapers! You're Jewish, aren't you?"

He wasn't sure if the two observations were connected. Before he could reply, she explained, "There weren't any Jews in the town where I grew up. Until I met some at UT Austin, I wasn't really sure that Jews didn't have horns."

He took her hand and put it to his curly head. "I'm not sure about the rest of them," he said, "but *I* don't."

She pulled away her hand with a frown of disapproval, but her eyes were bright. "I know that much by now. Though there's enough about you I don't understand. I hear you had a run-in with Bruce Haight in the lab today. I take it you were looking for me."

"Sorry about that," he said with a shrug. "I shouldn't have been there, I know. But he's a piece of work, isn't he? Is there something between you two?"

"Once," she admitted, "for fifteen minutes. Mostly because of the hyphenated name, Haight-Ashbury. But the sequence would've been wrong anyway. I'd be Elaine Ashbury-Haight. Why? What did he say to you?"

"He tried to chase me off his private hunting ground. Was he always like that?"

She laughed. "Bruce is doing a stint in pathology now. It makes him grumpy as a bear. Marsha says it's something in the basement air. We're counting the hours until his rotation is up tomorrow. I hope he didn't spook you."

"It was nothing, compared to Debs. But I'm feeling better, now. Thanks to you, Elaine. I think this talk has helped cool my heebie-jeebies."

"I can give you something more for those," Dr. Ashbury said, extracting from her bag a respectable syringe. "This'll help you sleep, and it should keep you from straining your heart, thinking about poor Mr. Debs."

It was not the response he might have hoped for, but Shelly accepted it stoically, unwilling to blanch at the sight of the needle. She swabbed the back of his upper arm with a cotton wad and stuck him. He bit the inside of his lip, feeling the cold liquid enter his arm. She pulled out the point, pressed another ball of cotton over the wound, and returned the device to her bag, advising him to count backwards from one hundred. By the time he reached ninety-two, he felt a tickling at the back of his skull, which turned liquid, sloshing around his brain.

Shelly wondered just what the hell she had shot into him, but his mouth was too sticky to ask. His perception was starting to wobble, too: there was a sharpness to colors he hadn't seen before and a blurring of outlines. Ashbury's face floated before him; hazel flames flickered in her eyes. He looked away, across the room, and thought he saw the spirit of Debs rising from the lump beneath the blanket on Nieff's bed.

Hallooo . . .

He must have groaned.

Dr. Ashbury followed Lowenkopf's stare to the next bed, then reached for the curtain bunched near his head, drawing it around its track until it closed off Nieff and the entrance to the room. It left them alone, imparting a peculiar intimacy to their being together, doctor and patient, in the small space around Shelly's bed. Elaine was by his head now, the folds of her skirt rising and falling in pleats. Her blue blouse was an ocean of calm, undulating dramatically. Above the open collar her face looked down kindly, brimming with compassion.

"Can I show you something?" he said.

She sat on the edge of his bed.

He shuffled through his newspapers until he found the one he wanted: the tent family in the lot, with the grasshopper. There it was, an enormous blur of legs and antennae, perched on a stalk of dry grass. Was it really as unfocused as it looked to him, he wondered, or had something been added or subtracted by whatever she had shot into his arm? He turned to Ashbury, looking up at her, poking his finger at the photo.

She didn't get it, glancing from the paper to his face and back again. "Very nice," she said tentatively.

He shook his head, stabbing his finger along the edge of the shot. "That's her," he said.

"Her?" Ashbury considered the woman beneath the tent flap: maybe fifty, black. The expression in her wrinkled brow asked, Her who? Not *her?*

Shelly stared at the picture. "Not her," he said, shaking his head violently. "Her."

His finger was pointing not at the woman in the picture but at the photo credit running up the left side of the shot: Mordred.

"You mean she took this?"

He nodded.

Ashbury stared at the picture. And then suddenly it became clear what was so troubling about it.

"You mean she took it *here,"* Elaine said. "In the Bronx. So she must be home from the Persian Gulf. But she hasn't come to see you yet. Is that it?"

She looked as if she had solved a particularly difficult round of charades; Shelly confirmed her guess and then waited out the self-congratulations with which she rewarded her own insight. When finally the significance of her discovery dawned on her, she turned to Lowenkopf, her face racked with sympathy and regret.

"You poor man! What an awful, terrible way to learn you've been abandoned!"

Shelly hadn't drawn quite so desperate a conclusion. But when he heard her say the word, it sounded accurate. *Abandoned.* That was it—like a rusted car at the side of the road, or a house of rotting wood. His chest filled with pity for himself. Elaine had said it, finally, aloud. Women knew all about these things, didn't they? He shook his head, and the woozy liquid splashed around his cranium. He looked at the photo, and his eyes filled with tears.

Ashbury took his head in her arms and rocked him while he wept. It was extraordinarily caring of her, but it made him crane his neck, twisting it. She seemed to sense his discomfort and sat up higher on the bed, leaning back against his pillows. She stroked his hair, his cheek against her bosom, trembling with loss and drug-induced emotion. Her physical presence exerted a powerful influence over him, less a solace than a stirring, which helped his breath grow deeper, more regular—deep enough for her to raise his head and look him straight in the face.

She pushed him away and slid off the bed, pausing at the curtain to glance back before disappearing without a word. Shelly hardly had the presence of mind to wave good-bye, let alone to apologize, and he lay in a swoon, face down in his sheet, knowing in some recess of his consciousness that he had screwed it up completely—just as Debs had said he would. The thought caught him unaware and filled his brain with remorse. He hadn't been trying to arouse her compassion, he told himself and whatever part of Debs was still in existence to hear his thought.

Oh, no? said a voice somewhere in the room. Debs. Shelly tried to sit up, lost his balance, and fell nose first into the mattress, where he sank into a bog. The effort to raise himself cost more than it was worth, and he decided to let it go for a while. His bed was coming loose from its mooring now, starting a lopsided spin. He closed his eyes to mitigate the dizzying rotation and found it didn't help. But opening them was out of the question. He lay clinging to the sheet by his fingers and toes until he was deeply asleep.

When he opened his eyes, all of the lights in the room were out, though a silver glow poured in his window. The window was open; a gust of air crossed his bed and lifted the hem of the curtain that separated him from Nieff, the corridor, and the rest of the world. He was unable to stir his limbs, though they felt utterly weightless, like blimps tethered in the moonlight. His eyeballs ached from a pressure behind them. And yet, despite the pain it caused, he shifted them toward the foot of the bed, where an unbelievable sight awaited him.

Elaine Ashbury was unbuttoning the cuffs of her blouse with precision. She looked up and met his gaze, holding it. Then, deliberately, she undid the buttons of her shirt. Beneath it she wore a red camisole with thin shoulder straps and a border of lace that revealed most of the upper aureoles of her nipples. She shucked off her blouse, folded it, and draped it over the back of his chair. She unzipped her skirt, stepped out of it, and folded that, too, on the chair. Then she sat down by his thigh at the edge of the bed, pulled off her pantyhose, and slipped under the covers, a warm presence beside him.

Her head was on the pillow; he had to rotate his body to join her. Her hair spread over the cotton pillowcase in soft curls of red. Her determined eyes were seaweed green, resting on him with equanimity. He managed enough control of his tongue to ask, "What are we doing?"

She put her finger to her lips.

Several thoughts raced through his mind at once. Was this the way Elaine expressed pity? Did it bother him, if it was? Could he possibly be misinterpreting her intention? No—he felt her toenail running the length of his calf; there was no other way to make sense of that. So were they actually going to engage in . . . what would a doctor call it? Copulation? Insemination? It sounded so technical. Could he manage? Would his heart stand up to the beating?

She leaned forward and kissed him, and none of it mattered. Shelly closed his eyes and surrendered his heart.

15

Lowenkopf awoke the next morning to the sensation of a ring around his big toe. He opened his eyes and found the sheet and pillow unoccupied beside him. But there was still a tug on his foot, and the feel of a sandpaper tongue licking his sole. He sat up and saw a chimpanzee squatting on the footboard, holding Shelly's ankle and tasting his heel.

He nearly leaped onto the pillow, his heart pounding. What the hell was going on here? He glanced over at the next bed to put the question to Debs and found Nieff sitting cross-legged on his blanketless sheet, playing checkers with another large chimp, and judging from the expression on Nieff's face, Shelly guessed that the chimp was winning.

The chimpanzee on Shelly's bed leaned over the edge, reached down toward the floor, and picked up the *Times*. He grunted three times at the front page and, crumpling whole sections in his big hands, turned to the real estate ads. Careful not to disturb him, Shelly leaned over toward his roommate's bed and whispered, "What is this? A new technique in primate research? Or is the hospital short on volunteers?"

Nieff made a move on the checkerboard before replying. "It looks like Liberation Day."

Liberation Day? What was it about that bed? It seemed to draw a certain sort of patient. Shelly decided he could find out faster for himself and swung his legs over the side, feeling for his slippers with his feet. He found them, all right, worn along the top—with a cold nose and whiskers inside.

Whiskers?

He looked down and saw an elegant white rat flee from one slipper to the other. He yanked his legs back onto the mattress and reached over carefully, lifting his slippers by the toes and shaking them both until one rat fell out.

Shelly heard a snort from behind him, half guffaw and half choke, and turned to his roommate sourly. The laugh might have come from the chimp, but it was Nieff who was grinning. "I don't suppose you know much about this either?"

Nieff opened his mouth, but before he could say a word in explanation, they heard a shriek from down the hall. Nieff sat forward and, pointing at the floor, counted, "Four, five, six. Uh-oh. Where is that little guy?"

There were two more shrieks, the crash of a fallen chair, and a soothing "It's all right! All right!" A moment of relative calm . . . and then the nurse Miguel came in, dangling a white rat by the tail.

"By the direction he was traveling, it looks like this might've started from here."

Miguel stopped in the doorway, took in the six rats running all over the floor and the two chimps on the beds, and started to laugh. The Austrian nurse, who was soon behind him, did not seem to share his view of the picture. She disappeared, returning a moment later with a long-handled broom, which she used at first to brush Miguel out of her way. Once the path was clear she eyed the white rodents on both sides, trying to make a judgment call which to sweep up first.

Nieff caught the glitter in her eye and leaped out of his bed, blocking her attack. "Just what do you have in mind, nurse? These are guests of mine."

One of the guests shot between Nieff's feet, making a dash for the hallway. The nurse swung her broom and sent it flying in the air, head over tail. It landed with a crash in a small plastic trash can. Nieff was divided between revulsion at the act of violence and admiration for the nurse's aim. But he recovered his moral ground when she moved to enter the room, blocking her once again with his outstretched arms.

"Enough violence! They are animals like you and me! They should not be imprisoned in tiny cages with electrodes stuck in their heads. What gives you the right to violate their bodies?"

The nurse nearly turned the broom on Nieff then, but was prevented from doing so by the sudden appearance of his doctor, Marsha Goodman, who came trotting down the hallway from the lab, her stethoscope flying over her shoulder. She set her hand on the broom at first, as if to quell a conflict between patient and nurse, then noticed the roomful of animals and turned on the nurse with a passion.

"What is going on in this room?"

The Austrian's temper cooled at the sight of Goodman's own, and she glanced around peacefully before answering.

"It appears to me, Doctor, that your patient Mr. Nieff has effected a mass escape and has offered a place of refuge to the animals from your laboratory."

Goodman turned to Nieff, who nodded righteously. "Not only refuge—sanctuary. We are all God's creatures, Dr. Goodman: me, him"—pointing to Shelly—"the nurses here, and all of the beasts in this room. Even you are a creature of the Lord's, like this rat. Look at him—look! Who has given you the authority to treat your fellow creature so cruelly?"

Goodman glared at him, her complexion darkening through two or three shades of crimson before she responded: "I'll tell you who gave me the authority, Mr. Nieff—the American Medical Association and the New York State Board of Certification. I am a medical doctor, which gives me the right to treat my fellow rat any way I damn well please. This is a hospital. You know what that is? A temple of medical science. I am one of the priestesses here, the holies of holy. Now, if you don't gather up my subjects as quickly as you can and put them back in their cages, pronto, I'm going to treat you as cruelly as I can. Capeesh?"

She turned and marched back to her lab. Nieff still stood facing the Austrian nurse, but Miguel slipped past them and took the chimpanzees by the hand.

Nieff stood his ground until the Austrian nurse walked off, returning her broom to its closet with a smug expression of vindication. Nieff moved to the center of the room and fell to his knees, opening wide his arms.

"Come to me, my little ones! You must return to your cells." The rats scurried around until he caught them one by one, seizing them gently around the shoulders and lowering them into his pillowcase. Shelly perched on the edge of his bed and watched the drama unfold. Nieff looked up at him and gave a little shrug, as if to say, You can't blame me for trying.

Miguel was walking out, leading the two chimpanzees, but halted in the doorway. "Here comes Nurse Hohenberg," he murmured to the chimps. "If we pretend we're just out for some exercise, maybe she won't notice us."

They disappeared, strolling down the hallway as innocently as they could manage, and the Austrian nurse returned to oversee the rest of the recovery operation.

"Don't touch them, please," Nieff said, scooping up a rat that had wandered into the range of her arms. "They'd rather be handled with kindness."

"How do you know that?" Hohenberg asked him.

"Wouldn't you?"

"Yes. But I'm not a rat, you see. There's a difference. We

human beings raise animals for our own purposes—for medicines, for food. People eat chickens; chickens don't eat people."

"I don't eat chickens," Nieff replied, "and I don't use any other animal products, either. No wool for my sweater or leather for my shoes."

"What are you, a supervegetarian?"

"A vegan."

A patronizing smile curled Hohenberg's lips. "I'm a human being. And for the sake of another human life, I would not hesitate to sacrifice a million of these beasts in scientific experiments."

Nieff shuddered. "A million lives for one? That does not seem to me good arithmetic."

Hohenberg said, "It's good enough arithmetic when it's your life at stake, isn't it, Mr. Nieff?"

"What do you mean?"

"You were admitted into the hospital three days ago after receiving treatment in the emergency room. You were found in your room in a diabetic coma."

"So what?"

"What do you think it was they shot into your arm? Insulin, that's what! And where do you think insulin comes from? Pigs and cows, that's where! So you are a user of animal products after all, aren't you?"

The triumph of her declaration went unchallenged as Nieff tried to make sense of what he had just learned. Shelly saw the sequence of shocks pass over his face. Diabetes, they had told him, it seemed, but insulin was new to him, and the source of the insulin in his bloodstream presented an inescapable problem. He climbed clumsily from his bed, nearly falling over as he struggled into his cotton tennis shoes. Then he walked past the nurse without a comment, without meeting her eyes, while she gloated, challenging him to make contact. When he wandered off down the hall, she turned smartly on her heel and took up her station at the desk.

Shelly did not see Nieff again for an hour, when he sailed back into the room with a fat book under his arm. It was a copy of the *Physician's Desk Reference*, which he must have stolen from a desk somewhere. Plopping the tome in the middle of his bed, he sat cross-legged in front of it, in the traditional pose of a seeker consulting an oracle. He ran his finger down the page, stopped in the middle of a dense column, and pressed his call button.

Hohenberg appeared, eager to confront him again. But this time he was ready.

"What do you want now?" she asked. "Steak and kidney pie?"

"They can make insulin from genetically engineered bacteria, can't they?" Nieff still pointed to the textbook, which lay open to the page describing insulin.

The nurse didn't need to check; she nodded.

"I want some," Nieff announced.

"That's up to your doctor," said Hohenberg.

"Get her."

Shelly thought the instruction would provoke a reaction from the truculent nurse, but she handled herself with remarkable aplomb—enough to make him suspicious. Nieff had her, didn't he? From the self-congratulatory expression on Hohenberg's face, Shelly knew she had something up her sleeve.

"I'll be happy to," she said.

That was it—delay. It would be days before she could find Goodman, days longer before Goodman could be persuaded to appear at her patient's bedside, especially after the riot he had caused in the animal room this morning. But Shelly found to his chagrin that he was wrong again. Hohenberg came marching back down the hallway from the laboratory with Goodman in tow not ten minutes after she had left.

The doctor moved faster than the nurse, and Hohenberg had to push herself to reach the room before Goodman. But she succeeded, just in time to announce the doctor's imminent appearance. "Mr. Nieff," she said formally, "you asked to see your doctor. Here she is. Dr. Goodman?"

"Yes?" Marsha asked pleasantly.

Shelly's antennae were humming. What was she asking about? Hadn't the nurse explained the reason for the call? Nieff seemed uncertain, too, because he hesitated before asking his question. But it was too late; he had unmade his bed and now had to lie in it. Squaring his shoulders, he began in a businesslike tone.

"Excuse me for interrupting your research, Dr. Goodman. But I understand you've been giving me insulin."

Goodman rubbed her eyes in a display of patience. "You've got diabetes, Mr. Nieff. That's what we give for diabetes."

"But there are different kinds of insulin, aren't there?"

"No, there's only one kind."

"I mean, there are different ways of manufacturing it. Different sources of insulin. Some of it comes from animals, and some is synthetic."

"That's correct."

"I want to be given the synthetic kind."

"Why?"

"Because I don't like taking things from animals."

"I see. Is that all?"

"What do you mean, all?"

"You have allergies or other conditions? Special sensitivities to medication?"

"Allergies? No. It's not a physical thing."

"Then I'm afraid it's not a medical consideration either." She gave the nurse a brief glance, which must have had a question in it, because Hohenberg beamed back approval. Goodman turned as if to leave, and Nieff sat up.

"Wait a minute! Does that mean you won't give me synthetic insulin?"

"It's not that I won't—I can't. There's no medical reason for a switch to synthetics."

"Does it have to be a *medical* reason? This is a moral issue, Doctor. Doesn't a principle qualify as a reason for a switch?"

"I'm afraid it doesn't, no."

"Why not?"

"Look," said Goodman, "are you a rich man? Do you have lots and lots of money?"

Nieff shook his head. "What's that got to do with it?"

"Your insurance carrier is paying for your care here, aren't they? And they'll have to pay for your insulin from now on, too—lots and lots of it."

"So?"

"Insulin produced by genetically altered bacteria is still more expensive than the kind we get from beef and pork. Your carrier covers synthetic insulin only when it's medically justified. Now, as far as I've heard, there is no medical reason to change your medication."

"I can change doctors, can't I?"

"Be my guest! But how will that make a difference with your carrier? If you're switched to synthetics, you'll have to pay for it yourself, for the rest of your life. That's why I asked you if you had lots of money."

Nieff's face blanched as his predicament coiled around him. He looked awfully fragile, a boy confronting two medical mothers. But there was determination in those pale lashes, too. He blinked a few times but insisted quietly, "I won't take it, then."

Goodman scowled. "What do you mean, you won't take it? You'll go back into a coma. How do you plan to maintain your blood sugar level without insulin?"

"By diet," Nieff said, with growing conviction. "I'll just keep all the sugar from entering me in the first place."

The doctor shook her head. "You can't do it. There's sugar in all sorts of things—an apple, say, or a banana. I assume you're a vegetarian, Mr. Nieff, aren't you? How are you going to give up fruit?"

"I'll do what I have to," he said.

"Then so will I." Dr. Goodman took a prescription pad from the pocket of her lab coat and scribbled on it quickly, tearing off the sheet and handing it to Hohenberg. "There, nurse, are my instructions, should the patient slip into a coma: an injection of insulin—from your normal supply. Mr. Nieff, your principles may be your own to decide, but your life is my responsibility. I'm going to see that you keep it."

Nieff regarded the slip of paper in Hohenberg's hand as if it were a death sentence. But his jaw set in resolution as he turned from Goodman to the nurse and then from Hohenberg to Lowenkopf. Shelly's heart went out to the diabetic vegan, caught between his morals and his medication. He would have liked to help him. But there was—as always in a hospital—nothing either patient could do.

16

It had taken Homer and Jill all night to go through the sales records and receipts in Mrs. Geffelman's coin shop on Fordham Road. Until about eleven the storekeeper had herself pitched in, supplying information about this or that document when a question occurred to one detective or the other. What did O.O. mean on the purchase orders? Original owner. And FTB on the sales receipts? First-time buyer. She had gone out and bought them some Kentucky Fried Chicken, which Homer nibbled and Jill devoured, and had finally kept them company in silence as they examined her business, document by document. They had gone through all of the current files by nine o'clock, without results, when Jill realized that the item they were after might have been sold by Geffelman to Pilson any time over the last few years, if the thief was himself following a belated trail of acquisition. So Mrs. Geffelman pulled out the boxes of files going back ten years, and Jill began to read through them. Homer, of course, had to do so, too.

At around ten-thirty Mrs. Geffelman had begun to yawn, a drawn-out feline purr that increased in frequency and infectious intensity for half an hour, until Homer sent her home. It was hard enough to keep his eyes open without her—he was still recovering, after all, from the shock of his swim. He had hoped they might follow her out for the night and pick up the case in the morning. But Jill said she wasn't tired, though she didn't mind at all if he went along. Which made him determined to stay, of course, and go through another few papers. The files gave out after seven in the morning, by which time they had turned up—nothing.

Nothing was something in itself, of course: they now knew that none of Mrs. Geffelman's documents referred to any of the items Arthur Pilson had reported as stolen from his collection of cinemabilia. It was hard to know what to make of that information. Perhaps Pilson would remember some additional tie clip or fingernail scissors that he hadn't noticed as missing on his first time through the mess of the burglary—which would leave them no choice but to go through the stack all over again. It might have been better to wait a little, just to make sure they had heard all they were going to learn from Pilson before they dived into the records. That, Homer felt sure, was what Shelly would have said.

Jill sat glumly behind the cash register, staring at four merchandise-description cards, culled from nearly eight thousand. They listed four sales made by Geffelman to Pilson over the last six years. The first described a string from Roy Rogers's guitar, purchased in June six years before. The second, dated eighteen months later, described a photograph of Eddie Fisher reported to have belonged to Janet Leigh. The third described a cigar clipper once owned by Edward G. Robinson, which had been sold to Pilson only a month after the photograph. The last card, the only important one from the file whose contents were now scattered over the floor, described the sale of a pair of jeans documented as having come from the estate of James Dean.

The discovery of this card had at first excited them,

though the item was not on Pilson's list of missing goods. They had called him and caught him home, only to have their hopes dashed completely. Yes, he had indeed bought the jeans from Geffelman's shop, but no, they were not stolen. He could see them hanging in his bedroom closet, undisturbed in their protective plastic. The heel mark found by Homer in that closet, in fact, was on a dress that had hung right beside the jeans. If the thief had been after those jeans, he would have seen them and taken them for sure. Yes, Pilson was certain they were the same ones—he could tell by the faded knees, where the pattern of washed-out color was quite remarkable and unchanged. The jeans were still there, passed over, as the thief searched for something else. Pilson was sorry to disappoint them, but appreciated their efforts on his behalf and advised them to keep hunting.

It was just the sort of disappointment to spur Jill on to further dedicated detective work. Having come so close to a big discovery, she wasn't about to go home without one. When she had turned over the last document in the last file with a sigh, what could she do but return to the ones they had pulled out and set aside? Especially the one that pertained to James Dean's jeans. The card had been on the floor in the wake of the break-in. The thief could certainly have seen it and followed the trail to the Pilson's apartment. It had to be the jeans. So why had he gone to so much trouble to find them, only to leave them in the closet?

Homer was ready to admit defeat, at least until they could think about it freshly in the morning. His head ached with fatigue, and every time he closed his eyes he saw floating wooden kitchen utensils. They should have been moving out, but Jill looked like a fixture behind the old cash register, immobile as the chandelier overhead. He came up behind her and waited a moment, staring at the card in her hand. Beside it on the counter was Pilson's list of stolen items:

dice used by Frank Sinatra in *Guys and Dolls*
sword used by Jose Ferrer in *Cyrano de Bergerac*

comb used by Edd "Kookie" Byrnes on "77 Sunset
   Strip"
comb worn by Greta Garbo in *Camille*
comb used to style Marlene Dietrich' hair for *Blonde
   Venus*
combs used off-screen by Gary Cooper, Errol Flynn,
   Cary Grant, Robert Redford, Clint Eastwood,
   Sylvester Stallone, etc.

Homer was surprised to see some of the names in the
comb collection. He hadn't been aware that Eastwood and
Stallone used combs, ever. But Jill was still struggling to
approach the page with some shred of professional interest.

"There seems to be a hierarchy to this list," she said,
running her finger down the column. "He saves the combs
for last because they're part of a special collection. But
within the combs, there's an order, too: on-screen combs
first, followed by dressing combs, with privately used ones at
the bottom."

Homer reread the list, and that was certainly the case.
"What do you make of it?"

Jill shrugged. "You're the sergeant. You tell me."

That rang in Homer's ears as a challenge. Tired as he was,
he took Pilson's list from her and studied it. "Well," he
began, not quite sure where he was heading, "that means the
items get more personal as you move down the list." It made
a certain amount of sense, though he wasn't sure it
amounted to more than a new way of stating her observation.

"So?"

"So the most personal items of all are probably right
down here." He pointed to the "etc." at the bottom of the
list. He meant it as a joke, but Jill took back the list from
him with renewed interest.

"Of course," she said. "How could I have missed it?
That's where it was all along."

Homer had no idea what she was talking about. But he

nodded and kept silent, figuring she couldn't keep her conclusion to herself for very long. She looked at him brightly, lit with inspiration, but, instead of speaking, she dialed the telephone.

"Who're you calling?" he asked.

"Pilson."

"Now? It's only seven."

"I don't think he'll mind the call. If it helps us get it back."

He almost said, Get what back? But then Jill's eyes slid away: someone had picked up the call. The Pilsons apparently had a phone on their night table, thought Homer. There had been time for only two or three rings.

"Mrs. Pilson? This is Officer Morganthal. Yes, I know, I'm sorry. But could I speak to your husband, please? It'll just take a minute." Jill spoke slowly, as if to a child. She chewed her lip while she waited, covering the mouthpiece to report to Homer over her shoulder. "He's home."

Where else would he be? wondered Homer, but he just nodded. "Good."

"Mr. Pilson? This is Officer Morganthal. I came to see you today. And I called you earlier, yes. I have just one more question for you. Do you mind if I ask?"

There was a pause during which her smooth brow furrowed.

"Well, then, will you answer it anyway?"

And uncreased.

"Thank you. The question is about your collection of combs. The list you gave us includes combs used by Gary Cooper, Errol Flynn, Cary Grant, Robert Redford, Clint Eastwood, Sylvester Stallone, *et cetera*. That means you had other combs, doesn't it?"

She shook her head.

"Yes, I know what 'et cetera' means. But that wasn't my question. The question is, did you have a comb used by James Dean?" A crooked half smile—Homer knew the one, glinting with pay dirt. "And did you by any chance find that comb in the pocket of his jeans?"

Homer felt sure if it had been possible for Jill Morganthal to throw up her hands and whoop she would have done so then, on the phone. But a gesture of unrestrained joy was not, apparently, in her repertoire, because the only thing she said to Pilson before hanging up the phone was "Thank you."

There was a sigh in that thank-you. Homer heard it and felt sure that Pilson heard it, too. But she had earned it, he had to admit, and he felt obliged to ask "Did he?"

She nodded. *He did!*

With her victory, Jill seemed to collapse, like a gambler who has seen a game through to the end. Her effort had paid off: they knew now that the thief had probably broken into Geffelman's in search of the comb that Geffelman had sold to Arthur Pilson. Why the thief wanted a comb used by James Dean was not a question for now, and Jill seemed to have little idea what to do with the new information. She had made good on her deductive surmise, and that was all that mattered for the moment.

"Very nice," said Homer, congratulating her.

Despite herself, she grinned. "What do we do now?"

"Go to sleep," he said.

"All right," she agreed, offering no objection for the first time that day. She walked straight out of the store, leaving to Homer the business of turning out the store lights and locking the hastily repaired door and gate. By the time he reached the Reliant at the curb and opened the driver's door, she was fast asleep in her seat.

When Jill Morganthal showed up at the precinct house at eight the next morning, Homer was already there, waiting and raring to go. On his desk were the jeans that had hung in the Pilsons' bedroom closet. Jill realized with a start that Homer must have been over to the apartment already that morning, picked up the evidence, and returned.

"I could've come earlier . . ." she began.

"Don't let it worry you," Homer said, halfway to the

door. He was back in his stride, two paces ahead, and wasn't about to allow her to overtake him again.

She followed him out to the car, but didn't say anything until they were seated, buckled, and moving. "Where are we going this morning?"

"You found a clue last night, didn't you? Well, then? We can't let it cool down now."

She sat for a moment, watching him rev the engine as he waited for a light to change. "How do we keep it hot?"

He knew the answer to that one from years of partnering Lowenkopf. "We've got to ask somebody a question."

"Who?"

"Who is there to ask?"

"The only people we know are the Pilsons."

"And Mrs. Geffelman."

"Sure. But she didn't know anything last night."

It was exactly what he might have said himself. And he knew Shelly's answer. "Maybe she will now."

Mrs. Geffelman was in her shop, rearranging her documents. She looked less than delighted to see the two detectives. "When I came in this morning, I thought I'd been robbed a second time. What did you do in here last night?"

"Found what we were searching for," said Homer.

Both women looked at him with some surprise at the tone in which he delivered the line.

"You found something?" asked Geffelman, an evident doubt in her voice. She was wearing a scarf today, the theatrical type he had expected on her the first time they met. Still a hand-knit sweater, this time in green, but over it a fringed scarf in a red and green arabesque pattern. Its presence made Homer more comfortable.

"We know what the burglar came to steal," he said.

"So tell me, already."

"Mrs. Geffelman, has anybody come in here during the last few weeks asking about James Dean?"

The woman laughed. "When don't they? Most of them are interested in James Dean and Marilyn Monroe. What else is new?"

"What do you say when they ask?"

"If I have something, I show it. If I don't, I don't. What are you driving at?"

"You sold a pair of jeans to Mr. Pilson. Did you show them to anyone else?"

The question seemed to strike her differently from the rest, and she thought about it for a while. "I was holding them for him, of course, because of the comb in the pocket. I knew with that comb in there, Pilson would want the jeans and pay a nice price for them. He tried to buy just the comb, but I made it a package deal. And he went for it, hook, line, and sinker, just as I knew he would." She tapped her head at the temple. "That's the way you work in the movie business."

"And while you were waiting for him to pick up the package, did anyone else stop in? Asking about James Dean—or about the jeans in particular?"

"Wait a minute," she said. "I'm thinking. . . . There was this one young girl who asked about James Dean, yeah. I had nothing to show besides the jeans, and they were sold. I told her she might be able to buy them from Pilson, which didn't please her much. She asked, 'Why is he buying them if he's willing to sell them already?' And I explained that what he really wanted was the comb in the back pocket. All of a sudden, she was very interested in the comb. But I had already committed myself to the sale and couldn't beg off on it then. A question of reputation. Pilson had already read me his credit card number over the phone. That's a done deal, in my book."

Homer could feel the excitement in Jill beside him, but kept himself calm and composed. "Can you tell us anything about this young girl?"

Geffelman shook her head. "Not a regular customer—

walk-in trade. I didn't pay too much attention. The only question I usually ask is 'Buyer or lookee-loo?' I had no idea you were gonna ask me about her this week."

Of course not—that was what Shelly always said: civilians never expect to be witnesses. So how did you make them remember what they must have seen? Jill was looking at him for an answer to that one, but Greeley was off his turf, treading on his partner's ground. So he had to think like Lowenkopf again. All right, how was it done? Shelly's strategy was to get them talking, answering questions about anything. If they answered one question, they'd answer another. The first one was always the hardest. Homer took a deep breath.

"You probably saw something you can't remember right now. Do you mind if I suggest a few ideas?"

Mrs. Geffelman waved one arm magnanimously. "Go ahead."

"Can you guess her age?"

"Young," said Geffelman without hesitation. "Younger than me, anyway—let's say under sixty."

"How tall was she?"

"Average—about as big as everybody else. Give or take a few inches either way."

"Weight?"

"I could make something up. But I didn't really notice."

"Eye color?"

She shook her head. "Never looked that close. You've got to actually *look* at people to see these things, don't you?"

Homer nodded. They were making about as much progress as he had expected: none. Jill's attention was wandering. But out of loyalty to his absent partner, he plugged on.

"Hair?"

"It was raining. She was wearing a hat, with her hair tucked up inside it. And one of those yellow raincoats."

"Open or closed?"

"Now that you mention it, I recall that it was open."

"You could see her clothing, then?"

Again, Geffelman shook her head. "Not really. It was covered by her other coat."

"She wore another coat? What kind?"

"A white one. You know, the kind they wear when they take blood from your arm. Like a medical technician or a dental hygienist." A memory must have drifted in, because she suddenly tapped his forearm. "Oh, yeah . . . she must've been something like that, because of what it said over her pocket."

"It said . . .?"

Mrs. Geffelman smiled, her grip on his sleeve tightening. She knew she had what he wanted. Prolonging her moment in the spotlight of his eyes, she paused as if she were about to pull a rabbit out of her scarf. "What did it say, you want to know? I'll tell you. It was embroidered in red script, and these eyes are not what they were. But I read it. It said Street Dudes Outcast Hospital."

17

News about the diabetic vegan on the third floor spread quickly through the hospital, eliciting a range of support and groans. Everyone seemed to enjoy the story of the chimpanzee playing checkers, though each side read it as illustrative of a different point. Those who were sympathetic to Nieff's point of view used the story to underscore how sensitive the man was; those who resented his interference with medical experiments used it to demonstrate what a dork he was.

Both groups apparently shared their opinions with friends and neighbors at home, because the next morning letters and packages of support began to arrive in the room Shelly shared with Howard Nieff. Several boxes of sugar-free chocolates and candy came in the morning mail, together with postcards and note cards—on recycled paper—encouraging him in his stand. Several supporters had enclosed pictures of their dogs and cats, with one picture of a pelican—all of which Nieff taped to the foot of his bed as an inspiration to him in his struggle.

But the most dramatic token of support was delivered to their room around eleven—a wreath of the sort awarded in the winner's circle after a race, with a six-pack of sugar-free cola suspended in the center by a wire and adorned with a silver bow. The florist carried the thing into the room and tried to set it at the foot of Shelly's bed, until Nieff summoned him over to his own. Nieff nodded but made no other gesture toward a tip; the florist wiped his forehead, tried to plaster down some spiky hair that stood straight up on top of his scalp, and trod heavily out of the room. Nieff climbed down to the foot of his bed and plucked a can of cola from the center of the wreath. He settled back into his pillows and popped the lid, releasing a delicious sizzle of carbonation into the medical air.

By the time lunch arrived, Nieff was prepared to eat nothing at all from the tray, subsisting instead on sugar-free chocolates and another can of sugar-free cola. Verna made some remark that Shelly could not hear and then presented him with his own meal: a tray compartment of green mush, another of orange, and a third of applesauce. There was also a plastic cup covered with foil that held some perfectly clear broth. As Lowenkopf watched Nieff drop another candy square into his mouth, he wondered about the advantages of his own diet. Nieff must have observed him, because, when Shelly came back from the bathroom, he found a can of diet cola and two chocolate squares wrapped in paper on his pillow. Shelly ate one chocolate filled with gooey cream and enjoyed the bitter aftertaste of sugar substitute. Not like sugar at all, he decided, but with its own kind of sweet; after the hospital food, it tingled on his tongue. He used the soda can to prop the postcard on his night table, setting the second chocolate on top of the can, planning to save it until later. But when the last sting of bitterness faded from his mouth and he had only three colors of mush to choose among, he threw caution to the wind and gobbled the second chocolate as well.

The visitors started to show shortly before one, when the nursing staff could no longer send them back into the elevators. They came marching into the room, anxious to see Nieff, a troop of print reporters with a lone camera from one of the TV stations. The cameraman commandeered the choice position at the foot of Nieff's bed, while the TV reporter took up her position near the pillow. A very bright light at the top of the minicam was all they seemed to need; the camera operator panned once around the room, brushing past Shelly, just before they went out. Then the print reporters and still photographers had their chance. One balding man in a brown suit left a canvas bag of lenses on Shelly's bed before he edged in, squatting, to take a low-angle shot of Nieff. Two others sat on his footboard. It was nearly two before they all cleared out, leaving Nieff feeling gratified with the significance of his principle, and Shelly not at all sure that he wouldn't have preferred Haight's burn victim as his roommate.

The four o'clock news break gave him some consolation when he saw, in a quick camera pan at the beginning of the story, himself in a hospital bed. The item was about Nieff, of course. A voice-over told the story, followed by a snippet of interview with the vegan and an even briefer snippet of Marsha Goodman refusing to comment on her patient's condition. A hospital spokeswoman in an expensive suit explained that the administration had contacted the insurance carrier and worked out an arrangement under which Mr. Nieff could be given synthetic insulin; but the patient was now refusing to accept that, too, on the grounds that its development was based on animal research. There were statements from leaders of animal rights groups, passionate about Mr. Nieff's courage, and sly, derisive comments from a medical doctor whose research on animals had produced tangible results: lifesaving patented medications. The reporters listened to both sides, commenting with a dry, professional humor that almost—but never quite—tilted one way or the other.

The staff members on the ward were themselves divided in their reactions. Miguel was delighted to see the place on the news. The arguments for research were persuasive, he said, but there was something to be said on behalf of the animals, too. The other nurses, to a woman, were solidly behind Goodman. Too many patients had died because of what medical science still needed to learn. When she came in with their dinner, Verna said nothing to Nieff, but complimented Shelly on his appearance. *He,* she stressed, had looked very good on the news. Nieff popped the lid on his fifth can of cola, not even bothering to glance at his tray. He wasn't looking too cheerful, though, sinking into his pillows. Shelly wondered if he wasn't wearing under the strain.

And then, around seven, another surprise: while Lowenkopf was reading his horoscope for the day before— "Attend to finances, and matters of the heart; someone close to you will present a problem"—he felt a presence at the side of his bed and looked up to find Mordred peering at him, her features screwed into an expression of concern and a small bag clutched in her fists. She was dressed in a leather miniskirt and a tight pink sweater with a poodle embroidered over her heart. She wore black stockings with her trademark crooked seams no doubt running straight up the backs of her thighs. Only without the Converses. Instead of her customary red sneakers, she wore shiny satin slippers with a definite Persian curl. He studied them for a moment too long—until there was no choice but to look her in the face.

"Shelly?" she said.

Her head was turned a bit aside, as if to avoid a direct blow, and she was watching him out of the corners of her eyes. They were the same eyes, smoky gray, with multicolored spangles in the lashes, but as openly frank as ever. Her lips were parted slightly, and he saw the usual stain of bright red lipstick on her upper front teeth. The same black hair, sloping from her left ear to her right shoulder, though the iridescent tint that sparkled in it seemed rather more purple than crimson. Most of all, there was still something irreducibly sweet about her face, in the tiny lines at the corners of her eyes and in the pull of her chin on her mouth.

"Hi," he said.

She frowned at him, not quite disapprovingly, with a smile twisted into the expression. "Is that all you have to say to me? 'Hi there, Mordred. What's up?'"

There were forty or fifty things he would have had to say at once, so he had opted for the best reserve he could manage. But she was never one to let him get away with standing behind a show of indifference. And yet things were different now, he reminded himself, anticipating the worst and resolving to take them one step at a time.

"How was your trip?"

"My trip? My trip was ginger-peachy, Shell. What the fuck are you doing in here, may I ask?"

"Recuperating."

"From what? A sickness unto death?"

He realized how gray he must have looked when all the blood rushed out of him at her sudden appearance. For some reason, he felt as if *she* had put him there, as if her postcard from Doha had done the real damage to him. That was nonsense, of course. What had Freylung called his condition?

"They're keeping me under observation to rule out a possible myocardial contusion. A bruised heart muscle. Otherwise, I'm feeling fine." He tried to sit up, to demonstrate, but couldn't find the stomach for it and after a minute lowered himself back onto his pillow.

"You don't look fine."

"You do."

She beamed. One of her best qualities, knowing how to take a compliment. Her whole face lit with pleasure, as if he had really done something splendid. It was hard not to join in that feeling of well-being.

"I was so worried about you!" she said, plopping down on the foot of his bed and crossing her legs Indian-style. "There was an old woman in the port of Doha. She said some awful things. About you, mostly. Didn't you get my card?"

He shook his head. Here it came.

She stared at him strangely and reached across to his nightstand. "Yes, you did. It's right here. Shelly, what's wrong with you?"

He shrugged. "A myocardial—"

"Contusion. Yes, I heard that. But it's not the wrong I meant, and you know it."

What could he say to that? She was prodding him to face facts, permitting no evasion, forcing him to confront the painful truth. In this, as in everything else, he couldn't resist her. He mumbled, "All right. If you've got something to tell me, you'd better get on with it."

Her face was at first perplexed, but she seemed to think of something and her brows narrowed suspiciously at him. "It sounds to me," Mordred said, "as if *you* might have something *you'd* like to tell me. Shelly?"

He met her eyes, despairing. What on earth was she driving at? Was he supposed to guess his own bad news? "I'm not the one who should have to say it."

"Why not?"

"Because," he said.

"Because why?"

Because it's not right, thought Shelly. He was growing a little angry at her coyness. "Look—I'm not the one who wants to end what we've got between us."

She sat up, suddenly catching the drift, nodding at the seriousness of the moment. She gave just the sort of nod he might have given during an interview, which meant simply, *Go on.* When he noticed it, he stopped and waited for a response.

Mordred shrugged. "Well, I'm not the one who wants that either! So it must be somebody else. Since there's only two of us involved here, why do we care what somebody else wants to stop happening between us?"

He was utterly lost. "What?"

"I said as far as I can tell, nobody wants to throw over anybody—or at least I don't want to chuck you. Where did you get that idea? From your horoscope?"

She picked up the newspaper, still folded to that page, and read her own horoscope aloud. " 'Confusion in the stars today. Your lover goes nuts, lying alone in a hospital bed.' " They do get it right sometimes, don't they?"

He looked at the newspaper, but of course it said nothing of the kind: "A friend will introduce you to someone new." At least that wasn't someone she had already met on a ship full of sailors, or a desert sheikh. Would she want to introduce him? The thought filled him with horror. But— was she denying it now? He looked up and found her staring at him with fondness in her glittering eyes.

"I don't have to ask if you've changed in my absence," she told him, taking his head between her hands. "You're still crazy as ever." She kissed his forehead, then his nose, and then his mouth, where her lips lingered to plant a little kiss in each corner.

The pressure of her hands felt gentle on his ears, warm and a bit clammy. For the moment he didn't care about her photo in the paper. What difference did it make how long it had taken her to come? She was here, wasn't she? He placed his big hands over her small ones, covering them completely, and lowered them tenderly into his lap. "I've missed you."

"I know," she said, grinning. "I brought you something to make it up to you."

She unsnapped the little clutch bag in shiny black vinyl and extracted a tiny box, wrapped in Persian paper. It looked like Persian paper—with the curving arches and dome of a mosque. He tore off the offending paper, ripping it to shreds, and opened the cardboard box. Inside was a ring, a slender strip of silver curved in front like a scimitar. The shape of it suggested a sword blade; it had been wrought so finely that its creator had eliminated any possibility that it might be seen as a moon or a sail or a banana. He tried it on his ring finger, where it didn't fit over the middle knuckle, then slipped it on his pinky, where it did. He held it up until it caught the light, reflecting back a single spark of pure white brightness.

"It's beautiful," he said, taking her around the waist and pulling her forward to kiss her. And then, in an instant of resistance before she gave in, he felt the old familiar doubt. This lovely girl, twenty years younger—what could she possibly see in him? It was a question he could never answer, and never managed to put out of his head. But she stroked the curls on top, chasing his doubts away. "And so are you—adorable. But what did your postcard mean, then? Why did we have to talk?"

She looked down. "I was frightened when I wrote that. A woman in Doha who said she could predict the future told me that my man was about to die. The only man I had was you. She also predicted our boat would be damaged, and two days later we nearly rammed into a mine. So I wrote that card to warn you. See, it says, 'Take care.'"

"Instead of 'Love.'"

"I thought you knew I loved you," she said.

"Then why didn't you come to see me sooner?" He reached for his newspaper and turned to her photo of the woman in the tent. "You've been in town long enough to have a local shot printed in the paper."

She threw up her hands in exasperation. "Shelly, I didn't know where you were. I called your apartment when I first landed, but you've been out. I left a message at the precinct also, but you never returned that either. I was starting to wonder if you were out of town, or maybe avoiding me, when I saw you on the evening news, behind your vegan friend, there. How's he doing?"

"Pretty good. Not talking much tonight."

She winced in sympathy. "He doesn't look so good to me." Sliding to the floor, she crossed the room, hands behind her back. Near the other bed, she whispered, "Mr. Nieff?"

No response.

"Try 'Howard,'" Shelly suggested.

"Howard?" She leaned closer until her breath would have warmed his cheek, had there been anything left in him to respond. When she looked up, her eyes were wide. "Shelly—"

Shelly leaped from his bed and ran over, inserting himself between Mordred and his roommate. Nieff was unconscious, in a state that was deeper than sleep. Shelly grabbed the call button beside the pillow and pushed it.

Miguel came immediately. "Just hold on there, Mr. Nieff. I'm coming as fast as I can. Some of the others at the desk weren't so anxious to hop on it, but I said—" He stopped cold when he saw the patient stretched out lifeless on top of the sheet. "Holy shit," he said, reaching at once for the artery in Nieff's neck.

Mordred said, "Is he dead?"

"Not yet," replied Miguel, "but close."

He ran out into the hall, shouting toward the desk, where Verna appeared a moment later. "What is it?"

"Who's on call?" Miguel asked.

"Dr. Ashbury. She's downstairs in the cafeteria. Should I get her?"

"No time now. Where's that prescription Dr. Goodman left, in case Nieff went into a coma?"

"Pinned to the bulletin board," Verna said. "Right here. In case of an emergency."

"That's what we got right now. Fill it."

In a flash, Verna was in the room, with a small bottle of insulin and a syringe, measured off in red. "I've got it," she said. "You go page Dr. Ashbury. Don't stop to explain it. Just get her up here in a hurry."

Miguel took off, and Verna slid the needle into a jar of clear liquid, retracting it carefully and reading the amount on the calibrated cylinder. She checked the prescription slip again to make sure she had drawn enough, and injected the medication into Nieff's arm. A moment later he spasmed, relaxed, and stiffened again. The surprise on Verna's face told Shelly he wasn't supposed to react that way. Something was wrong. She put her ear to Nieff's chest, listening, until her mouth tightened firmly. She climbed up on the bed and leaned on his back, rocking back and forward while she murmured words of encouragement to the corpse.

By the time Dr. Ashbury reached the ward, Howard Nieff had been dead for over a minute. Elaine knew it as soon as she examined him. But she did whatever she could to bring him back. None of it made a difference to poor Howard Nieff, whose moral crisis was now finally resolved. The papers would have a story to pick up in the morning—the end of their hero. The cause of death was later determined to have been insulin shock, resulting from too large a dose of the proper medication, administered to break a coma he never should have gone into. The reporters would not, however, hit upon one sensational angle that now absorbed Shelly more than the death itself.

Mordred had turned to him and was now weeping in his arms while Elaine Ashbury watched them and wondered about what he had told her and what sort of man Shelly was. Mordred looked at least ten years younger than Elaine. Had he neglected to mention that? There was no way for him to explain, with Mordred wrapped around him, pressing against him for comfort. And in Elaine's eyes he saw all of the personal anguish she had done so much to relieve in his own.

18

By nine o'clock, Mordred was gone and Howard Nieff's bed was once again stripped—the pillows uncased, synthetic blanket tossed into the laundry—and then made up fresh, the pillows recased, a new blanket folded tightly into the smartly cornered sheets. As Verna was tucking in the last corner, Martin reappeared, once again pushing Bruce Haight's burn patient into the third-floor room. The patient's condition had evidently deteriorated, since he was now attached by a tube in his neck to a respirator, a metal contrivance of dials, digital readouts, and blinking lights that fed air into his trachea between his Adam's apple and his collarbone. The machine on the other end of the tube was larger than a bread box but not much, resting on its own cart. Verna glanced at the patient, eyed Martin shrewdly, and said nothing, offering no objection when the bandaged man was hoisted into the bed by the big orderly as effortlessly as if the patient were ancient or newborn.

Verna had more pressing things to worry about. It was she, after all, who had injected the dose in Howard Nieff's arm which had sent him into insulin shock. Nurse Hohenberg verified that Marsha Goodman had prescribed medication should Mr. Nieff drop into a diabetic coma; but according to the buzz on the ward, the resident was denying she had prescribed more than ten units per cubic centimeter, while the dose administered had contained a hundred units per cc of insulin. Verna admitted loading the larger concentration into her syringe, but swore that Goodman's scrawl on the prescription slip unambiguously specified as much; three times she was asked if she could have misread it, and three times Verna shook her head. The slip itself had been confiscated at the command of the director of medicine, when news of the death reached him at his home in Scarsdale. The public interest in Mr. Nieff lent this case considerably more attention than it might otherwise have received from the hospital's upper management.

By nine-thirty they were alone together, Shelly and the new man. After Debs's relentless conversation and the uproar over Nieff, Shelly found their replacement an agreeable change. The respirator hummed gently in its soothing monotone, while the patient himself groaned and cried out in barely audible whimpers. The enforced intimacy of the sleeping arrangements, together with the reassurances of medical science, had misled Shelly into a false sense of confidence in which he had struck up acquaintances with roommates, only to have them die abruptly in his presence. He was not inclined to take that risk so easily again. There was a wonderful anonymity about the new patient, his face obscured by bandages, his voice hardly more than a whisper, his consciousness utterly absorbed with his suffering. Shelly did not ask his name and did not offer his own. It lent an illusion of privacy to their semiprivate room.

At ten, Elaine Ashbury returned to take a final reading of Lowenkopf's heart after all the excitement of the evening. She did not speak at first, pressing the cold metal cone of her stethoscope against his chest until it had put quite a chill in him. Only then did she put it into her bag, after coiling up the black rubber hoses with unconscious skill. For a moment it looked as if she might withdraw without further comment, but she lingered after closing her black leather bag and Shelly decided to try to break the ice. "Working late tonight?"

She grunted assent.

This was not going to be easy. "You doing the autopsy on Howard Nieff?"

She shook her head. "I signed the death certificate. Can't do both. Besides, my tour in the basement doesn't start until tomorrow. Brucie's still on the hook tonight."

"Touchy one, huh?"

She nodded, without interest in the subject. He knew where her thoughts had to be, but still had no ready answer when she asked, "Shelly? Was that your girlfriend I saw in here earlier? The one who wrote the postcard?"

"It was all a horrible misunderstanding—"

"You don't have to explain to me," Elaine said primly.

"I think I should," he said, inviting her to absolve him one more time of that awkward necessity.

"Go ahead, then."

Shelly took a deep breath. "That's Mordred: very skeptical about some things—sentimental things—but awfully credible about others. A Gypsy woman in Doha told her I was going to die, and she was trying to warn me about it. That's what the postcard was supposed to be, a warning. It made no difference, of course. I was caught in the explosion anyway. But the feeling of imminent danger came through in her card. When I thought—"

"She dumped you—"

"I thought she meant to throw me to the dogs. I had no idea things were so good between us."

The last line was delivered with undisguised bewilderment; Ashbury couldn't suppress a smile. He could see her resentment dissipate as her estimation of him fell. His only excuse was his ignorance, which was too easily believed. He could read her thoughts on her visage, while she struggled to maintain a frown: this was no way to treat women, playing one against the other, but he hardly seemed in control of his wayward heart. It was an organ banging around in his chest, smacking into the rib cage, ricocheting against the spine. Just try to imagine him scheming to capture another!

Elaine said, "All right. So you didn't lie. I believe you. You've done nothing to me that I didn't invite."

That should have been satisfying, but it wasn't, really, to Shelly, who insisted on more. "I would never have misrepresented myself to you, Elaine. It was you who said I was abandoned"—she winced at the word—"and it sounded right to me at the time. I thought I was abandoned. And now I'm abandoning you."

The thought seemed to strike him so glumly that he lapsed into morose silence. Elaine said, "You are not abandoning me. We shared one night of mutual solace—that's all, Shelly. The biggest risk was medical. I should never have taken a chance like that, with your cardiac condition. But . . . there is something you ought to know—a consequence of that night."

His heart leaped into his throat. A consequence? Her voice was full of foreboding.

"It was all so spontaneous," Elaine said. "Neither one of us had a chance . . . to prepare for our encounter. It was stupid—what could we have been thinking? But neither one of us was thinking much, were we?"

He knew it—she had AIDS. Now he had it, too. He would never get out of the hospital again. Never, never, never, never, never. And how was he going to explain this to Mordred?

"So I . . . took a blood test today. Just to make sure nothing went wrong. And of course—it always does. Forget about the odds. When you're smart enough to know better and you act like you don't, you always get nailed for the lapse."

Shelly sat for a moment in stunned silence. Above all, the irony stung him. Had he survived so many shoot-outs with bad guys, so many crashes and explosions, to fall victim to a night of passion in a hospital bed? It made no sense, none at all—which made it fit so naturally with every other turn of his life. "How long have we got?"

She gave him a peculiar expression—raised eyebrow, grim lips—which read *Are you kidding?* Why would he be kidding about something like this?

"Nine months," she said quietly. "Minus a day. Just like everyone else."

Nine months? But he thought some people had survived for years. Nine months was only as long as it took to have a . . . and then, as if an oxygen line had been pumped into him, he felt a great lightness in all of his limbs—his knees weakening, the base of his spine tingling, his arms rising weightlessly into the air. His hands came to rest on her soft upper arms, where they gripped her gently.

"Elaine, are you pregnant?"

Exasperated, she propped her fists on her hips. "What do you think I've been trying to tell you?"

But he wasn't thinking anything anymore. "But, after only two days, you *couldn't* have missed your—"

"You're not listening, Shelly. I didn't say I missed my period. I was concerned because we hadn't taken precautions. And I just had a funny feeling, you know? So I decided to make sure there was nothing to it."

"But after two days? There aren't any tests—"

"You're not up on cutting-edge research! There is a test now, not routinely given but medically available. I had a friend in a lab who owes me a favor run a radioimmunoassay analysis, a very sensitive test for HCG—the stuff an embryo secretes into your blood. And he found some."

A radioimmuno . . . what? Shelly's mind, which had been struggling to encompass the news, gave up the effort completely, his thoughts replaced by a bright yellow glare that washed out all comprehension. He sat dully, in a stupor, unable to react. His chest was so full he could hardly breathe. After eleven years, he was about to become a father again. Or was he? He looked into her eyes.

"What are we planning to do about it?"

That *we* seemed to strike her pleasantly, and she pushed him back into bed. "Nothing tonight," she said. "Get some sleep. You look as if you need it! I'm still your doctor, and I have to say I'm not at all pleased with the progress of your recovery. You haven't been getting much satisfying rest, have you, Sergeant Lowenkopf? Try not to dwell on the news tonight. We'll talk about it tomorrow."

With her humor restored, Elaine skipped out, pausing in the doorway to snap off the lights. In the momentary flash, his whole life passed before his eyes: Mordred, Izzy, Ruth, Thom. Each one represented another problem in breaking the news—all versions of the same problem, really. How could he explain what a schmuck he had been? Shelly stared after Elaine for a minute, his gaze broken only by his need for a blink and a change in the hiss from his roommate.

What was it? A pause, some kind of break in the constancy of the man's groan. He listened, but it did not recur. He heard only the respirator's hum and the mewing groans of the man connected to it. What was a man in his condition doing in this room? Shouldn't he be in Intensive Care? The proximity to his doctor's laboratory provided some justification, Shelly had to admit, but was that really for his good or for his doctor's convenience? A bilious liquid started to burn the lining of Shelly's stomach. He reminded himself not to pay attention, not to get involved. He stopped listening, swinging his mind around to the daunting consequences of Elaine's revelation. A bottomless pit gaped at his feet, when he suddenly heard another hiss—this time quite distinctly.

Hney! Hney!

It might have come from the glowing machine, a sigh of released air pressure. But it was uncomfortably irregular and unmechanical, as if effort were somehow involved. The man in bandages lay on his back without stirring, one hand at his throat where the tube from the ventilator entered below the Adam's apple. His fingers closed around the tube, squeezing it off. And then the noise came again, this time even more disturbingly human in timbre and duration, distressingly—speech.

"Hey! Hey!"

There was no way he could ignore it; Shelly climbed from his bed and crossed the room to stand beside his roommate. From this distance, it was only too clear how much damage lay beneath the bandages. The head was wrapped down over the forehead, and a strip of gauze crossed the nose. The face was framed entirely in white, bandaged under the chin and over the head, covering all but a slit of the mouth. And yet shadows in that slit seemed to stir with life, with undeniable intention. The ventilator tube disappeared into a crisscross bandage above his collarbone. All of his attention was focused there, on his throat and mouth and the air that flowed between them. The muscles of his limbs and torso lay still. But there was no mistaking the shift in the eyes, which came to rest on Shelly.

"You want something?" he asked.

The burn victim's head seemed to tip slightly, the merest stir of a nod.

"I'll call the nurse," Shelly said.

No! The message was communicated simultaneously by a wince of the eyes and, despite obvious pain, a slight shake of the head.

"All right," Shelly agreed, just to stop the man's movement, "I won't. Is there something I can do?"

The burn victim's eyes slid to his right, toward the respirator at the side of the bed. Shelly followed them to a red button beneath a glowing red light on the front of the panel, where they definitely were focusing. He reached over tentatively toward the machine until his hand came to rest on a switch below the light. The burn victim's eyes flared in their sockets—that was plainly the one to adjust. Shelly leaned over and, peering through the darkness, read the label below the switch: On or Off. It was set to On.

He looked back at the man in the bed, whose eyes were now comfortably closed. Shelly stared as the eyes opened and filled again with pain, contested only by a wavering hope, which fixed directly on him.

"You want me to . . .? No," said Shelly. "Absolutely not. There's no way I can do that for you."

The man's eyes pleaded for a moment, full of longing and dread. But he must have seen they would not suffice to make his case, because with a grimace of anguish that seemed to increase with every syllable, he forced his lips to speak.

"Agony," he muttered.

Shelly shook his head. "I'm sorry. But I can't—"

The eyes winced again, and Shelly cut himself off, to spare the burn victim the necessity of speaking any louder. His fingers closed again on the tube running into his neck. There was a shudder in the shadow of his mouth and another hoarse whisper.

"I . . . can't either." It took all of his breath to utter the words, and the effort seemed to exhaust him. But he closed his eyes, bracing himself for an even more demanding task, and continued, "My . . . life . . . is . . . pain. Nothing but pain, here. But there is . . . another place. I . . . see it, when I close my eyes. I . . . want to go there. Help me."

The last thing Shelly needed was a theological discussion of the afterlife with a dying man. That was not the way to stay uninvolved. He looked toward the door, praying for Verna or Miguel, and shook his head when neither of them appeared.

"You don't understand. I'm a police officer. I can't help a person voluntarily end his own life. You really should talk to the nurse or someone."

Again the burn victim tipped his head, with that minimalist shake. No escape. Shelly sagged.

"You're still alive. There has got to be something they can do to help you."

"I . . . am . . . burned . . . here." His arm muscles tensed alongside his hip, as if to indicate the whole area. "I . . . won't . . . live this way."

There was nothing Shelly could say. But he wasn't about

to kill the man either. He looked down at his bathrobe, put his hand in its pocket, and noticed the plastic water pitcher on the nightstand. He poured some water into his room-mate's cup and offered it to the bandages where his mouth should have been. The burn victim raised his head a fraction, and Shelly poured water into the slit, spilling some onto the gauze over his cheek and chin. Shelly blotted the spill with the man's sheet, feeling an inch of springy cotton over the sinews of his face. How badly the covered skin was burned he could only guess.

And then he saw the man's hand, lying on the coverlet, stir again, inching away from the hip. It seemed to go limp, falling to one side, and then it moved again, creeping toward the edge of the mattress. It took Shelly a moment to realize its goal: the switch beneath the red light on the respirator.

Shelly stared at the hand straining toward the life-support machine. All he had to do was reach out and hold it; the man in the bed could hardly have resisted even the slightest restraint. Just hold his hand, in a gesture of comfort and support. But Shelly didn't do it. Instead, he returned to his bed, climbing in without doffing his bathrobe.

The hum of the respirator was louder now, the red light glowing brilliantly. Its glimmer of crimson burned a hole in his vision as the room grew darker around it. In his mind's eye he saw the trembling hand straining, spasm by spasm, across the sheet. But the real difference was the groans. Each gasp of the burn victim now shook him, too, gripping the muscles of his stomach and wringing his bowels. His own breathing repeated the rhythmless, patternless intake of air hissing across their room. Shelly crossed his arms over his head, covering his ears with his biceps, trying to concentrate on something less distressing—Elaine, for example. He moaned.

Shelly knew he should warn the nurses about his room-mate's request. But what could they actually do? Tie down the man's hands? But that would only increase his agony, and Shelly hadn't the heart to add bondage to the man's suffering. Instead, he listened to the groans in the darkness, until the sharp exchange of gasps and sighs finally put him to sleep.

His dreams were full of crabs, sidling across white sand. And children, plenty of noisy children, running up a winding staircase. It was in a lighthouse on a rocky promontory at the end of a deserted beach. On top of the lighthouse, a beacon turned stubbornly, emitting a dull red gleam.

He woke up suddenly in the middle of the night, startled by the silence. The groaning had stopped. Peering over, Shelly saw that the red light on the respirator was out. His roommate did not seem to notice. Shelly listened to the quiet, holding his breath, waiting for the alarm on the respirator to go off . . . and heard only the seconds ticking away on his watch. The alarm had been disconnected, then. When he had heard no cries of pain for two full minutes, Shelly rolled over and plunged into a dreamless sleep.

19

Bruce Haight stopped by before seven the next morning to look in on his patient, and found the man dead, hanging over the side of the bed, where he had fallen after the last desperate lunge at the switch on the life-sustaining machine. Shelly was awake but lay with his back to the other bed and the door, waiting for someone else to begin the day with the heartrending discovery. It was Haight who happened to snare the bait, checking the chart before glancing at his patient, then moving in for a closer look. It took him about three minutes to realize that the respirator had been shut off before the death occurred. When he spotted the extinguished light on the control panel, he loosed a bellow down the hall that shook the nurses' station—a surprisingly loud and angry shout, considering his size. But the measure of a physician was not taken in inches, and the summons brought forth a worried Miguel, who poked his head into the room, bracing himself in the door frame.

"You called, Doctor?"

"Who turned off this machine?"

Miguel considered the patient hanging half out of his bed, and turned to Lowenkopf.

Shelly thumbed toward the inert form. "He did."

"I did not," said Haight. "I just got here."

"Not you," said Shelly, shaking his head. *"Him."*

Miguel considered the body grazing the floor and moved to hoist it onto the bed. Shelly almost objected, but remembered it was not a murder investigation; professional habits were hard to break. From the stiffness of the limbs, he could see that the man had been dead for hours.

The suicide was not easy for Haight to accept. From the wrinkles on his brow it was clear he was by no means certain that his patient could have managed the stretch by himself. Or he might have found it impossible to believe that his patient wanted to kill the light—especially since Bruce Haight was his personal physician. Death itself was hard enough for a doctor to accept; the deliberate suicide of one's own patient verged on the fantastical. He shoved Miguel aside and stared at the patient a moment before covering the face with the sheet in a gesture he had learned from the movies. Then, turning away with a practiced scowl, he ordered, "Get him out of here."

The staff was very good at that, Shelly noticed. Not fifteen minutes later, there was no sign of the man. The bed that once supported him, like Debs and Nieff before him, was empty again, stripped of its occupant's identity along with his sheets. Fresh linens now covered the mattress; no remnant remained of any of the men who had so recently died there. The staff, of course, might remember them, though they did their best to forget, having long ago learned what had just dawned on Shelly: that the occupants of this room were not secured for intimacy or a personal sort of care. You had to develop the ability to care for the patients as suffering human beings without caring for them as people. Which left Shelly as a witness on the scene who had struck up three friendships before each had been struck down in turn.

Shelly was asked to serve as a witness of another sort soon after. A pleasant young woman in a slender blue suit and frilly collar drew up a chair by his bedside and asked him again for his story. Had he actually seen his roommate turn off the respirator? Then how did he know he had done so? Shelly asked and was told that the woman, Ms. Manner, worked for the hospital's legal office and had some questions about the incident. He told her what he had heard the night before: groans and a request for assistance, which he had refused to provide. She nodded at that, her hair bobbing furiously as she scribbled on a long yellow pad. Was he willing to sign an affidavit, testifying to what he'd just told her? He supposed he was willing, he said. She would have one typed for his signature, she promised, as soon as it could be arranged. She fairly ran out of the room.

So he had spared the hospital a lawsuit—they should have been grateful for that. And it seemed that they were, for no sooner had the legal aide left than a man entered the room. He studied the empty bed, checked his work order, and crossed to the foot of Shelly's bed. He was black, with a mustache, in white overalls—a cartoon protagonist for an affirmative-action video game. He knelt, disappearing behind the footboard. Shelly leaned over and saw the man sprawled halfway under the box spring, from which a series of grunts emerged.

"Hmmn! So it's not . . . hmn! All right, lessee here."

Shelly called down, "Something wrong?"

The handyman withdrew his head. "You complained about the bed, didn't you?"

Shelly stared. "You must have somebody else—"

"Got your name right here on the order. That's you, isn't it?" The name on the work slip was Lowenkopf, S. "The number on the bed matches, too."

"I don't remember the problem—"

"Something about the head section there not rising?"

The mechanism—of course. Isabelle's instructions to Nurse Hohenberg had worked themselves through the system. The button that raised and lowered the upper part of his bed was about to be fixed. "That's right! By all means, go ahead."

The handyman screwed up one eye but said nothing, sliding back underneath the mattress. It took him only a minute to check out the bottom before he resurfaced, making a note with a stubby pencil on his work slip.

"Nothing to it, really. We'll have it done in a jiff. Long as it takes to settle you in over there."

Shelly wondered at the use of the *we*—editorial or royal prerogative? But the man's good news took an unexpected turn in his last two words: *over there?* "Over where?"

The handyman thumbed toward the newly made bed. "The other bed over there. We can't get at this mechanism with you lying on top of it, can we? It's lucky the other one's free. We'll just lug you across and have at it."

Shelly regarded the bed so recently vacated with a tingling sense of uneasiness. Three men had died on that mattress in so many days. There was no significance to that, of course, but he couldn't entirely suppress a superstitious reluctance to follow in their place.

"I don't want that bed," he said.

The handyman gave him the screwed eye again. "We'll move you back again as soon as we're done, if you like. I don't think there's another bed free on this ward." He glanced at the door, and Shelly saw the other half of *we*, as Martin, the orderly, loomed in the frame.

"Gimme a hand here, Martin, will you?" said the handyman, tipping his head.

Martin took a giant step toward Lowenkopf, who shrank into his bedding. But there was no escape. The big man approached, blotting out the day, filling all the space at Shelly's bedside. He would have been dug from his blankets, hoisted into the air, and dropped into the triple-time deathbed had not Homer entered at that moment and uttered a quiet observation that froze the two employees in their tracks.

"Moving the patient might be contraindicated at this time," he said.

The handyman looked to the orderly for confirmation of the newcomer's status, but Martin was not himself sure. From the cut of Homer's expensive suit, he could certainly have been a physician—pure silk, navy blue with a thin green stripe, flatteringly but inobtrusively styled. He had the arrogance of a doctor, his lip ready to curl, his jaw ready to thrust, his temper ready to flare at their recalcitrance. They couldn't ask him, because the question in itself might be interpreted, if he chose to be offended, as a challenge to his personal authority. He probably wasn't a doctor, since he didn't make it plainer, but neither man was prepared to take the risk. So they withdrew from the room with a backward glance at Lowenkopf's broken bed, biding their time, opting to wait out his visitor.

"It's good to see you," Shelly said.

Homer nodded. "How are you holding up in here?"

"Fine," said Shelly. It wasn't really an answer, but then again, Homer hadn't really asked a question. It was just one of those exchanges between partners, where each one knew what the other expected to hear.

"I, uh, saw on the news the other night—you had a little excitement in here, with that vegetarian fellow."

He meant Nieff—Lowenkopf had almost forgotten about him. In the aftermath of the suicide, it was hard to keep track of those earlier fatalities. "You don't know the half of it, Homer. We've got enough action around here to keep a squad busy. If you had stuck to your bed in this place, you'd have found plenty to distract you, believe me."

Homer responded defensively to an odd interpretation of the comment. "I've been assigned to a case, more or less. Stolen shoes and things—a comb. Not exactly the Boston Strangler, but I'm not sitting around on my duff, either."

"No, I mean *action*," said Shelly. "There was a suicide here this morning—in this room. A couple of days ago, another man's heart burst open—in that bed. You've heard what happened to the vegan, haven't you? And the doctor who runs the lab in the annex on this floor hasn't been seen for a week."

Homer paused. "You think there's a connection?"

It occurred to Shelly when he heard himself speak that the list of fatalities was probably longer than it should have been, even for an unfortunate hospital. He hadn't even mentioned the incident at the refrigerator—he hadn't heard the outcome of that. He shrugged. "Maybe we should look into it."

He knew it sounded crazy, but there was a real advantage to the suggestion: it would give them a way to be with each other. They were partners, after all, and in the absence of a case, they didn't have a whole hell of a lot in common.

Homer said, "What would we look into?"

"Well, there are three deaths to start with," Shelly said. "Make that two—I know all about the suicide. Or we could begin with the missing doctor. Work our way into it, easy like."

"Has anyone reported this doctor missing?"

"I don't know. Her residents are covering for her here, so there probably hasn't been any formal request filed with the local precinct. At least, not by the hospital."

"Does she have any family?"

"I don't know. Maybe."

"Maybe we should leave that to them, then. What about the deaths? What did those people die of?"

Shelly approached this more carefully now, remembering the careful professionalism Homer brought to a case. "Let's see now: the first one, a man named Debs, died of cardiac failure a short time after heart surgery."

Homer hesitated. "I'm not sure that counts as a suspicious circumstance."

"Wait!" said Shelly, reaching under his pillow to produce a newspaper. The headline was printed in a script that resembled Hebrew or Persian but was clearly distinct from both. He handed the paper to Homer. "There's this."

"What does it say?"

"I don't know. It's in Georgian. But I think it says something about liberation."

"Shelly," said Homer, "every paper from Eastern Europe says something about liberation. I'll get it translated, if I can. But it's not exactly evidence that anyone's been murdered. What about the next one?"

The next one? Of course—now they were on to something. "Insulin shock. Resulting from too large an injection, either overprescribed by the doctor or overfilled by the nurse."

"They don't know which?"

"The doctors are having a meeting to talk about it on Monday. A regular thing—an M and M conference."

"Like the candies?"

"As in 'morbidity and mortality'—why people die. They hold them once a month in this place."

"Then why don't we wait and see what they find out? These physicians are a lot more talkative to one another than they ever are to us."

That was undeniably true, and it surprised Shelly a little that Homer had thought of it. Anticipating what people might say in an interview was usually his department. Was Homer starting to pay attention to these things?

"All right," Shelly was forced to admit, "that makes sense to me."

"So," said Homer, summing up, "we have a cardiac patient whose heart gave out and an incident the hospital's looking into. That doesn't leave much of a case, here, does it? I mean, not one that we can follow. Lots of people die in the hospital, Shell. That's the place most people do it."

"Not like pins in an alley," replied Shelly. But Homer's assessment was certainly fair—there wasn't a whole lot to go on, so far as a case was concerned.

Homer didn't enjoy disappointing him. "Well, what about the last death? You said there were three."

Shelly shook his head. "I said two, really. The third was a suicide. I was kind of in on that."

Homer nodded—there was nothing he could say. But it put the kibosh on their investigative plans. Neither one of them was particularly anxious to explore just how much Shelly knew about a suicide in his room, when he learned about it, and what he might have done to prevent it. An awkward silence stretched out in the space between them.

Shelly said, "So—tell me about your case."

"It's nothing much," explained Homer. "Somebody broke into a store and stole a pair of dancing shoes. He read the receipts in the file and followed one to the apartment of a film nut, where he stole James Dean's comb."

"Big money case."

"You'd be surprised. We've been working on it for two days now, tracking down leads."

" 'We?' " said Shelly. He hadn't expected Homer to sit around waiting for him, but still, it came as a surprise.

"The captain gave me a new partner," Homer explained, "just until you get out. A plainclothes cop, to train in detective work."

"How's he working out?"

"She's pretty good."

" 'She?' "

"Jill Morganthal. You must've noticed her."

"Morganthal?"

"She scraped up a lead. A week before the first burglary, a woman came into Mrs. Geffelman's store asking to buy this very same comb, which wasn't for sale anymore. We haven't got much of a description of her—just a few doubtful words. We spent all day yesterday tracking them down."

"What words?"

Homer shrugged. "The best our informant could remember was the script on a lab coat. We've been checking out every possible clinic and neighborhood doctor who might be serving the streets, because the name stitched over the pocket was Street Dudes Outcast Hospital."

Shelly couldn't contain a crooked smile. "I'll bet you tried all the phone books and couldn't find the place. And then all the bookie joints, and no one heard of it, either."

"Right."

"And then you went for informants—also a bust."

"Not that it surprised me," Homer admitted. "I couldn't help but suspect our informant's memory. But Jill, she's determined, Shell. You can't imagine what it's like to work with somebody like her. She wouldn't let us quit."

Shelly glanced quickly at his partner, who seemed to be speaking without irony. "I can imagine a partner like that," he mumbled, but Homer still didn't get it. It occurred to Shelly that each of them only noticed the other and hardly ever noticed themselves. He said, "You want to know where it is?"

Homer looked up slowly. "Where what is? You mean you've heard of the place?"

Shelly nodded, suppressing a smile.

Homer tapped his chin. If his partner had heard of it, he must have also. They always traveled together on the job, and Homer was the one with a memory. But where? When? He couldn't remember—and Shelly could? It was plain from Homer's expression he couldn't quite believe that. And yet if there was a chance it might be true, he clearly wanted to know.

"It's a clinic, isn't it?"

Shelly shook his head.

"What, then? An abortionist?"

For an answer, Shelly rang for the nurse. Miguel responded, poking his head into the room before Shelly could put down the call button. "Sergeant Lowenkopf? You called?"

"Come here, Miguel, if you don't mind. I'd like you to meet my partner, Detective Sergeant Homer Greeley. We'll be conducting a secret investigation on this ward, but I think we can trust you."

"Yes, sir, you can. Thanks for getting me off the hook before. With the suicide."

"I couldn't leave you to swing for it. Homer, say hello to Miguel Santiago, one of the best nurses on this ward."

Homer shook the offered hand, but said nothing, waiting for the point of this encounter. His gaze wandered over the nurse and then stopped dead, inches from his heart.

"Nice t'meetcha," said Miguel, trying to release his hand, but it was trapped in the officer's grip.

Homer's eyes lifted, peering hard into Miguel's. But when he spoke, he addressed himself to his partner. "Shelly? Why don't you tell me that story again? About your case. Then I'll tell you mine."

My case? thought Shelly. Suddenly I have one? But he knew what had changed Homer's mind. The blond detective was still staring at Miguel, though not at his face, exactly. His gaze had dropped again and was fixed a few inches above the pocket on Miguel's white uniform where elegant red embroidery spelled out in cursive script a barely legible name: St. Jude South Coast Hospital.

20

The name of the hospital didn't really provide much help, but it gave Homer a good deal more interest in poking around the wards. Shelly knew his partner was less interested in the local crime scene than *he* was, but he was willing to take what he could get in the way of assistance. The alternative, after all, was to say good-bye to Homer, sink back into his bed, and allow Martin to carry him to the deathbed.

Once Homer agreed to investigate the events on Shelly's ward, it was no trouble convincing him that they ought to start with Marsha Goodman. It had been her instruction that had brought on insulin shock in Howard Nieff; that alone made her a reasonable suspect in one of the possible crimes. Shelly knew his partner always felt better interviewing reasonable suspects. It helped him feel they were making progress on a case. Shelly did not underestimate the advantage of his partner's feeling good about their work.

First they paid a surreptitious visit to Freylung's office, which was unlocked and in reasonably good shape—not really neat but tidied, so that a superficial patina of order reigned over whatever disorganization might lie just beneath, with a stack of four magazines on the round coffee table in front of three upholstered chairs near the door: two medical journals, a travel magazine, and an upside-down *Newsweek*. The walls were hung with clippings from newspapers and magazines, touting the accomplishments of the research wing of the hospital, simply framed in black wood and glass, which reflected the light from a window against the rear wall. Beneath the window that looked out over the parking lot stood a small rosewood desk matching the coffee table, and a chair of the same wood, with an upholstered seat that did not quite match the print on the three chairs by the door. Shelly found no photographs, but saw several uneven stacks of papers on the desk, in no discernible order, yellow lined pages sticking out between typed white sheets and line graphs, in the middle of which a glass ashtray overflowed with the filters of long, skinny cigarettes. This evidence of a vice condemned by the medical community convinced Shelly that the desk was where Freylung did her personal work, receiving visitors at the coffee table near the door. But hadn't she felt the need to cover up her habit by dumping the butts when she left for the day? He picked up the phone on the desk and pushed the automatic re-dial button. The telephone made a series of beeps and groans until someone at the other end picked up with a click and a voice mumbled, "Internal Revenue. One moment please."

Was that what Freylung was doing before she disappeared? Calling for tax advice?

Homer interrupted Shelly's thoughts with a soft tap on his shoulder. "There's someone down the hall."

They found Dr. Goodman alone in her laboratory, hunched over a microscope. It was a large room lined with wooden shelves on which racks of test tubes were arranged in groups of six in chronological order. Each was carefully dated on a square of white tape. Most of them were about a quarter filled with milky liquid, and all of them were stoppered with cork. Next to the microscope was a wooden rack of six. Goodman uncorked the last tube, sampled it with a cotton swab, and wiped it on a slide, which she slid beneath her lens. She did not look up when they entered, though Shelly stepped noisily on the parquet floor and Homer cleared his throat twice.

"Dr. Goodman?" Shelly said. He had made an effort to shape up his appearance to something closer to a profession-al standard, but the best he could manage was to tie all the strings in back of his gown and bind his bathrobe securely. Something about slippers marked the wearer as casual, no matter how crisply he walked.

The doctor measured a squirt of brown liquid into a dropper and squeezed it, drop by drop, onto the slide. "You should be in bed, Sergeant Lowenkopf."

He was gratified to know she remembered his name, but his radar went up just the same. Of course, she must know that her insulin had caused the death of Howard Nieff. He had heard that she denied writing the fatal slip, or writing it as it had been administered. And yet questions of negli-gence, not to mention malpractice, gathered round her professional reputation—at least until the M and M confer-ence cleared her, if it cleared her. There was always the chance of criminal charges, too. It must have been a bad night for Marsha Goodman, Shelly decided. And, from the shapelessness of her hairdo and the blue bags under her eyes, he gathered that she had spent it peering into that lens.

"Sorry to bother you, Doctor," Shelly said quietly, so as not to startle her. "We know you're busy, here. But if you could spare a few minutes for us, we might be able to clear up one or two things."

It was a shameless temptation, and she looked him straight in the eye. But he kept himself from blinking and knew he had her. She could doubt his intentions and ability, but she couldn't help desiring a miraculous deliverance. He was a policeman, wasn't he? And wasn't that what they were supposed to do—save people who were wrongly accused? It was a powerful bit of psychology, easier to recognize than to resist.

"All right," she said, in spite of herself, "a few minutes. What do you want to know? How many units of insulin I wrote on that prescription?"

"Not yet," said Shelly. He could see that she wanted to tell him about that, but he knew he would learn more if he made her wait to say whatever she had in mind. "First I want to know about Margaret Freylung."

"Margaret? What about her?"

"When was the last time you saw her?"

"Tuesday."

"The day of your fight with her?"

"What fight?"

"In the research annex. Over the sperm samples in the lab refrigerator."

"You know about that?" Her eyes glinted with new respect. "That day, yes. But our fight, as you call it, was not the last time I saw her on that day."

That caught him unexpectedly. "It wasn't?"

"No," she said, gratified to be springing the surprises once again. "I came back to the lab to see her again, later—around nine, I think."

"Why?"

"To apologize. I had spoken in anger earlier in the day, Sergeant, and said some things I regretted. I wanted her to know that I did."

"What did you regret?"

"A lot of things. The tone of my demands, first. But I had also made a discovery that changed my feelings about the theft. You see someone had stolen a prepared sample of sperm, from which the DNA string had been removed. It looked at first as if the test tube had been refilled with somebody's personal squirt. But that's not what it turned out to be."

"What was it?"

"Chimpanzee sperm. Some of my experiments are done with it."

She winced as if expecting a blow, and Shelly could imagine how much ribbing she must have taken about it. He tried to keep his own response wholly professional.

"So your accusation was premature? I mean, the error might have been yours? Mixing up test tubes?"

She rolled her eyes and sighed. "It might have. I don't think that happened. But I wanted to tell Margaret. That's why I came back to see her."

"Did she always work so late?"

"Often. She was obsessive that way and usually expected the same dedication of others. But I knew she'd be here Tuesday night because of the microscope."

He glanced at the table. "This microscope?"

"No. An electron microscope she was trying to persuade our principal sponsor to purchase. The request had been denied twice, and she planned to take another whack at the man who ran the foundation."

"Do you know his name?"

"She never troubled us with politics or business, but took care of that herself. We were hired as researchers and practitioners. She tried to keep the money men away from us. As much as she could."

"Didn't she succeed?"

"In my case she did. You'll have to ask the others about their own situations."

"So you wanted to apologize and knew she'd be here. And you found her in."

"Yes. She was evidently in a foul mood, but accepted my apology without a fuss. She said she always felt a share of responsibility for what her residents did. Even when we most disappointed her. Gracious she always was—I should say 'is.' You don't know where she is, do you?"

"No. Has she ever done this before?"

"Disappeared? Once—for a week. Her daughter in California had run into some complications during pregnancy. I've called, and she isn't there."

"Any other family?"

"A son, somewhere in Europe. She doesn't know where he is. A husband in a grave here on Long Island."

"Can you tell me something about her research?"

Goodman laughed. "You bet—she doesn't do any. She signs her name as an investigator on the papers of her residents, and she likes to be cited in the literature about clinically produced anesthetics. Not plant-based, but synthetic: the kind they make from genetically altered bacteria."

"The way they make insulin."

"Exactly. But Bruce has been doing all of that work, including the research design. She's listed as a collaborator on some of my papers, too. But have you nosed around her laboratory lately?"

"Why?"

"It's an office, now. No lab equipment in active use—not even a Bunsen burner. That should tell you something about a scientist."

Shelly looked around with a shrug. "I don't see a lot of burners in here."

"You see plenty of samples, though, don't you, Sergeant? Each one has to be collected, labeled, and studied. That's work, any way you tackle it."

"What are you trying to find, exactly?"

"Start me on that and I'll chew off your ear for an hour! The short story is: I'm trying to fertilize a living egg without a sperm cell—that is, without a traditional impregnator. Do you know what I mean?"

He nodded, although he didn't understand. Not that the pretense helped, since she clearly didn't believe him.

"There needs to be genetic material from two divided cells, and nature's delivery system relies on the sperm. But we're into the cell structure now, and there's no reason in principle why a DNA string from a divided egg can't be joined with a match from a source other than a sperm. There's no reason in principle why a DNA string from a skin cell, for example, couldn't be tied to one in an egg to create a viable new life.

"Imagine what that might mean, Sergeant! Birth without a sperm. Eggs would still be essential, of course. You need a site for the fertilized ovum to attach itself to and grow. But the father's contribution would no longer be confined to donors of the male sex. Women would be able to 'sire' children in each other. Think about that! We'll have to invent another word for it, won't we? That's my research. That's what I was hired to do here. I was not hired to overdose patients on insulin."

Shelly risked another nod, indicating assent. It might have been interpreted as confirmation, agreement, or simply as a sign of understanding. It kept people talking until they noticed the ambiguity. That was when he asked a question.

"You didn't write that prescription for a hundred units?"

"No, I didn't."

"Do you know where the slip is now?"

"Sure. Matahashu has it, the chief of medicine. But I've seen it. It shows a prescription for one hundred units of insulin."

"In your handwriting?"

"Not quite all of it. I wrote a prescription for ten units. Somebody else added the zero. Look," she said, reaching into a drawer beneath the microscope. "See this?" She held up a capless pen with the name of the hospital printed on it. "That's what I used. You have any idea how many of these are floating around this hospital? Or how easy it would be to copy my zero, and add another beside it?"

"Any idea who would do something like that?"

She sat silently for a moment, thinking it over. "That would be homicide, Sergeant, if any doctor did it. You don't

192

up a dosage by a power of ten as a practical joke—not if you know anything about medicine. I'm not ready to accuse anyone in particular of murder."

"They may accuse you. At the M and M conference next week."

"We'll see who does the accusing, then, won't we?"

She was not prepared to say any more about her suspicions, if indeed she harbored any. With that prospect to stimulate them, Shelly and Homer decided to poke around the rest of the laboratory annex after their interview with Dr. Goodman. The door to Bruce Haight's room was locked, and all they could see through the double window was an untrimmed hedge growing in a planter box on the far sill. The blinds were drawn, admitting almost no light, but the medium-size shrubbery sprouted a profusion of white flowers, bright red berries, and attractive leaves—pointed, smooth-edged, oval in shape, three inches long, six to eight on each stem off the main branch. In addition to his medical skills, the man had a green thumb—that much they could see. And nothing that would mark him as a murderer. They had better luck at Dr. Ashbury's door, which they found open. But it wasn't Elaine they discovered inside.

It was a cadaverlike man, who seemed able to hold himself upright only by leaning on the handle of a mop, which he swished around the floor between his feet. He was performing a delicate balancing act, keeping the mop handle beneath his center of gravity while the ragged gray mop head flung scum lines of dirty water across the tile floor. What they saw of the man himself was the top of a head, almost entirely bald with a few strands of feathery white clinging gamely to the sides. He was dressed in jeans and an open flannel shirt over a T-shirt, both of which looked as if he had been lying mummified in a grave for two or three thousand years. When he looked up, his face confirmed the impression—hairless eyelids and grizzled cheeks, pinched lips and a wavering chin. Prominent bones stuck out from his cheeks and protruded over his eyes so that the whole skull gave the impression of a demonstration sample that had been passed from class to class of anatomy students since the founding day of a medical school.

"Mr. Griegg?" Shelly held out his hand to the skeleton and was surprised at the grip. "My name is Lowenkopf. This is Homer Greeley. We're police detectives looking in to some things that might be going on around here."

Griegg laughed soundlessly, a convulsive bobbing. "Oh, they might, might they?"

"What do you mean?"

"What do *you* mean?" said the old man.

Shelly turned to Homer, whose shrug said plainly, He's all yours, partner. Shelly didn't mind that at all. But he knew he had to find an avenue of interest for the man. The mop in his hand was a clue. Shelly looked around, taking in the furniture: a soapstone sink with gleaming taps, a desk like a schoolteacher's in blond wood, coat closet, on the door of which hung a sign of Ashbury's Texas origins—a photo of a lanky cowboy lying across the front seat of a convertible, while behind him a lone ranch house sat on a desolate landscape. The cleaning man's eyes followed Shelly's with pride around his spotless domain.

"You clean up the lab after hours, don't you? Most days of the week?"

"Can't really clean much on weekdays. Too many people around. Saturdays—that's when you got to do the real work." Having reminded himself, he put his back into the mopping again, swabbing the floor in front of Lowenkopf.

Shelly let the bubbles dribble toward his shoes, expiring before they reached him. "I'll bet you see a lot, then, Mr. Griegg. Who stays late every night, working in the labs. And who hangs around until the boss doctor is gone and then cuts right out of here."

Griegg dropped the mop noisily into his bucket and ran the sodden head through his wringer. "I see enough."

"Did you happen to see Dr. Freylung working late Tuesday night?"

"Maggie? That's what I call her. What she told me to call her. Sure, I seen her Tuesday. Monday, too."

"But not since then?"

"No. She's been on vacation."

"How do you know?"

Griegg made a face that said, What an ass you are. "If she wasn't, I woulda seen her Wednesday, now, wouldn't I? And Thursday night and last night also."

"Are vacations the only times you don't see her?"

"Unless she goes off to see her daughter in California. She did that once. And she's got a son, too."

"We know. He's someplace in Europe, but she doesn't know where."

Griegg grinned, showing missing teeth on both sides. "Then you don't know much. He's in Algeria."

That put Griegg one up on their last informant, and Shelly wondered why Freylung had confided more to the custodian than to her resident. Perhaps Griegg had learned about the son on his own, somehow. Or perhaps he was lying.

"Can you think of a reason," Shelly wondered, "why anybody around here might bear a grudge against Marsha Goodman? Or want to stir up a bit of trouble for her?"

"You mean like switching that scum in the freezer, eh?" Griegg seemed to think it over, then spoke with care after a pause. "Not a grudge, exactly. But it's easy to see how someone might be tempted to play a little trick on her now and then. She takes herself awful seriously. It makes you want to tweak her nose. Her schools were all the best schools, to hear her tell it, and her teachers the best doctors, too. Her research is the most important research, naturally, and her work the hardest there is. And then, when it comes time for her to do it, what do you see? She's in the animal room, jerking off the chimps."

He flushed to hear himself say those words out loud, but he set his lip grimly. He wasn't about to let politeness keep him from addressing the kernel of the matter.

"Collecting samples," Shelly prodded.

"Don't doubt it," said Griegg, nodding sagely. "That's what she calls the stuff—samples. She's the doctor. But you had to see her collecting the stuff. Quick and efficient as a damned machine. Ever seen her husband? No wonder the poor bastard's so shriveled."

"Sergeant Lowenkopf?"

They heard the voice behind them and only then became aware that Marsha Goodman was standing in the doorway of the lab. From her expression, it was impossible to tell how long she had been standing there and how much she had heard. Shelly felt an unaccountable sympathy for the woman who tried so hard to make herself unsympathetic. He didn't dare express it, since he felt sure she would cut him to ribbons for presuming to harbor such a sentiment.

"Yes?"

"There's a call for you on my telephone. Transferred from the one beside your bed." *Where you should be,* her tone implied, *instead of nosing around our labs.* "You can take it in my room, if you like."

He followed her silently and picked up the receiver, pressing the cool plastic against his ear.

"Hello?"

"Can you explain to me," a familiar voice hissed, "why you are signing affidavits now?"

It was Madagascar, speaking as he did when he was too full of rage to find his vocal chords.

"There was a suicide in my room," Shelly explained, wary of the captain's anger. "A man turned off his own respirator. I couldn't let them hold the nurse responsible."

"You couldn't do that," Madagascar gasped, choking on his restraint. "If you did, we might have been able to arrest a man every now and again."

Shelly hesitated. He knew he was missing something, but

couldn't figure out what. Homer kept telling him to keep his mouth shut, but there was no other way now to fill in the blanks. "There was no reason to arrest Miguel, Captain. He had nothing at all to do with the incident."

"Miguel? Who's Miguel?" hollered Madagascar, finding his voice at last. "Who cares if *he's* free? You idiot! I'm talking about Freddie Santino."

21

Elaine Ashbury never looked forward to her rotation through pathology, where her medical skills were used not to save lives but to analyze how the hospital staff had failed to do so in one case after another. She was not enjoying this rotation in particular. Her first corpse of the morning had been a young man who had died, without doubt, of AIDS, but still the examination had to be done and the exact cause of death determined. So her mood was unusually edgy after coffee when she stopped by Shelly's room to listen to his heart before returning to her duties in the basement. Her annoyance was consequently that much greater when she discovered that both beds were empty.

She rang for a nurse and stood in the doorway, tapping her toe until Martin strolled in. "Where is Sergeant Lowenkopf?" she demanded of the orderly.

He looked at the bed Shelly had occupied, then at the other, and shrugged. "Somewhere on the ward."

"What do you mean *somewhere*? This patient is suffering from a myocardial contusion. He is not supposed to be roaming the halls."

"Oh, he's not roaming," Martin said. "He's investigating."

"Investigating? Investigating what?"

Martin scratched his ear. "I dunno. He was awful excited about it."

The doctor's face turned crimson. "Excited is precisely what he is not allowed to get."

Martin's lips pulled back in a vindictive grin. "You want me to tell him that for you?"

"I want you to find him and bring him back here. Whatever else excites him. And I want you to see to it that he remains in his bed. Do you understand me?"

"I understand, all right, Doc. I'll haul him back and keep him here. Don't worry."

He turned and went out, heading for the laboratory. Elaine watched him march down the hall, swinging his giant fists. She did not enjoy treating patients this way, but Lowenkopf certainly had it coming, and not just in his cavalier attitude toward his medical condition, either. It was just like him to wander off and leave her waiting at his bed. Well, there was no reason she had to be there when Martin dragged him back from who knew where. He could wait for her this time. She had patients to see, and it hardly mattered that some of them were dead. She stormed off to the staircase and stomped her way down four flights to the dank pathology lab.

Shelly, in the meantime, was still in the research annex, trying to digest what he and Homer had learned in the short, angry call from Madagascar. The district attorney had informed the captain that Freddie Santino's lawyer, Zbigniew Jones, had come into court and presented a judge with paperwork documenting Freddie Santino's death. He had been caught in a terrible accident, it seemed, an explosion on a boat, and had died five days later in the hospital. All of the papers were apparently genuine. The death certificate was signed by the attending physician, and a report from the pathologist had been included as well. But the signatures of physicians were sometimes for sale—any insurance company claims adjustor would swear to that. The document that had really clinched the decision was an unusual one: a deposition from his roommate, a police officer, testifying to the details of Freddie's suicide.

"Freddie?" Shelly said to Homer. "That was Freddie Santino? I can't believe it. He didn't look anything like him."

"All we really knew," Homer reminded him sullenly, "was that Freddie had a funny-looking mustache."

"This guy didn't."

"But, Shell, he was burned, remember? All of the hairs on his face must've sizzled off in the blast."

The gauze-wrapped face filled Lowenkopf's memory, and he recalled the shadows above the slit of the mouth. Had there been the trace of a mustache between the bandages? "Was that really him?"

"They would have sent his file to pathology along with the body. There must be something in there," Homer said, "that could be used to confirm his identity. X rays or something."

"Right," agreed Shelly, warming to the prospect of further inquiry. "To the morgue, then. In the basement."

The two detectives headed for the elevators, but met with an obstacle once they entered the ward from the bridge—Martin, who spotted Shelly immediately and moved to block their path.

"Excuse me, Martin," said Shelly, trying to step around him. "You're standing in our way."

"Not *his* way," said the giant orderly, thumbing at Homer. *"Yours.* Doc says you belong in bed."

"And I'll go straight there," promised Lowenkopf, "just as soon as we pay a little visit downstairs."

Martin shook his head—like a sheep's. "You're going now."

The big man picked Shelly up by the hips, tossed him over

200

one shoulder fireman-style, and carried him toward his room. Homer followed at a respectful distance, then stood in the doorway as Martin dumped his partner into the bed that had been occupied in turn by Marvin Debs, Howard Nieff, and Freddie Santino. The handyman was already working on the mechanism under Shelly's own bed.

"Now stay there," said Martin, brushing an invisible residue from his hands.

"You bet I will," said Shelly.

The orderly looked doubtful, but couldn't stand sentry; he had other duties on the ward. With a suspicious eye on Homer, he lumbered out, his back obscuring most of the hall as he headed for the desk.

"The coast is clear," said Homer.

"Let's go."

The two detectives slipped from the room and made tracks for the back staircase. As the door closed behind them, they heard a shout of discovered betrayal from Martin, which redoubled their speed down the steps.

They heard the squeak of a hinge overhead and his heavy tread on the steps behind them, half a flight back. On the lobby level, they fled one staircase and entered another for the last flight down to the basement. The orderly must have expected them to run for the front door, because he followed them out to the lobby but could not find them among the crowd awaiting admission to or release from the hospital. In the basement stairwell, the two detectives stopped, listened, and heard nothing. They had lost him, for the moment. Shelly sighed.

"Which way to the bodies?"

Homer pointed to an arrow painted on the concrete wall, indicating that the pathology lab was to their left. They followed the damp corridor around to a steel swinging door, pushed their way in, and found Elaine Ashbury. She was wearing a white smock like a butcher's, similarly smeared with blood, wielding a formidable pair of scissors.

"Shelly?"

"Elaine!" he said. "We haven't much time. Do you still have the file on my last roommate? The recently diseased Freddie Santino?"

"The suicidal burn victim?"

"That's him."

"I suppose it's here somewhere. No, wait, they took it away this morning. His lawyer subpoenaed it for use in a hearing."

"Then the D.A. must have seen it," Homer said, "and would've gone over the details with a fine-tooth comb. If the patient in that file was anybody other than Freddie, the D.A. would have blown sky-high the motion to dismiss our warrant. Freddie Santino's X ray must be in there."

Elaine was trying to stay with him. "You mean the identity of the dead man? I'm sure it was correct. Why?"

"He was wanted for murder," Shelly said. "The brother of a big fish in a very dirty pond. We heard noises that Freddie might be willing to talk. We could have learned a lot from him."

"It's always like that with a suicide," murmured Ashbury, shaking her head. "So many things the person could still have contributed! It's terribly sad, even when they were despicable human beings. It's so much worse when they weren't."

"We're responsible," Shelly said.

"No, you're not!" insisted Elaine. "That's one of the hardest things, even for doctors to learn. We do what we can to help; that doesn't make us responsible when it fails to prove enough."

The detectives exchanged glances.

"You don't understand," Homer said. "We let him slip away. We had him in our custody and lost him. We've been after him ever since. That's why we jumped in the bay. Shelly doesn't quite believe he's dead."

"Oh, he's dead," Elaine assured them.

Shelly looked at the wall of steel drawers in which the bodies of the dead were kept refrigerated. In the high polish he saw Homer, Elaine, and himself, weirdly elongated, like children in a fun house. Behind this facade, the corpses lay puckering. "Which one is he?" Shelly asked.

"Oh," said Ashbury, "he's not here anymore. We do what we need to do and send them on their way."

"Where?"

"To a mortuary, Shelly. So their families can mourn over them, say good-bye, and bury them. Or cremate them and sprinkle their ashes around the yard. Or keep them in an urn over the television set. Or whatever people need to do to help themselves feel better about their loss."

"Freddie's people are great believers in concrete," muttered Homer.

"Which mortuary?" asked Shelly.

Elaine shrugged. "What difference does it make? He's not going to testify now, one way or the other."

"Which one?" he insisted.

She made a face. "I don't remember."

"You must have a file in which you keep track of the bodies that pass through here. Where is it?"

She bit her lip, thinking about what he wanted to know. "We don't keep file cards."

"There's a computer terminal on the desk," Homer observed. "There might be something listed in it."

"Could be," Elaine said. "But I don't know the system, if there is."

"It's usually pretty apparent," said Homer, flicking a switch on the side of the computer. The monitor lit, amber letters on black, and a box of options filled the screen.

"There we go," said Shelly, pointing at the third line on the menu. " 'Releases.' "

Ashbury nodded.

It took Homer less than two minutes to work through a series of prompts, which led him to the record of one Frederico Santino, deceased earlier that day and released to the Seaside Mortuary, located about two miles from the hospital. Homer wrote the address on his notepad along with other information the amber screen provided about the patient, the physicians involved in his case, and his finances. No health insurance, and no wonder: what company would have been willing to insure the life of a Santino? Were there actuarial charts for gangsters?

"Let's go," said Shelly.

Elaine caught his arm. "Where?"

"To pay our respects to the dead man. He was my roommate. Not for long, but I feel I owe him that much, at least."

"Shelly Lowenkopf!" said Ashbury as his doctor. "You climb right back into your bed. You are a sick man—or at least you might well be. Do you want to kill yourself? Leave police work to your partner or to anybody else, and take care of your own self, for once."

Her concern touched him. "I will, Elaine," he promised. "Just as soon as we look in on Freddie."

But she didn't release his arm. "I'm serious. If you go running around after dead men, you're in real danger of becoming one yourself."

"No running," he swore and did a silent imitation of careful walking as he pulled himself gently away from her.

She picked up the phone. "I'll call an orderly on you, if I have to."

"We'd better be off," he told Homer.

Ashbury dialed.

Shelly went through the door. Homer was beside him a moment later. "I mean *off,*" said Shelly. "If Martin finds us, we'll never make the door."

It took them fifteen minutes to reach the Seaside Mortuary, situated high above the dunes on the shoreline. As they approached, a veiled widow was sprinkling ashes over the sand. Two or three steps behind her, a young man in a suit gripped a boy around the shoulders. Two cars and a hearse waited in the drive.

Inside, the lobby of the mortuary was dimly lit, paneled in deep brown and furnished in green leather. A lectern to one side of the entrance supported an open book and a pen, in which a few names had been illegibly inscribed. A short man in a tuxedo crossed the lobby to greet them. He stopped two steps in front of them and bowed, rubbing his hands together before offering a dry palm to Shelly.

"Are you here for the Gruenwald affair?"

Shelly felt an impulse to tip the man. "We're not here for any affair, actually," he said. "We're police officers. Looking for a body."

The man smiled with patient understanding. "We do have some here, of course. But I don't think they're available, even for our fine police forces. If you wait here, I can ask if there are any that might be spared."

"No," said Shelly, "we're looking for a particular body. It was released to this mortuary earlier today by Saint Jude South Coast Hospital."

"You must mean Santino," the man replied.

"Exactly! Do you have him on display? Or are you still preparing him for the family?"

"He's prepared," the man said, "but not for public viewing."

"Why not?"

"The wishes of the family. Santino will not be displayed. He's slated for cremation. Any moment now. We have our own facility, right on the premises."

Shelly leaned his face very close to the mortician's. "Can you take us there immediately, please?"

"As soon as the outdoor service is concluded."

Shelly shook his head. "Now."

The mortician thought for a second and peered out the door, estimating the degree of grief on the shore. "I think we have a few minutes, if we move quickly."

They followed him downstairs to a room in the cellar where everything glowed red. A furnace stood in the center, its black wrought iron filmed with heat. Its sheen was picked up as a design scheme. In front of the furnace was a table covered in red velvet, trimmed in black satin. On the table was a pine box, stamped with the logo of the hospital, all four corners of its lid nailed down. A man in black overalls was sitting on the table, snacking on a tuna fish sandwich laid out on a napkin on the box.

"The fire's almost ready," he told the mortician, rapping on the wooden box. "We'll have this baby burning any minute now."

"Who is it?" asked Shelly.

The man in overalls shrugged. "They don't tell me. I just shove 'em in."

"Open the box," said Lowenkopf.

The man finished his sandwich, looking to his boss in the tuxedo. The mortician nodded, and the workman reached under the hem of red velvet plunging over the table's edge. From a toolbox stowed below, he brought out a hammer and, one by one, pried out the nails.

Inside the belly of the furnace, something pinged against the wrought-iron side.

"It's ready," said the man, touching the belly lightly with his palm, testing the heat. Then he turned back to the casket and angled the claw of his hammer between pine boards. The first one came up cleanly. The second splintered a bit. He had to lift three boards before they could see the face—calm, composed, collected in death. Comforting, in a way.

Except it was the face of Margaret Freylung.

22

If Margaret Freylung was lying in the casket that should have held Frederico Santino, where was Freddie himself? That was the question Shelly and Homer turned to after they had called for a deputy coroner to collect the doctor's body. The discovery had been a shock, but once Shelly became acclimated to the doctor's gray visage and felt some sadness over her death, he found it reassuring to know that they actually had a case to investigate. Flat on his back in the hospital, watching his roommates expire, it had been easy to believe he was manufacturing a role for himself to play. But a body meant a case, clean and simple, and that meant something for him to do.

Homer did not say much, but he seemed quite happy to leave the questioning of janitors and morticians to Shelly, with his impulsive sentiments. This allowed Greeley the freedom to do what he enjoyed: concentrate on the *things* in a case. Which was just what he began to do when the casket was opened and he bent forward to peer at the corpse until the deputy coroner arrived and claimed possession of the remains. When he and Shelly were alone again, Homer sat up on the table in front of the furnace, crossed his legs, and picked invisible lint off the knee of his pants.

"It happened Tuesday night," he said.

"Well, no one's seen her since then," Shelly agreed. "But it could've happened Wednesday morning. She might've come in early and been dispatched before anyone we talked to had a chance to see her."

"She might have, but she didn't," insisted Homer. "She was killed on Tuesday night."

Shelly sighed. "All right. How do you know?"

"The makeup," Homer said with evident satisfaction. "Heavy mascara and shadow on the eyes, plenty of dark red on the lips. Women don't wear makeup like that first thing in the morning."

"Mordred does. Sometimes."

"Mordred," said Homer, as if her name were enough to explain the anomaly. "Women like Mordred wear makeup like that *because* women like Margaret Freylung don't. That's my point. Besides, you can see how smudged it was—a fourteen-hour smudge."

Shelly could not see, because the body had been taken away by the deputy coroner and he hadn't noticed when it was there. So he had little alternative but to nod in agreement and ask his partner, "Any idea how?"

Homer shrugged. "Hard to tell without touching her. My guess would be strangulation."

"Because there were no bloody bullet holes?"

"Because of the muscles in her neck. Didn't you notice how strained they were? Bunched together like knotted cords. She tried to scream, but couldn't manage it."

Lowenkopf thought of the corpse's throat, trying to remember if he had seen bruises there. He hadn't looked closely enough. "All right," he said, "so tell me already, if you've got it all figured out. Who killed her?"

"That's a lot to call without lab results, a long limb to climb out on. It had to be someone connected somehow

208

with Freddie Santino. Because someone stuck Freylung in his box."

That made enough sense to help them decide the next place they should go: the Santino compound on the south shore, a few miles farther out on the Island. They needed a warrant to burst in looking for Freddie, and they called the captain to have one requested from a judge. The call came back half an hour later: no luck. Freddie Santino was officially dead; Lowenkopf himself had testified to that fact. Why were they searching for a dead man? The assistant district attorney assigned to the case had been forced to admit the possibility that, despite Lowenkopf's affidavit, Mr. Santino might still be alive. But that did not convince the judge, who knew more about the Santinos than the assistant D.A. expected. Freddie had never actually resided on the grounds of the family compound, built by his father years after both sons were fully grown. If the stories on the street were true, and his brother Francis was trying to kill him, the compound would be the last place Freddie would go for sanctuary. It smelled like a fishing expedition to the judge, who wasn't inclined to issue a license. Lowenkopf had done enough fishing, he said, off the sailboat in the bay and the power boat that exploded at the pier.

When the news reached Shelly and Homer at the mortuary, it ended their hopes of a surprise strike at the Santino compound. And yet, even without a warrant, the compound was their best bet. No one had even reported Margaret Freylung's absence; her corpse in Freddie's casket was their only real clue. It wasn't a bad one, as clues went, because it gave them a way to keep the case alive. Without it, Shelly saw no alternative but to return to Martin and the deathbed in his room. He held out a hand for the car keys. "I'll drive."

It wasn't as easy as he had anticipated. The sensations of noise and color on the road assaulted Shelly's senses with palpable intensity. The grass at the side of the highway seemed piercingly green; the blue sky and white clouds glared brilliantly, forcing him to blink. The chrome of car bumpers was inordinately shiny; the horns and grinding engines of the traffic grated against the back of his skull. Traffic lights swung precipitously on overhead wires. Shelly found himself swallowing, not because his throat was dry but because he needed air. Breathing was difficult, and his chest . . . he did not want to think about his chest.

When they reached the Santino compound, the guard at the entrance closed the black iron gate, told them to wait in their car, and called ahead. Shelly didn't give their names; he merely said they were policemen. Since he hoped to pique Santino's curiosity, he figured that the less they said in advance, the better would be their chance of gaining entry. Without a warrant, they had no alternative but to talk their way in as guests of the house. But, looking at the fortifications that confronted them, Shelly was not altogether displeased that the judge had refused them a warrant. Prospects for an unexpected assault would not have been promising. Busting through an iron fence was not his idea of fun, especially with sharpened spikes aligned along the top. The living quarters were set well back from the road and the entrance: the time it would take them to cross the lawn would spoil the surprise anyway.

The guard murmured respectfully into his phone, almost in reverent prayer. He pushed a button that opened the gate and waved them up the hill. Shelly rolled forward but stopped for directions at the guardhouse, revving the Reliant's cylinders. The guard gave the car a derisive smirk, and Shelly squealed out, burning city rubber. It wasn't his own Volkswagen square-back, but it felt good to be back behind a wheel.

There was a sleek Corvette in front of Francis's house, and another guard on the porch. When they arrived in the Reliant, he stood from his chair, rubbing the small of his back. The chair was made of wood without a seat cushion, straight-backed and uncomfortable—the sort of chair no one would choose to sit on for hours. Saint Francis believed that personal comfort dulled a man's fighting edge. None of his men could afford to be dull; he saw to that himself. Sacrifice and self-denial were the keys to personal fitness— to physical, mental, and spiritual strength. All of the men who waited on him, or guarded him or his family, kept the same Spartan regimen Francis had chosen for himself. After rising in the early dawn, eating a single piece of toast and a raw egg for breakfast, he would run around the compound three times, clocking himself over the miles. His resolution was to improve his time each dawn over the morning before. When he did, the day began in balance; when he failed to do so, woe to the underling who crossed his path.

Francis did not believe in the comfort of anger, an emotion he considered self-indulgent. But he did believe in the curative power of righteous indignation. It was he who decided what was righteous and what was not; his anger was invariably the curative kind. It helped to cure spiritual ills in particular. His cures would often result in physical injury, but what was pain of the body compared to pain of the soul? It was a question that called for careful judgment, since a wrong answer was corrected with a shotgun's *booyah*. So much Shelly knew about Saint Francis Santino. If his brother had stirred his righteous indignation, Freddie might well be dead.

"Where do you suckers think you're going?"

The guard on the porch raised the barrels of his shotgun at the two plainclothes detectives. If he saw anything unusual in the red plaid bathrobe worn by one, he didn't make a stink about it, but relied instead on his innate hostility to see him through the encounter.

"We're expected," Shelly said. "Ask Francis."

The shotgun did not waver from their chests, but the guard kicked the door open behind him. To someone inside they could not see he muttered, "Tell Francis his guests are here."

A moment later the slim, balding heir apparent of the third largest extortion racket in lower New York State stepped out onto his porch. He wore black yoga pants with a drawstring waist and a black T-shirt that showed to advantage the wiry muscles in his forearms. He was shod in Chinese slippers, strapped, without socks; his feet curled forward to grip the floorboards as he moved soundlessly across them. He seemed surprised by the red bathrobe, but, resisting any cheap cracks, put two and two together.

"Sergeant Lowenkopf?"

"Yes."

"Then you must be Greeley. Tasteful suit. How can I help you gentlemen?"

"You could tell your gunsel there to lower his barrels," said Shelly, just as pleasantly.

"Does it disturb you?"

"It might go off accidentally. And that would disturb the whole neighborhood."

"It's a nice neighborhood," agreed Francis, inhaling the crisp suburban air. The guard turned the shotgun toward their car and retreated to his straight-backed chair.

A bead of sweat cooled Shelly's spine when the shotgun moved away. But he struck an attitude of indifference. "We hate to drop in unannounced. But we're planning to make an arrest here today. We thought you'd want to know."

Francis nodded appreciatively. "Who're you planning to bust?"

"We hoped you might help us decide."

The mob leader smiled. "Hope springs eternal. But there must be a charge."

"The charge is murder. A doctor, one Margaret Freylung, who directs the genetic research annex at a nearby hospital."

Francis seemed to consider the name but at last shook his head, turning from the guard to another man who stepped uneasily onto the porch, wearing a three-piece suit. An attorney, for sure. Shelly thought he recognized Zbigniew Jones. The guard imitated the shake of his boss's head; the lawyer said nothing, studying the two policemen.

"Never heard of her," Francis said finally.

"We found her body in the coffin that was supposed to hold Freddie. Your brother. Ever hear of him?"

Francis's eyes grew darker, more forbidding. But he kept control of his voice. "You are a guest here today. Frederico's death was a terrible loss to my family, Sergeant. I expect you to respect that."

"I would. If he were dead."

"Isn't he?"

"Why don't you tell us that, Mr. Santino? Where is Freddie now? In your father's house? Or yours?"

"Cremated this very afternoon."

"No, he was not. We interrupted the cremation of the body in his box. But it wasn't his body inside."

Francis glanced at his lawyer, who was plainly surprised to hear it, but refrained from comment.

"It wasn't?" said Francis.

"No. It was Dr. Freylung. How do you suppose her body found its way into your brother's casket?"

"I have no idea. The people who work in those places— morgues, and so on—are not the best and the brightest, are they? Mistakes are made from time to time. I will find my brother's body, rest assured of that. I thank you for calling the error to my attention."

"You're welcome," said Lowenkopf. What else could he say?

Santino headed for the door, to Jones's evident relief. The attorney considered any talking with police an unnecessary risk. But how did he advise a client who liked to cross swords now and then, for the exercise? Now the duel was over, with no palpable hits—unless Lowenkopf could find a way to prolong it.

"Wait!" he said. "Since you have nothing to hide, would you mind if we poked around?"

"I can't have you disturbing my father."

"Here, then. Inside. Just a quick peek through the rooms of this house."

"You have a warrant?"

"Not yet. We could get one, if we need to."

"If that's true, you'd better do it. There's no reason I should permit you to do what a judge will not."

"Perhaps there is."

"And what would that be, now?" His voice was just a note sharper, but it was the difference Shelly had been waiting for—the first sign that he was losing his saintly calm.

"Self-interest. Your own versus Freddie's. I'm betting you'd rather have us arrest him than you."

"Me?" Francis smiled again, with no mirth in his face. "On what grounds could you possibly arrest me?"

"Murder," said Shelly.

"I've never heard of your Dr. Freylung."

"There's Debs and Nieff," Shelly said. "Two more."

"Who?"

"My roommates at Saint Jude. The prior occupants of your brother's bed."

Francis looked blankly at his colleagues before turning back to confront the police. "Listen to me," he said carefully. "You seem to imagine that I'm aware of everything done in my name. But no one could run this business that way. A man in my position has to delegate authority—which, I admit, sometimes slips away. This seems to be one of those times. I haven't the slightest idea what you're talking about."

"I'm talking about your brother," Shelly said.

"So I understand—accusing me of killing him, directly or indirectly. But I had nothing to do with that. Business is business—that goes without saying. But he was still my brother. Strange as it might seem, I'd rather have him alive and talking about me than dead in his grave."

"Oh," said Shelly, "I'm not accusing you of killing him. I'm accusing you of saving his life."

Francis blinked. "Pardon me?"

"I think it went like this," Shelly said. "Your kid brother found his wife in bed with another man. So he shot him,

214

neat. No thought about getting away with it, and no precautions, so the police found what we needed to put him away. His big brother Francis heard about the scene too late to help him get off by any of the usual means. So you reached for a new idea: you had your mouthpiece call us and suggest Freddie might be willing to sing all the songs he learned as a kid growing up in this family.

"Which amounts to a reason to kill him! A reason for us to believe in. You dropped a loose word and waited for it to reach us. Then you tipped us off to your boat in the bay here. My partner and I took our seats on the sailboat—we were cast as the witnesses to Freddie's death. We see the boom go off with plenty of noise and smoke. We might have assumed nobody could've survived the blast. Except I was aboard at the time, and survived. So Homer started to wonder, Whatever happened to Freddie's corpse? And someone on your payroll must've overheard him wonder—in an elevator in the hospital, say.

"You knew we suspected your brother might still be alive. So you switched to a backup plan: Freddie's painful recovery, which unfortunately led to his suicide. And this time you had a witness—a policeman, yet—to swear to the authenticity of the death. That's where I came back into the picture. Except you had to get Freddie into the room with me, and somebody was already in the other bed. A man named Debs. So you arranged to have him vacate it early.

"You tried to have Freddie transferred into Debs's empty bed—and discovered that my roommate had already been replaced. Howard Nieff was installed and looked as if he'd be staying for a while. So you found a way to move him out, too. It required two murders, but it worked, didn't it? Freddie managed to occupy a bed in the same room as me, where he could play another scene for me to witness.

"You had a couple of things going for you, and I was one of them. Drugged. And stupid. And those semiprivate rooms—it's hard not to notice your roommate, after a while. You also had some damn good information, I'll say that for you. Killing Debs with a newspaper declaring the independence of his homeland! Awfully clever, but it left as evidence the murder weapon itself: the newspaper with a false headline. That had to be printed by a printer somewhere. We'll find him, Santino. Believe me. Don't think you're off the hook on that one."

Francis shook his head. "Fantastic. Fascinating! Do any of you fellows know about this?"

The guard shook his head.

Zbigniew Jones hesitated, reluctant to break his silence, but unwilling to allow Shelly's narration of events to go any further unchallenged. "Even if such a printer could be found, Sergeant, what would your case amount to? Someone sent the man a joke gift, meant to entertain him after surgery. Unfortunately, a heart patient recovering from an operation is likely to keel over at the least provocation. Especially when he's so old and emotional a man."

"Howard Nieff was not old," said Shelly. "And his death was not caused by his feelings."

Jones made little tsking noises. "A terribly sad case, that one. An error on the nurse's part—or was it the doctor's? The hospital is still deciding which, I understand."

"It was nobody's error," Shelly said. "Someone added a zero to the physician's prescription, while it was pinned to the wall in the nurses' station. That doesn't happen by mistake."

"No, it doesn't," agreed Jones. "But it can't be done by outsiders, either. Surely you're not suggesting that Mr. Santino here altered the prescription himself?"

That was a problem for Shelly—how did the Santinos finish Nieff? Anyone other than hospital staff would have instantly been barred from access to the nurses' station. That had to be someone who worked in Saint Jude's. So what evidence did they have tying the death to Santino?

At that moment, right on cue, Homer stepped forward

and murmured into Shelly's ear two words that made no sense. Shelly squinted and Homer repeated, "The cola."

"What about the cola?" Shelly said uncertainly.

"What cola?" demanded Francis.

And suddenly Shelly understood: they had physical evidence—supporting the postcard near his bed. "Six cans of diet cola were sent to Nieff by some unknown supporters, to help him stave off a dose of insulin. Only they didn't help him stave off anything. He drank five cans and plunged into a coma. That doesn't sound like diet cola to me."

"It should be difficult," Jones observed, "to differentiate the effect of that soda pop from all his other food."

"I doubt it," said Shelly. "The cans of soda were practically all he consumed—those and some chocolate candies."

"Perhaps it was the chocolates, then? I'll bet it's hard to be sure, now that the sugar has been wholly absorbed into his bloodstream."

"No," said Shelly. "I tasted those chocolates. They were artificially sweetened, take it from me."

"Ah," said Zbig Jones. "An expert witness."

"Don't worry," Shelly said. "There's no need to argue now. I have a can of that cola Howard was drinking. He gave me one. Our lab will be able to tell if it's diet or sugar. Which would make it a second murder weapon, wouldn't it?"

Jones whispered something into Francis's ear; Francis nodded to the guard. The man looked uneasily at Lowenkopf and Greeley and went into the house with his shotgun.

"Unfortunately," said Jones, "there's really no way to know who sent those mismarked cans of cola. So many people feel so strongly about the issue Nieff was protesting! It might have been any crackpot who decided to enter into the debate about animal rights with a fatally dramatic contribution."

"It might have been. But I doubt if we'll have much trouble finding out. Those colas arrived in a wreath delivered by a florist, who must have parked directly in front of the building. The nearest parking lot is too far away for anyone to lug a wreath that big. The security cameras posted over the hospital entrance will have the name of the florist on tape. Maybe his picture, too."

Francis moved forward, but Jones restrained him. "The name on a florist's truck is hardly conclusive evidence of anything you've attributed to my client."

"You see, Francis?" said Shelly. "You're a client already. Would you rather face these charges or hand over your brother for questioning? You know as well as I do that he's not about to sing. But somebody's going to stand in the box."

Francis stood silently, glaring at the detectives, thinking or waiting for something. Then the guard returned to the porch with a man Shelly had never seen. He was dressed in a brown suit with a Rolex on his wrist and two-tone tap shoes on his feet. His face was long and foxy with a tremor at his nostrils, as if he smelled something frightening in the air. The man saw Francis and straightened, staying alert, on the balls of his feet.

"Chester!" Francis called him. "You should hear the story these gentlemen have been telling. Fantastic! About cans of sugar cola and Russian-language newspapers. I thought you'd find it entertaining."

"I heard it. Upstairs," said Chester, a minimalist.

"And perhaps before?" Francis mused.

Chester did not seem to like the sound of that, but didn't protest, either. Francis waited to make sure that none would be forthcoming before turning to address the police.

"Sergeant Lowenkopf, this is all news to me. But you said one thing that did ring a bell: a florist shop. Chester owns a florist shop, you see." Francis shrugged. "My job is a little like being the president: you never quite know what all your men are up to. I suppose it is possible that Mr. Gafarian might have overstepped some bounds in performing what

I'm sure he considered his duty to me. I apologize on his behalf for my organization. You'll have to take up further particulars with him. Chester, you have our full support—whatever legal counsel money can buy."

Gafarian said nothing, leaving Shelly to puzzle out the deal Francis was offering. "What about Freddie?"

"He's not here," said Francis. "In my house or my father's. Chester is. You can take him or leave him. Without a warrant, he's the best you're going to do."

It occurred to Shelly that Francis had taken another leaf from the presidential book: an organizational structure providing immunity to the man at the top while a second rung of operatives carried out his wishes. But there wasn't a lot Shelly could do about it, and he opened the Reliant's back door.

"Come on, Chester. Time to go for a ride." Homer began to read the man his rights.

Gafarian looked at Francis, whose expression was stern but forgiving, like a father leading his son to the woodshed. There was a debt to be paid, Francis seemed to say, but atonement was possible once the punishment had been suffered. Gafarian looked at the armed guard and at Zbigniew Jones, who stood like sentinels on either side of Santino. Homer led Gafarian to their car and secured him by cuffs in the back. Francis watched with pity but said nothing.

Jones stepped off the porch, tapping at the window of the police car. "I'll be at the station to talk with you soon, Chester. Don't say a word until I get there."

Gafarian nodded, looking back in silence at Francis as the car pulled down the long drive. He said nothing as they made the turn and headed for the street. But as soon as they cleared the front gate, he leaned forward toward the detectives. Chester prided himself on his loyalty and his fine sense of distinctions, which told him when to be loyal and to whom. He was a man who saw where his interests lay, and, as he had done when Francis Santino first entered the mattress factory twelve years before, Chester saw that his interests had once again changed.

"So," he said amiably to the two detectives, with the winning smile of an agreeable middle manager, "do you want to know or don't you?"

"What?" asked Shelly, turning the wheel.

Chester's face soured. Would he have to manage the whole business himself? He sighed. The brunt of the job, as usual, fell to him. "What do you want to know?" he said. "Who killed Margaret Freylung? I can tell you that. Listen to me."

23

Homer dropped off Shelly at the hospital and drove Gafarian on to their precinct house in the Bronx. After his single tantalizing question, the mob middle manager clammed up, holding out for a captain and a deal. His implication was plain: they had a foreign-language newspaper and a can of soda pop they might be able to pin on him. Would they trade that in on a murderer, offered up in a collection bottle?

It was clear that Gafarian maintained careful distinctions in his loyalty. He was unlikely to give them Francis Santino, and Freddie was questionable, though he clearly felt he had someone to trade for himself. The two detectives could hardly decide to accept or decline his proposition without the participation of their captain and an assistant district attorney. There was no choice but to drive him home to Madagascar—too far from Shelly's hospital bed for him to make the trip and return.

By the time he reached the third-floor ward, news of the death of Margaret Freylung had already made the rounds. When he stepped off the elevator, he could feel the melancholy glumness of the sentinel at the nurses' station. For once Hohenberg didn't seem to care who visited whom outside of specified hours. She sat in front of a computer screen, sniffling and blowing her nose into a handkerchief. Marsha Goodman stood over the nurse murmuring words of solace.

Behind the desk, Elaine Ashbury was thumbtacking an index card to the bulletin board with a red plastic pushpin. When the elevator door opened, she looked up hopefully, and Shelly could see how red were her still-brimming eyes. Whatever her faults, Margaret Freylung had inspired powerful feelings in the hearts of her residents. Shelly wondered if those feelings had played a part in her murder.

"I'm sorry," he said to Elaine, when she put down her pins and faced him. "About Margaret, I mean."

"We're having a memorial service for her. In the chapel downstairs. Tomorrow. You can come, if you like."

"I would like."

"And we're naming the microscope after her. The Margaret Freylung Center for Electron Microscopy."

"She persuaded the sponsors to cough up all that money?"

"Almost. Bruce is in there right now, trying to settle the deal. Margaret's death makes it a sure thing. Foundations love to donate commemorative funds." Elaine smiled bitterly and tilted her chin toward the bridge to the annex, with "LDS Research Facility" stenciled on the door. Shelly read it again—he had thought it was "LSD." Like a tiny gear that slips into place, enabling all the bigger gears to engage, the reversal of letters started a sequence of connections in his mind. He strolled over to the door and peered through the glass. No one was on the bridge, and no one was watching from the nurses' station, so he crossed the span, turned left at the corner, and walked until he stood in the hall outside Bruce Haight's room.

Inside, the doctor was conferring with a lean young man in an expensive suit, who reached out one delicate hand to touch the leaf of a plant, blinking his long eyelashes as he felt its texture. Bruce responded to his interest, giving him hints, no doubt, for his garden in Greenwich, Connecticut. Or in the Hamptons. Something about the young man made Shelly think of lazy summer afternoons around a tennis court.

And then the lean young man did an extraordinary thing: he plucked the leaf and ate it.

Lowenkopf must have registered his surprise with a movement, because both men looked at the door, and Haight crossed to open it. When he saw who was outside, he began to close it again but decided against a gesture his sponsor might view as treating a patient rudely. Instead he moved into the open space, blocking Shelly's view of the room behind him.

"What can I do for you, Lowenkopf? I'm busy."

The lean young man looked up at the name, and walked toward them until he stood directly behind Haight.

Shelly said, "I heard you had a visitor."

"That's none of your business," Haight muttered through his teeth, still trying to interpose his body between the detective and the sponsor.

"Don't say that," said the lean young man. "He's a patient here, isn't he?"

Haight sneered. "More or less. This is Detective Sergeant Shelly Lowenkopf of the New York Police Department. He was hurt in a boating accident nearby."

"Patients are the people we're trying to help," the sponsor explained to Haight. "That's why we give money to this hospital: to build facilities that might improve patient care." He offered his hand to Lowenkopf. "I'm Eliot Hardwick," he said. "From the foundation that funds this laboratory."

Shelly accepted the hand, but did not let go after shaking it firmly. "From LDS?"

Hardwick glanced at Haight. "That's right."

"I'm glad to meet you," said Shelly. "It's a wonderful lab

you've contributed here. I've been wondering what the initials stand for."

"The initials?"

"LDS."

"Louisa DeSoto," said Hardwick. "She was the wife of our principal contributor. She died in this hospital, after every effort had been made on her behalf. Our contributor was grateful for their labor. The foundation's intention was to thank these people for their dedication."

"DeSoto," mused Shelly. "Is that the *D?* Or the *D* and the *S* in your name?"

"DeSoto was her maiden name, actually," Hardwick clarified, instead of answering the question. "Why do you ask?"

Shelly shrugged as if to suggest his question had nothing behind it. "I only wondered," he said, "if the final *S* might've stood for Santino."

Hardwick looked at Haight, who scowled deeply, shaking his head to mean *I told you.*

Shelly wandered over to the plants beneath the windows and plucked a leaf from a branch. He held the leaf between them, studying its shape. "This is *Erythroxylon,* isn't it? The coca plant. And they say that money doesn't grow on trees. What's cocaine selling for today on the street, Mr. Hardwick? Have you any idea?"

"I'm afraid I don't."

"I'm sure you do. They're your real interest in the work done here—the work that Dr. Haight does, at least. Isn't that why you sponsor him?"

"What do you mean?" asked Hardwick. But Haight was already backing toward the door.

"Synthetic anesthetic—that's what Goodman told me Haight does. But cocaine was once an anesthetic, wasn't it? And cocaine grown by bacteria—what would that be worth? Producible in American labs, without all the headaches of smuggling it into the country? Imagine what a contribution that would be, for a boy who married into a mob family."

The last words stung Hardwick particularly. But he wasn't ready to abandon his pose as a philanthropist.

"What are you talking about? Bruce, do you know what he's talking about? You're crazy, that's what it is. Bruce, isn't he a patient? Isn't there something you can prescribe?"

"How about a bullet?" Bruce suggested.

Hardwick reached in his jacket and produced a small handgun. "I was hoping you would think of something else."

Shelly reached instinctively for his own firearm and felt nothing in the space between his waist and underarm except the radio transmitter in his holster and the flannel of his bathrobe on his knuckles. He ducked behind the doorjamb just as a bullet crashed into it. What had he been thinking? Talking tough was a helluva lot smarter when someone on your side was well armed. Oh, sure, he could convince a mob boss to hand over an underling, but doctors and foundation reps were another class entirely; they never went down without a crash. Confronting them with unpleasant news was like interrupting a fight between a scorpion and a spider, who could put aside their differences long enough to divvy you up between them.

Shelly did not feel like being divvied. His heart was racing in his chest—was that what they called palpitations? He crawled backwards across the hallway into Ashbury's room just as the two desperadoes ran from Haight's. They fired three times vaguely in his direction, missing but driving him back into the lab. He saw them run around the corner and heard them crash through the glass door, then tramp over the bridge.

He steadied himself against the door frame as he stood again, waiting for the dizziness to clear. It didn't, quite, so he ignored it, rushing after his suspects with abandon—well, he decided, not really with abandon. He moved quickly back to the ward but exercised caution when he entered the hall. There were two men nearby. One of them was armed, and both of them wanted him dead.

They were not in the corridor that led to his room at the other end of the hall. Of course he had heard them running there. But which way? Halfway to his room, on a short stretch of corridor, the nursing desk faced the elevators. Would they risk going that way? Or head straight back past his room, to the staircase at the end of the hall? He heard a grind of sliding metal and a sudden burst of voices—the elevator doors opening. He ran around the corner in time to see them close, with Hardwick and Haight among the passengers.

Shelly headed straight down the hall to the stairs. He had to beat the elevator down. From the nurses' station, Martin saw the blur of a red plaid bathrobe, made a belated connection, and bellowed, leaping to his gigantic feet and heading after Lowenkopf. By the time Shelly's shoulder hit the staircase door, he heard Martin's stomps shake the floor behind his own floppy slippers.

But there was no chance to stop and explain—he had to keep ahead of the orderly and beat the elevator downstairs. He flew past the second floor door, as the grunts grew closer at his back. Martin was gaining. As Shelly passed the door, he made a feint for the knob, which the big man inexplicably repeated. It took Martin a few seconds to realize there was no reason for him to do that and a few more to zero in on Lowenkopf. But those seconds were enough of a delay for Shelly breathlessly to reach the main floor.

From above he heard a voice—not Martin's, but gentler, the voice of a woman, filled with concern. It reached him through a buzz in his ears, but he knew it for Elaine's. Of course, she must have seen him racing by the desk, ignoring her instructions, as usual. But he had no time to answer her call with Martin behind him and Haight and Hardwick still on the loose.

To his left was a flight down to the basement; in front of him the door to the lobby, metal with chipped green paint. He burst through the door and raced around to the elevators, discovering with enormous satisfaction that the car which had swallowed Haight and Hardwick was still descending. For an instant he enjoyed imagining their surprise, until the door slid open and they weren't inside. He made sure they weren't in back and then realized they must've stopped on the second floor and were winding through some back way to the ground. Where was it? Shelly wondered for less than a second. Then he had no choice but to run again when Martin loomed suddenly behind him.

He turned left—for no reason except that Martin was coming from the right. The corridor cornered there into another long hall, with an emergency exit at its end. Still closing. Someone had gone through. An alarm went off that drowned out the noise in his head. He lowered his shoulder and went through that door, too, emerging in a small parking lot filled with BMWs, Mercedes, and Porsches, Porsches, Porsches. With MD plates, every one. Darkness was falling; through the dim light, he saw two figures climbing into an open convertible. One was dressed in a three-piece suit and the other in the flashing white lab coat of the medical trade. The ignition roared and the headlights glared as the Porsche backed up with a squeal. There was only one path through the lane of parked luxury cars. Shelly flung himself toward the center of that aisle.

Out of the corner of his eye, he saw another blur moving, bigger than he was—bigger than the car. Martin. He must have known where the left-hand corridor emptied and headed around to cut Shelly off at the lot. He was coming straight at Shelly from the far side of the aisle. But there was no other way to intercept Haight as the Porsche came roaring between them. Shelly ducked his head into his shoulders and leaped, and the blur across the lane did the same.

Shelly landed on the hood. But Martin was in the front seats—sprawled across them, and the two men seated there. Haight tried to beat the orderly's hands from the steering wheel, while Hardwick hollered, brandishing his gun. Shelly clung to the windshield, watching the struggle under his pressed nose. Hardwick pointed his weapon toward Lowenkopf on the hood, hesitated, and redirected it at the big man in his lap. But there was no way for him to shoot at Martin without risking a hole in himself or in Haight, at the wheel. Martin seemed to be enjoying himself, taking things easy. He grinned at Lowenkopf, growled at Hardwick, and let his huge ham of a fist find Haight's jutting jaw. The blow fell gently as a caress, and the doctor collapsed into his seat and the door.

Hardwick reached over and grabbed the wheel as Haight's foot slid from the gas. Martin reached under the dashboard and leaned against the brake. The car screeched to a halt, turning almost completely around before piling into a Saab. How it had found a Swedish car among all those fellow Porsches was a mystery to Shelly. But it couldn't have come at a better time for him. His fingers came loose and he slid from his perch, toppling across colliding fenders and rolling over the hood of a fully restored Thunderbird. The convertible crumpled sideways, slamming into the T-Bird with a sickening crackle, like aluminum eggs broken by the dozen. A thousand dollar paint job ruined in seconds. Boy, will its owner be pissed, Shelly thought.

He landed in a heap between two cars, missing the make and model as he went down. Darkness in the crevice between two hulls—for a moment he thought he was underwater. Further sounds of crashing floated by. Tinkling glass and the hiss of released air. Steam obscured everything in sight. He tried to stand. There were people crossing the lawn, running between the rows of cars, their feet pounding on the tarmac, pounding in his ears, in his chest. And then he felt a sharp pain and thought he'd been stabbed in the arm by a shard of glass from Haight's Porsche or the Saab or the T-Bird.

But there was no shard of glass in his arm.

He looked down stupidly and saw there was no blood. But the pain still ran down his arm like a fire in the tissue. And then the source of it changed. It came from his shoulder. Not his shoulder, really. From his chest. He sat down in the roadway, clutching under his arm. But the pain was striking from under his solar plexus. Like a hand gripping him there. Its fingers reaching out, driving nails into the nerves around his heart.

There were people around him, over his head. Two or three, he couldn't make them out. Presences, shadows. He couldn't look up while white lines of agony shot into his lungs. He would have screamed if he'd had breath. But he could draw no air into his chest. There wasn't room for anything but pain.

And then the earth rocked with its own spasm as the Porsche went up in a roar of flame behind him. People were rushing in every direction. He heard a groan from Martin, like a harpooned whale. And the black tarmac around him sparkled red and yellow with bits of broken glass on every side. Smoke, in thick gray clouds that seemed to pass him by, blotted out the building overhead. He knew he was in danger. Elaine had told him so. And Mordred's Gypsy woman in Doha. But like this, in a bathrobe and slippers, in a parking lot reserved for physicians . . . ? He had hoped for something a little more heroic. The smoke entered his eyes, stinging him, bringing forth involuntary tears. He put his hand to his temple, shielding one eye, and took it down, sticky with his blood. All right, there was a cut someplace. That could be patched up. Air was what he needed now, oxygen in his lungs, which weren't taking it in for themselves. He tried to make his chest expand, to force in air, but a piercing stab under his ribs ended that attempt.

It was ridiculous, drowning on dry land. But he couldn't capture the oxygen around him. What he gulped burned in his lungs. He tried to stand, to raise himself where the cool night air was, floating over his head with the crowd. Something—a hand at his elbow—was helping him to his feet. No, pulling at him as he tumbled to the ground. The tarmac would not lie still beneath him now, but spun its black cocoon around his limbs. He tried to free himself but couldn't stir, sinking into the soft, sucking ooze. Like quicksand. Don't struggle. You'll only sink deeper. No hope but to call for help. His stomach was in his throat already, gurgling aloud, in the oldest of all ancient tongues. A woman called him Shelly, from a distance, through a fog. A spike went cleanly through his chest, front to back. Like a vampire. In a coffin. Trapped at noon. Penetrating the tissues of his heart.

He thought of Thom, of Izzy, of Mordred, and of Elaine, with a tiny seed uncurling in her belly. His gaze fissured, splintered, prismed. And then dimmed, burning at the edges like a cloud. Ten thousand swords of fire glinted in the roadbed when Shelly Lowenkopf died.

24

It required no effort. On the contrary, like a helium balloon suddenly let slip, it was easier for him to go than to stay. One minute he was writhing in horrible pain; the next, all sensation ceased. He neither felt the cramping of the muscle in his rib cage nor saw the ground glitter with flame. Yet his sense of presence continued in unbroken awareness from the moment his eyelids closed. Shucking his life like a soiled suit of clothes, Shelly loosened his hold on muscle and bone, on nerves and senses and breath. He surrendered the habits of his body and his mind, the rhythms of pulse and thought. No darkness and no light: neither did the sun burn nor the moon reflect, but both hung with equal magnitude in the gray heavens. As if the laws of refraction and gravity had been suspended, he lifted through an unencumbered sky. Chunks of his memory fell from him like ice: he wandered lonely as a cloud, a bear after honey, passing through shimmering silver linings. A cotton whiteness muffled all sound. On the ground, miles below, Elaine Ashbury straddled his waist, pounding her fists into his chest. Behind her, a crew from the hospital sprayed extinguisher foam on the Porsche, where Haight's and

Hardwick's charred corpses smoked. Martin groaned on a stretcher halfway to the emergency room. But all of them dwindled, as Shelly's attention was drawn irresistibly to another crowd collecting overhead.

He did not know their names, but they were as familiar as the members of his family. As a parent will sometimes call one child by the name of another, so Shelly felt he had forgotten those of the souls who gathered above him, gesturing for him to ascend. But he knew them all, mothers and fathers throughout the years, awaiting their time to be born. Behind them, a cool blur of blue light wavered, like the sun seen from a depth of water. He swam up into it, up among his family, and broke through a surface of liquid silver into the streaming light of a hall. Its walls were lined with portraits of the same face, cast and recast through generations. At one end, in a vaulted chamber suffused with light and crowded with murmuring presences, a group of bearded men and silent women gathered around a painting strung on wires that fell from an immeasurable height. A wind blew at once chilling and warm. Moving among them, children carried brimming goblets of clear sparkling fluid shot through with colors. A boy passing in front of him turned to meet his gaze, and Shelly recognized his father.

There was music—a Russian peasant tune, balalaika and drum. Was that what they listened to in heaven? Or was it just what *he* heard, since a woman in a dress like a desert wrap swayed to an entirely different rhythm. Shelly would have preferred to hear what she must've been hearing, and maybe even to join her dance, but as he moved toward her, she disappeared, and he found himself among the group by the painting, studying it with appreciative murmurs. It was exactly like dozens he had seen in the hall outside the vaulted chamber: a family portrait's mother, father, two sisters, and three brothers grouped in formal poses. None of their faces looked familiar to Shelly, and yet he knew every one. The youngest boy was Homer—that was clear at once. The middle boy could only have been Shelly himself. It took him a moment to recognize the eldest as his own son, Thomas. The younger daughter was Isabelle; the elder daughter, Ruth. The father resembled his own mother. But the eeriest resemblance was unmistakable: in the center of the portrait sat an ancient crone with a beaded shawl and a face like the Sphinx—and it was Mordred.

Mordred?

Shelly opened his eyes and saw Elaine Ashbury bent forward, leaning over him. Her right hand was clenched into a fist, which she had evidently been pounding on his chest. It hurt like hell, inside and out, tingling steel needles with each breath. But the expression in her eyes showed enormous relief, even joy, when he blinked. He allowed his own to close again but could not recover his dream.

"Shelly? Can you hear me?"

The sound in his ears was like cannons. Hearing—a rough, approximate sense. But the smell of burning gasoline in his nostrils carried all the sweetness of life. He opened his eyes, waiting until they adjusted to the contours of Ashbury's face. And the colors—another phenomenon.

"Am I alive?"

"I should think so. Now."

"Was I dead?"

She hesitated. "If you mean, did your heart stop? the answer is yes."

"But you started it again."

"Yes, I did."

He laid a careful hand on his chest, feeling for tremors. "It's not throbbing anymore."

"You had a heart attack. Not surprisingly. I told you you couldn't run around."

"I owe you my life, then, don't I?"

"Among other things."

She nodded to some orderlies, who laid a canvas stretcher on the ground beside him and started to ease him aboard. When he was raised, with all his weight, to a height between them, Shelly reached over and touched Elaine's arm. The movement strained a muscle in his chest, but he kept his hand on her sleeve.

"We need to talk," he said.

"I'll be in to see you. Try to sleep."

He did not want to sleep, but as usual his body had other ideas. His eyelids dropped at the doctor's command, and the orderlies carried him away.

But Elaine was as good as her word: when he opened his eyes again, back in his bed, she was sitting near him, listening to his heart. He lay in silence for a moment, feeling the circle of cold metal against his chest. When she removed it and gently resettled his gown, he said, "Thank you."

She seemed taken aback by his unexpected awareness, but knew how to cover her surprise. "Don't mention it. I'd do the same for any of my patients."

It was a veiled reference to something more between them, and Shelly didn't want to let it pass. "I'm not just one of your patients—and then again, maybe I am. That's not my baby you're carrying, is it?"

"What do you mean?"

"As much as I enjoyed our night together, and as much as I flatter myself—your decision to climb into bed with me wasn't entirely impulsive, was it?"

"It was deliberate, if that's what you—"

"No, that's not what I mean, and you know it. I'm talking about the comb."

She blanched. "What comb?"

"James Dean's comb. Some people went to a lot of trouble to get it for you."

"James Dean's . . . Why would I want something like that?" Her tone implied impatience, but she wrapped the rubber tube of her stethoscope around the tips of her fingers and had to wrap it again.

"The best that I can figure is that you needed it for insemination. Tell me if that rings a bell."

She shook her head in denial—too wildly. "What are you talking about?"

"You told me your research involves using the DNA of dead cells as a blueprint for making live ones. Marsha Goodman told me her research involves fertilizing eggs with cells other than sperm. If you put the two together, it's not hard to see: you use the cells that stuck to the comb, extract the genetic codes, and insert the stuff into some special sperm that's already had its own DNA string removed—by Marsha Goodman—and stored in the lab refrigerator.

"You were the one who stole her samples and replaced them with chimpanzee sperm. You needed them to carry James Dean's genes. That's what you used to impregnate yourself. And then you used me as your cover. So you could carry a fetus for nine months without anyone getting suspicious. Until delivery, when you announced to the world that you were the mother of James Dean's baby."

She covered her face with her hands, perched on the edge of his bed. The mattress trembled silently beneath her weight. "I wasn't planning to announce it to anyone. This was not a bid for professional recognition. I just wanted the baby, for myself. Can you understand that?"

Sure, he understood that well enough. He nodded and started to ask her what she did to get it.

Before the words were out of his mouth, Elaine cut him off, going on with her story.

"It seemed so simple. I had no idea that all of this would happen . . . to Bruce and Eliot Hardwick! You don't think it's my fault, do you?"

She looked up at him with swollen red eyes, and he couldn't help reassuring her. "No, I don't think so. Not the car crash, anyway."

At first he assumed she was merely afraid of punishment. But Elaine was evidently equally concerned about the judgment he would make, about the sort of woman she had become. She opted for the course that made her feel most comfortable—confession to a sympathetic man. "They said they just needed a signature, on my rotation through the basement, to back up Bruce's description of the cause of death. Bruce couldn't sign both, of course—as physician and pathologist. They needed a second signatory; I was on the shift, and they were willing to pay any price.

"Any price! I refused, at first. I thought they meant just money. But that man, Gafarian, helped me think about it another way. What did I really want, he asked, that I could never get for myself, working as I did within the law? He was willing to step outside and do what it took to bring back whatever was in my heart. It was easy to turn down money, but this was something else. He was willing to do *anything*. Has anybody ever made you an offer like that?"

Shelly shook his head.

"It's incredible. It makes you start to think. What did I *really* want, of everything I could imagine? To tell you the truth, it was hard to come up with something. And then a memory of something that I wanted and couldn't have filtered into my head. Just a few days before, I had tried to buy a comb from a woman on Fordham Road. But she said it had already been sold. It should have been a simple matter of offering a better price, but nothing that I offered made a difference. It was a matter of principle to her, of business ethics. So there was no legal way to get what I wanted.

"Now here was a man offering to grant my secret wish! And all I had to do was sign a form. No one would be hurt by it, Gafarian said. He was trying to help his friend save his life. There were mobsters or somebody trying to kill him. Saving lives is what I've devoted myself to, and all this required was a fast scribble on a pathology report, like endorsing a check or signing a petition. His friend would be able to escape the mob, Bruce and Gafarian would be grateful to me, and as a token of their friendship, I would get my comb.

"How I wanted that baby! It wasn't just an idea anymore, a procedure no one had tried. I've told you already what youth means to me. James Dean is all of that, made living flesh and blood: the embodiment of everything I never permitted myself while I was studying medicine. Lazing around in the afternoon, a hat over his eyes, thinking about nothing but sex and romance . . . you don't get much chance to do that as a medical resident, when your shifts run back to back through the night."

Lowenkopf nodded again, to keep her talking. "I saw that photo from *Giant* over the desk in your lab. It made me feel like kicking back for a while."

"That photograph! I should've torn it down. But I couldn't have kept my sanity without it. Whenever it became impossible here, I would gaze at that wooden ranch house in the middle of an empty plain and imagine he was waiting for me inside. Doesn't it sound ridiculous? A woman my age! And yet it was my age, of course, always preying on my mind.

"I was staring at the picture one day when I should've been watching my rats. Marsha came in, complaining about one of the chimps. And suddenly the whole idea occurred to me at once, in all its personal and scientific beauty. It was hard to chase from my mind once it came, and I started to wonder if it would be possible to find a cell of James Dean's. I started asking local dealers until somebody mentioned his comb. From then on, I knew I had to get hold of it.

"Can you imagine my frustration when I finally tracked it down, and that woman refused to sell it to me? I tried to outbid the previous buyer, but to her, it was a question of honor—'a done deal,' she called it. What does that mean, now? Is there anyone who needed the damned thing more? Who had a better use for it? But she wouldn't budge, and the irony made me crazy. The comb was so close at hand and yet utterly unavailable. She told me to wait until the purchaser claimed the comb and then try to strike a deal with him. But he never got around to it. And the waiting, day by day, was driving me mad.

"Until Bruce Haight led Gafarian into my lab, and he offered to obtain for me whatever on earth I wanted. And all he needed in exchange was my name on a form that would save his dear friend's life. Perhaps I should've questioned him more closely about it. Perhaps? Of course I should have! But I didn't. It was my only chance to get the comb and the child that I could produce from it, given my awesome medical training. He offered me his hand in a gesture of friendship. I took it—and all that the handshake implied."

She seemed to come to a rest, so Shelly asked, "Did you know that the handshake implied the death of Marvin Debs? And Howard Nieff?"

"What? How do you mean?"

"Gafarian killed Debs to clear a bed for Freddie Santino. And Bruce did the same to Nieff. All it took was a zero on Dr. Goodman's prescription, pinned to the nurses' bulletin board."

"No! Bruce wouldn't do anything like—"

"Wouldn't he? Have you any idea how long he kept Margaret Freylung's body on ice?"

"Margaret?" Elaine stared at him. "You're wrong. Bruce may be a bastard, but his own career was too closely tied to hers for him to have hurt Margaret Freylung."

"He didn't," agreed Shelly. "He just kept her under wraps. Eliot Hardwick murdered Dr. Freylung."

"Eliot Hardwick? President of—"

"The Louisa DeSoto Santino Foundation. Do you know who she was? The wife of a notorious mobster. She was killed in an explosion meant for him, in an elevator not far from here. They were both brought here afterward. He recovered; she didn't. Salvatore Santino found his second wife here, working on the nursing staff. Her name was Daphne Hardwick. She changed Sally's life, got him out of the business. But his eldest son Francis was broken up by the loss of his mother. He started a commemorative fund, to keep alive her memory. When Sally asked him to find a legitimate job somewhere for the son of his new wife, Francis made Eliot president of the fund. Some joke.

"But Eliot wanted into the *illicit* side, where the real big money was. So he looked for his opportunity the only place he could: among the recipients of his foundation's research grants. He found out that Chester Gafarian was holding the paper on Bruce Haight's gambling debts—maybe Chester put in a good word for him when Haight applied for the grant. It must've been exactly the news Eliot had been waiting for, since it gave him the leverage he needed to persuade Haight to work on a method for bacterially synthesized cocaine. It was a natural pairing of like-minded souls: the assignment was right down Bruce's alley research-wise, and Eliot promised to get Chester's collector off Brucie's back. The idea probably appealed to Haight, as a way to use his medical training to make some real money fast. So they worked out an arrangement—but Margaret discovered it. Marsha Goodman told me that Freylung always felt responsible for what her residents did. She must have confronted Eliot Hardwick when he came here late Tuesday night to discuss the grant request for a new electron microscope. She must've tried to scare him off by threatening to expose them all—Bruce, Eliot and his whole operation. Do you know the last call dialed on Margaret Freylung's office phone? The IRS—guardians of the non-profit status. How do you suppose Francis Santino would've felt about Internal Revenue poking around his mother's memorial foundation? Dr. Freylung must've turned her back to make the call at the telephone on her desk. And to show Eliot what she thought of him. He panicked—he had to stop her talking into the mouthpiece, to cut off her voice. So he stepped up and strangled her.

"Then he did what kids like him always do—made his way to a pay phone and called home for help. The job fell to Gafarian to clean up after him. And then Chester had a better idea. He could use Freylung's body to help Freddie disappear—if he could make me witness the suicide that you and Bruce would endorse. He had to find your price tag, which he did, Wednesday night. He must've brought you the comb late Thursday. Which meant all he had to do was install Freddie in my room. Debs and Nieff just happened to be in his way."

"You don't think I knew anything about those deaths, do you? Shelly, I swear, if I'd had any idea—"

"No, I don't think you did. But it's hard to separate them out now, isn't it? If I bring you in on the fraudulent form, they'll charge you as an accessory. To the murders—all of them. They might do it anyway, since your name is on the computer in the morgue, as the pathologist who signed off on Freddie Santino's suicide."

"You're not going to . . . bring me in?"

"It hardly seems the gentlemanly thing to do," he observed, "considering you've just saved my life. Besides, nobody's asking me. These deaths are out of my jurisdiction —out of my city, in fact. My only clear purview is Freddie Santino, who escaped from us in the Bronx. You haven't any idea where he is now, do you?"

She shook her head.

"I didn't really think so," Shelly said. "But it never hurts to ask."

Elaine was overcome; she couldn't quite believe she was free of guilt and punishment—or punishment for guilt, which was something else entirely. But that distinction eluded her for the moment. "Do you mean that our local police might be out here in the morning, asking all these questions again?"

"They might," said Shelly, "but there's no reason why they should. Unless someone here decides to call them in. Bruce is dead, and Eliot's dead—I don't see a call. Technically, there is no case: people die in the hospital. If there's anything out of the ordinary, you're supposed to call. There's no provision for medical murderers. You're having a meeting tomorrow on morbidity and mortality. Whatever you and your colleagues find there will probably be the end of it."

25

When Mordred came to visit him the next morning, Shelly was awake but subdued. She was wearing a beaded shawl with long silken fringe over a hot-pink leotard with a plunging neckline and a skirt of Persian design. She struck a model's stance and turned in a small circle for him, spinning the fabric and fringe of the shawl around her as she whirled. When she stopped, it took her a moment to recover from dizziness, and she seemed to wonder about the funny smile he gave her.

"What's up?"

"I'm springing this place."

"Released?"

"Just a transfer," said Shelly.

"To where?"

"Anywhere in the Bronx."

Mordred grinned. "I see. You want to trade in these quiet suburban surroundings for the crack of bullets whizzing by in the halls."

"The surroundings are pleasant enough," he said, glancing at the sunny window. "It's the roommates that unnerve me."

"Oh," said Mordred. "You're looking forward to sharing your bedroom with a Bronx gang member and sharing visiting hours with his friends."

"At least they sleep at night."

"Then I'd better get you packed," she said. Mordred got a plastic garbage bag from the nurse's station and packed it with the things Izzy had brought: his books, tapes, bathrobe, and some clothes. He watched her as she placed it carefully on the floor, rearranging the items inside. There was something gentle in how she handled each book, folding the dirty red bathrobe at the waist. Almost maternal, he noticed. How had she acquired such a tender touch? Shelly leaned forward to better view her face, remembering how it would look wrinkled. She felt his gaze and asked, "What?" and when he shook his head, asked, "What?" again, more suspiciously, propping her fists firmly on her hips.

"I was just thinking," he murmured, "what a grand old lady you'll make."

She seemed pleased by that. "At least you're not thinking how young I am. We're making progress, aren't we?"

Homer stopped by just before lunch, looking in on his partner. He reported cheerfully that Freddie Santino had been arrested again—in the back of his carpentry shop on the parkway. "Can you believe it? He was sitting there just like before, with his eyebrows and mustache singed off. Half the police force looking for him, and he goes right back to the very first place we would look."

"Except it wasn't the first place," Shelly said. "It was the last place we looked for him."

"They're always in the last place you look, Shell. After you find someone, you end the search. But that shop *should've* been the first place we looked. After all, what does Freddie actually do? Nothing but work in wood. I don't think he'll mind prison a bit, if they let him use the wood shop."

"What about your own case?" Shelly asked. "With your substitute partner?"

Homer shrugged indifferently. "We got the shoes back from Gafarian, at least."

"And the other burglary?"

"We know Gafarian was behind it. But he absolutely refuses to give us the name of his hired hand."

"Too bad."

Homer shook his head in rueful acknowledgment of the one that got away. Shelly could only imagine how unsettling that particular unsolved case must be.

Schnork Szabo was afraid to return to the florist shop on Hempstead Turnpike. As a falling star loosed from its mooring burns up the earth where it drops, so Schnork anticipated a dreadful knock any minute on the door of his room. He had told his mother he felt sick this morning; he had no idea what he could say the next day. But no hostile fists beat at his door, and by noon he felt enough confidence return to risk bringing out from the foot of his closet the secret shoe box in which he had hidden his hoard of ill-gotten gains.

Gafarian's reaction to the dancing shoes had affected Schnork very deeply. Never before in his life had anyone rewarded his efforts with a clearer demonstration of gratitude and respect for his personal potential. When he had stood in the Pilson apartment, surveying the collection on the surrounding shelves, it occurred to him that other people might respond as well as Chester to a gift of movie memorabilia. In looking for the comb, he had kept an eye open for other things that might be welcomed as gifts. No big money items—Gafarian had warned him that the dollar amount could raise the charge of the crime and so attract more attention and effort from the cops. But there was a lovely old pair of dice he felt sure his father would enjoy. And a slender French sword that would make a perfect birthday present for his kid brother. When it came to the combs, he decided against going through them all on the spot, looking for that one marked "James Dean's." Instead, he took the whole damned case along with him, planning to find the one he needed later and to give the rest of them away.

But later, in his room, when he had identified the comb used by James Dean, he began to wonder about all the fuss. Somebody must've wanted it awfully bad to put him through all this bother. He wondered what was so special about the comb. Then he thought of the hair standing straight up from his forehead, and figured, Who the hell was gonna know? He ran the valuable comb through his hair— and it stayed down where he combed it.

It stayed!

That was all Schnork needed to know about the comb, the extent of its powerful magic. He peered closely at the comb in his hand, examining the teeth and the hard black rubber. It was just like the comb in his own back pocket. That was when he had an idea. Just like the kind that Chester had—an insight. Only it was Schnork's very own.

It occurred to him that the paperwork mattered more than the comb itself. If a letter signed by the hairdresser on the set of a movie swore that a certain comb had been used on James Dean's coif, that comb carried the hairdresser's authority with it. But there were no actual signs on the comb itself that could not be duplicated by a reader who possessed the letter in advance. He read the letter of testimony again, more carefully. It referred to a nick near one end of the comb, in the thicker section that held the teeth. With great care, Schnork took out his pocketknife and carved a nick just like the original into the hard rubber of his own comb. The third smaller tooth was broken, and he matched that on his copy. Then he set the two combs side by side, to make sure they were identical.

He felt a twinge of guilt when he handed the replica to Chester together with the documentation. Gafarian was pleased; he compared the comb to its letter description and slipped both together into his shirt pocket. Schnork worried that its final recipient might be someone who could tell the difference, who might fling the fake back at Chester. He practiced a few excuses he might offer in that eventuality. But there was no reason for him to worry: without the original for comparison, there was no reason for anyone to suspect that the comb presented as James Dean's came from Schnork Szabo's own pocket.

So there was no way for Schnork himself to know, nine months later, that a child christened James Dean Ashbury, Jr., had been born to a mother on the south shore of the Island. The baby had a strange crown of dark black hair. It stood straight up from his forehead.